PARADISE CITY

JOE THOMAS is a visiting lecturer in English and Creative Writing at Royal Holloway, University of London. Prior to this, he lived and taught in São Paulo for ten years. *Paradise City* is his first novel. The second book in the series – *Gringa* – will be published by Arcadia in 2018.

PARADISE CITY

JOE THOMAS

A

Arcadia Books Ltd
139 Highlever Road
London W10 6PH

www.arcadiabooks.co.uk

First published in Great Britain 2016
This B format edition published 2017

ISBN 978-1-911350-16-3

A catalogue record for this book is available from the British Library.

Typeset in Garamond by MacGuru Ltd
Printed and bound by T J International, Padstow PL28 8RW

ARCADIA BOOKS DISTRIBUTORS ARE AS FOLLOWS:

in the UK and elsewhere in Europe:
BookSource
50 Cambuslang Road
Cambuslang
Glasgow G32 8NB

in Australia/New Zealand:
NewSouth Books
University of New South Wales
Sydney NSW 2052

In memory of Elizabeth Mary Pond

Woe unto you, scribes and Pharisees, hypocrites! You are like whitewashed tombs, which indeed appear beautiful outwardly, but inside are full of dead men's bones and of all uncleanness. So you also outwardly appear righteous to men, but inside you are full of hypocrisy and iniquity.

Matthew: 23:27, 23:28

Time doesn't stop.

Cazuza, *O tempo não para*

PART ONE

Pai rico, filho nobre, neto pobre
Traditional saying

Every man for himself and God for all

Favela Chic –
São Paulo, 2012. Operação Saturação –
500 Military police from Batalhão de Choque and from 16º Batalhão de
Polícia Militar Metropolitano (BPM/M) installed in favela *Paraisópolis*
– Paradise City – in response to escalating violence in the city.
Result:
In one month –
107 detained.
67 caught in the act.
24 traficantes *on the wanted list sought out and captured.*
16 teenagers apprehended.
Result:
In one month –
18 weapons, 407 rounds of ammunition, 1 grenade.
Result:
In one month –
59 kilos of cocaine, 344.3 kilos of cannabis, 783 grams of crack.
Result:
In one month –
Homicides fall threefold, incidents of theft drop, no cases of rape.
Fucking result, they say.
Stray bullet collateral: a consequence, know what I mean –
Não tem problema nenhum.
Absolute fucking result –
Happy fucking days, amigo.

Paraisópolis, Paradise City, the largest *favela* in central São Paulo – November 2011

The streets pounded with Baile funk, and flip-flopped men in dark glasses stood around the car, watching the five dirt roads that joined at the junction. The sun slipped down out of sight of the *favela* crater, below the line of the city. Naked bulbs were scattered about the rooftops of the surrounding houses, each illuminating a few circular feet. Rusted tin doors squeaked, opened into the gloom and faint rectangles spilled on to the street, were still for a moment and then vanished.

Renata left her legal aid office an hour later than normal. She'd been helping a man with a dispute over land. He was expecting another child and wanted to extend the rough house his family lived in. But a bar owner and a tyre shop were unhappy with the plans. Renata had slipped easily into the space of the disagreement, fluid, empathic, and negotiated a compromise. The man had just visited her office to bless her and offer his respects. He'd talked for a long time.

She didn't like leaving after dark.

She scanned the street. A cockroach zipped out from the back of the *por kilo* restaurant where she ate her lunch every day. The owner – a large woman – stepped out from behind the counter and in three steps had crunched it under her plastic sandals. She smiled at Renata, who waved and dug her keys out of her bag.

Fireworks spat and crackled, and the men standing by the car turned, recognising the warning from the top end of the *favela*. Police. Renata tensed, struggled with the padlock to her office, dropped it. She glanced nervously at the restaurant owner who stood with her arms crossed, shaking her head, clicking and sucking her teeth, before stepping back behind the counter and pulling down the metal grille. Renata looked over her shoulder, watched as the men skirted around the cars across the road, crouched. Someone was shouting instructions to one of the younger boys. The Military Police would be here soon. These invasions were becoming commonplace, but this one was earlier in the evening than normal. Should she go back inside or try to get to her car? She told herself not to panic, that she had a little more time. The door was locked now. But better to get back inside, she thought. Surprised by a single siren-wail and blue-red flash she fumbled her key, watched it fall into the gutter and bounce towards the uncovered drain. The men drinking at the bar flinched then ducked under the tables.

She pulled at the padlock.

The maids and nannies walking home carrying their *céstas* of rice and beans started and scattered down the side roads.

The heat pulsed like a heartbeat, the clouds thickened and cracked. More shouts. Running. Renata froze. She looked across the road. The Military Police were advancing. Men in flip-flops ran from shadow to shadow. One was carrying a pistol, arm lowered.

Then, an unholy rattle. Renata took a step towards her car, limbs pushing though water. *This is happening.*

Gunfire. Strobing light.

And Renata glimpsed him – the last thing she ever saw. A teenager with gold teeth grinning, his rifle too powerful for him to control, police moving towards him from all sides.

One year later

Leme sat in his car on the edge of Paraisópolis, sweating in the fattening sun. Workers gathered by the bus stop, forming a queue that stretched up beyond the tyre shops and burnt-out cars, sipping at coffee they'd bought from the usual woman. Leme watched her drag the table up the hill from her home every day.

He traced the dust in the car window with his fingertip. He drew a heart and then smudged it, glanced in the wing mirror. His sunglasses hid his hollowed eyes. He stared at the street and shut everything else down. He'd sat here, or close, almost every morning for a year. No one knew. It was his own routine, part of his own struggle: automatic now, a way of not forgetting, not giving up. Anything he had got in life was in part down to his persistence, his wife, Renata, included.

And so here he was.

Again.

The stink of rubbish drifted up the road, but he left his windows open at the top. Slum-happy dogs nosed about in the mess, pulling out scraps. This was Morumbi, only a five-minute drive to Leme's own apartment block, with its swimming pool and tennis court, its sauna and its restaurant. Renata's apartment.

He'd moved in with her and now it was his, alone.

Across Avenida Giovanni Gronchi, the school gates opened and security shifts changed over. Cars crawled up the hill from the other side, turning left towards the city. Morumbi was empty once. São Paulo crept out from its centre like a stain.

Trucks rattled past. On the forecourt of a garage on the corner to Leme's left, a temporary Military Police post was manned by two officers standing next to motorbikes, lights flashing, hands on the guns at their sides. He hadn't told them he'd be there. This was theirs, the *favela*, not his. It was foreign, frightening. He did not belong. He did not want to be there. He had no choice.

The queue thickened. Men and women greeted each other, slapped hands, shuffled forwards, chatting. Leme only half-listened;

he'd heard the conversations time and again. 'Another day, *ne? Fazer o que?*' they said, laughing about the night before. '*Porra, meu. Que bacana, eh?*'

Once, Leme had pitied them, knowing that they would travel hours to a menial job to earn a laughable wage.

Now he envied the sense of community that he didn't feel at home.

He blamed the *favela* for what happened to Renata, killed by a *bala perdida* one year before. 'It's just bricks and mortar,' his partner Lisboa always said. 'It's people who are to blame, not the place they're from.' Leme disagreed with that. He went silent whenever Lisboa brought it up. Lisboa, Leme knew, thought his silence meant he agreed, would do nothing more and try to move on. But for Leme, Paraisópolis was alive. Toothed brick walls and jagged roofs: uneven, unregulated shapes diced, chopped and left where they fell. Most people who lived there were honest and diligent and Renata had worked hard to protect them. But not all.

A group of young men walked past the car, flip-flops slapping on the road. Leme raised his hand to his face, but the boys didn't notice. They looked harmless enough, none of the posture and entitlement of the dealers who worked the *bocas de fumo*. They laughed and one of them kicked at a rubbish bag.

Leme looked straight ahead as the cars zipped past, lines of grey and black.

There were shouts coming from behind him.

The noise of a car backfiring.

Leme swivelled in his seat, looked over his shoulder but saw nothing. Another bang. Fireworks? No, too early. And then again, this time three cracks in succession.

Gunfire. He knew.

More shouting. The queue for the bus rippled with fear and a number of people walked quickly away towards the main road. Leme stuck his head out of his window and sensed the tension. He made to start his car. He should leave. It didn't start first time.

Another engine growled. Leme looked again in the mirror: the boys scattered and swore, waved their arms, middle fingers. '*Vai tomar uma, eh!*' A black SUV careened up the road in a drunk stagger. Leme flinched and pulled at the door. It powered past, taking his wing mirror with it, and shot across the junction, into the traffic. Moments later a Military Police vehicle followed. An arm hung from the passenger window, gripping a revolver. This was the sound Leme had heard. He'd been to the firing range enough times to know.

Leme saw the two Militars by the motorbikes exchange a look. The SUV veered left, the wheels locked, there was a screech and it hit something on the road. It flipped and slid, crashed hard into the wall on the other side, buckling on impact. A group from the queue ran past Leme, shouting. The two Military Police were next, radios out. Traffic slowed and commuters climbed out of their cars and looked on from behind the open doors. Shaking of heads, looking at watches. '*Babaca*. Driving like that? *Filho da puta.*' In moments, a widening bottleneck. The three Military Police in the vehicle jumped out, hands on their weapons, surrounding the SUV.

Leme stayed where he was. A couple of cars swerved around the SUV and drove off quickly. One of the officers blocked the traffic and the other tried to open the vehicle, rattling the door handles. More shouting. Questions. 'Who was inside?' 'What were they doing in the *favela?*' 'An SUV, *porra.*'

Leme waited. When he heard the sound of sirens – police and ambulance – he climbed slowly from his car and walked over. He nodded at the Militars, the hint of a smile the pretence he belonged there. He flashed his badge: detective, Polícia Civil.

They examined the car as the engine steamed. The windows were blacked out and bulletproof, the doors securely locked. People paid well for this impregnability.

They couldn't get inside.

Leme hung back. The fire brigade arrived. They cut into the side of the car with a circular saw. He edged closer. When the door came off, he flashed his badge again, and leaned in as close as he could.

The young man in the car was dead.

Two spreading bloodstains, one on his right shoulder, one on his left thigh.

One of the Militars pushed Leme back, eyed him, noted him, it felt, and threw a blanket across the man's body.

He looked at Leme again. 'Nasty crash,' he said.

Leme nodded slowly and backed away. He wasn't supposed to be there.

The driver wasn't killed in the collision, he was sure of that.

There was a dark nucleus at the centre of each bloodstain. Whatever the Militar wanted him to believe, he'd investigated enough murders to know gunshot wounds when he saw them.

Mid-morning. Leme sat at his desk, distracted. He didn't want to have to answer any questions as to why he'd been in the *favela*, why he'd left the moment the body was recovered. He could explain it as a shortcut on his way to work if need be, but he didn't know if anyone had seen him sitting stationary in his car in the half-hour or so before the incident. Or any other morning, in fact. News of the young man's death would come through soon enough. He'd have to think about how he'd play that.

He struggled to put it out of his mind. He didn't have a capacity for distraction when something bothered him. '*Batendo na mesma tecla*,' Renata always said. 'The same question again and again and again.' He envied those friends of his who could compartmentalise, let the hours tick by immersed in work without the angst.

He logged into the secure archive and clicked the link to the case he was working on: The Gabriel Murder. Time to look over the transcripts of his interviews with the two suspects he had brought in. Two lowlifes. Real pieces of work. Not a great deal of contrition – they'd shrugged, smiled even: what were we supposed to do? they seemed to be saying.

The story was: robbery gone wrong. Familiar enough. The victim was Sergio Moreira, a man in his late fifties who lived alone in a smart, low-rise house on Rua Gabriel Monteiro. No security, no alarms – it was a smart neighbourhood with little history of crime. It wasn't late at night and the house had appeared empty, according to the statements from the accused. They'd broken in through a side door and were stripping the place of valuables when Moreira had surprised them in the living room. They struck him over the head with a heavy table lamp and he died later that night in hospital. The suspects called the ambulance themselves, *after* they had fled. They claimed self-defence – Moreira was, they said, carrying a baseball bat. The guy was almost seventy. It was his house.

Fucking self-defence –

It hadn't been too hard to pick them up. There were fingerprints all over the place and the two had a history of robbery. Leme brought them in and they confessed. Straightforward. Not something a detective of his experience needed to agonise over, perhaps. But he lingered.

Where the fuck was Lisboa?

They'd been partners for fifteen years and school friends before that. They joined up and were promoted together. Lisboa's father had been a detective in the Polícia Civil, and it was his influence that led to their recruitment. 'It's a worthy and rewarding profession,' he always told them as they were growing up. 'You use your head, you think, but you're out and about, *doing*. Not many careers offer that combination. Solving other people's problems is a fine way to live.' Both Leme and Lisboa were sold. Neither had designs to go to college and neither of them wanted to spend their days behind a desk. And the Polícia Civil didn't have the danger of the Military Police. They wouldn't be fighting battles with *traficantes* in the *favela* and they wouldn't be spat at in the street. They'd worked hard and had built up a reputation as both competent and fair. What they had discovered, though, after their last promotion, was that competence and fairness meant there was a ceiling on how far you could rise.

It was this realisation that left Lisboa disillusioned. He had a family now, two children, and the job had been shunted into second place. Leme tried to understand. And while Lisboa was content to simply *do*, Leme had begun to find that he was spending more and more time with his own thoughts.

After Renata's death, Lisboa had looked after Leme. In the first paralysing weeks, he saw him every day, slept over at Leme's flat, neglected his family to take care of his friend. Perhaps now he was simply making amends at home? Leme knew he was being selfish, but it had only been in the last few months that he had settled back into the job, and it was through hard work that he was starting to feel like he could function again. He wished Lisboa had the same attitude.

He studied the transcripts. Procedure was that once up in the secure system, the audio recordings were archived and took time to get hold of, so Leme had no choice but to read the transcript instead. His head ached, his eyes were tired; he shook from caffeine and lack of sleep. The problem with reading rather than listening was gauging tone. He'd mentioned this before to Superintendent Lagnado but he'd been waved away. 'Nothing I can do,' Lagnado had said, which

was pretty much his stock response to any query. Blindly following directives from Magalhães, the Delegado Geral, was one way of
securing your position. And salary. And, most importantly, benefits.

Despite his hangover, there was a line that jumped out every time
Leme read it.

We'd been told he was there. I mean, wasn't there, entendeu? *You
know, rumours. Easy mark, we heard. Yeah, it was a surprise,* sabe?
Faz o que, ne?

This bothered Leme. He remembered the way the guy had glanced
at the door, as if needing corroboration. That perhaps it hadn't,
in fact, been a surprise. There was no way of proving this; it was
intuition.

He leant back in his chair, scratched at his chin. If he didn't
act now, it would be too late. Confessions were in – he had to tell
Lagnado what he was thinking before the case was signed off and
passed on to the legal departments.

Leme left his office, crossed the open plan space, ignoring the
greetings of a couple of colleagues, and took the lift up to Lagnado's
floor. He had long ago realised that there was never any point in
ringing first to check his availability – according to Lagnado's secretary, he was never available.

He walked past her, knocked on Lagnado's door and went straight
in.

Lagnado was sitting behind his vast, oak desk, examining his
reflection in a small mirror, picking at a piece of tissue on his chin.
He didn't bother to see who it was.

'Shaving accident?' Leme asked.

Lagnado grunted – hostile. 'Fucking thing won't stop bleeding.'

'Don't pick at it, *querido.*'

Lagnado looked up. 'Oh, it's you. Thanks for the advice. Rich
though, *ne?*' He paused. Smiled – snide. 'You look like shit, Leme.
Your skin's the same colour as your fucking hair.'

Leme said nothing but thought this a bit unfair. He was only
greying at the sides. Lagnado was dressed in his usual dark-blue
three-piece suit. Wiry black hair cut short. Eyebrows low and thick.
Aftershave stink.

'Fuck do you want anyway?' Lagnado said. 'I told Moira I was busy.'

'I never asked.'

'I'm sure you didn't. Let's make this quick.'

Leme didn't sit down. Lagnado wasn't going to invite him to, and he decided he might have antagonised him enough.

'Those confessions,' Leme said, 'for the Gabriel murder. Something I'm not sure about. I want to talk to them again.'

Lagnado breathed out heavily. 'Really?'

'Yes. Not sure I trust what they've said.'

'Well, they're criminals. That's the whole point.'

'So you'll let me?'

'No, I won't. It's done. *Acabou.*'

'What do you mean?'

Lagnado grimaced, then smiled. He was a squat, square-shaped man, and his upper body strained against the suit so that it seemed he was always slightly uncomfortable, as if suffering from backache. It always looked to Leme like it was difficult for him to move.

'Exactly that,' he said. 'It's done. You're off it. Been passed on. We've got the confessions. *Então. Chega.*'

'But I think they knew he'd be there.'

'Think what you like. It's done.'

Leme took this in. 'Since when?'

'This morning.'

'So that's it?'

'Yep. Nothing I can do.'

'What does that mean?'

'None of your fucking business.' He stood awkwardly.

Leme sighed.

'Talk to Alvarenga when you can about that dentist robbery in Alta do Pinheiros. It's murder now. Both of them died of the burn wounds. He's going to need some help, OK? You and Lisboa can be it.'

Leme nodded. This was a nasty case. The dentists tied up and all their equipment and drugs stolen and the room torched. It was the second time it had happened in a month. Dentists both times. Why dentists?

'I'll talk to him,' Leme said. 'Soon as I can.'

'Oh, one other thing,' Lagnado said. 'You live near Paraisópolis, *ne?*'

'You know I do.'

'Rich kid called Leonardo Alencar died in a car crash there this morning.'

Leme tensed. Fuck. He picked at his lip. Did Lagnado know he was there? So it *was* a rich kid. Car accident, Leme thought. Right. How much might Lagnado know?

Leme said nothing.

'Best you keep out,' Lagnado said. He leaned forward. 'For your own good, actually. I hear you were there this morning. We all know why you have this … fascination with the *favela*. It's not healthy. Leave it, *certo?*'

Leme nodded. 'You say it was an accident?' he said. 'Nothing suspicious?'

Lagnado waved his arms in exasperation. 'Drunk kid in a crash. *Nada, entendeu?*'

The room was cool, spacious, wood-lined, in complete contrast to his own cupboard on the lower floor. Lagnado was a stooge, always had been.

And this is what it got him.

'*Certo*, Sr Superintendente,' he said. '*Valeu*, eh?'

'It is what it is, *porra*. Nothing I can do.'

But there was a violence contained in that Neanderthal body and Leme knew better than to push it too far.

He turned to go.

'Don't be a cunt,' Lagnado muttered as he left.

Back in his office, Leme logged into the archive but couldn't access the transcripts this time. He tried again. Nothing. Denied. Odd, he thought. Clicked again. Still nothing. Maybe there's a system error. He rang the IT department and spoke to a technician. No error, apparently, the level of classification changed, that was all. You know how it is. Leme didn't.

He hiked up the stairs to the central archive and rapped on the desk. A harassed-looking man came from out of the back office.

'I need the transcripts and tapes for the Gabriel murder,' Leme said.

The archive guy whistled. 'No can do. Sorry.'

'Eh?'

'Restricted.'

'Since when?'

'About ten minutes.'

Leme said again. 'I need the transcripts and tapes. Do your fucking job.'

The guy said nothing and looked down at his desk. 'I don't make the rules,' he said.

Leme nodded. 'You want to do me a favour? Who *can* access them?'

The guy smiled. He looked up at the ceiling and made a face. 'Who do you think?'

Leme raised his eyebrows in thanks. '*Valeu.*'

He took the lift back to his own floor. It had happened quickly. Almost as if Lagnado was expecting him. Like he was prepared. Could be nothing, the suspects had confessed after all, but as the lead detective, he should have been able to get to the transcripts. It didn't make sense. But that wasn't what he was thinking about: he was wondering why this rich kid Leonardo Alencar was in the *favela*. And why no one seemed to be mentioning the fact that he'd been shot.

Lisboa showed up around lunchtime. 'You ready?' he asked Leme.

'Fuck have you been?'

'You know.'

'No, I don't. Ready for what?'

'Lunch, *porra.*'

Leme laughed. 'That why you come to work now, is it? Lunch?'

Lisboa sat heavily on his chair. He'd put on weight and was irritable. His wife was making him diet, exercise. He was a man of appetites, liked to live well, enjoy himself. He liked to laugh, was always sociable. One of those people who innately understood that if something was beyond his control then there was no point worrying about it. Having children was testing that philosophy. And physically it was showing. He'd never been vain and had always been perversely proud of his softening belly. And he dressed and moved elegantly, so it didn't seem to matter. Not today. Today he looked like he'd been drinking too much on an overnight flight. Crumpled and exhausted, like the suit that slipped off him as he sat down.

'Don't fucking start, *certo?*' he said. 'Been a tough night. I've slept about two hours. Teething and fucking night terror.'

'Aren't you a bit old for that?'

Lisboa ignored him.

He eyed Leme for a moment. Leme knew that he was aware they'd reached the limit of their potential in the department and while it didn't bother him so much any more in a professional sense now he had a family, he needed the money to support them. Not that he ever said anything. And Leme understood that.

Probably best he didn't mention what had happened in the *favela*.

Leme didn't feel like having an argument. He'd stop by at the *lanchonete* on the edge of Paraisópolis on his way home, have a word with a guy he knew who worked there.

He'd tell Lisboa when he needed to.

Leme sat up at the counter. It was one of those twenty-four-hour places. Clientele changed as the hours passed. Early morning was workers drinking bitter coffee, eating eggs fried in a deep pan of oil and slopped into a grilled French stick; rich kids stopping off on the way home after a late night, the proximity to the *favela* giving a little transgressive buzz.

Early evenings were different. Families having dinner, groups of kids with tennis racquets, flushed from training at the club next door, the odd couple – though it was too early and too basic a place for a date – a few men on their own, crumpled shirts and loosened ties. Leme fitted in at least.

He ordered a *chopp*, which came in a pleasingly large, frosted glass. The beer here was good; it was why the place was so popular at either end of a night out. He looked at the menu, but nothing grabbed him. He looked around. Mountains of fries dusted in salt. Hot dogs spilling extras: cheese, eggs, bacon, ham, sweetcorn, onions, *batata palha*. His stomach tightened.

He called out to the guy serving behind the counter.

'*Mini-pastel*,' he said. 'Cheese.'

The guy nodded. Jotted it down on his pad, turned, ripped off the ticket and stuck it on a board by the grill.

'*Oi, vem ca.*' Leme waved him over again. 'Sr Luis working today?' he asked.

The guy nodded again.

'Call him for me?'

'*Certo.* Be a while though.' He indicated the tickets lined up on the board. 'Busy, *entendeu?*'

Leme nodded. '*Tudo bem,*' he said.

Luis was once the chef in Leme's condominium's restaurant. Leme had got to know him pretty well – what happens when you spend evenings and weekends sitting around eating and drinking with other men in one place. Luis lived in Paraisópolis. He didn't mind talking about it when he worked in Leme's condominium, but he'd become more reluctant now he was outside its gates, and they weren't exactly in private. He wasn't an informant – never had been – he just seemed to know people, hear things. He was friendly, but guarded, trustworthy in his manner and reliable in his job. People confided in him, including Leme every now and again.

Leme figured he might have heard something about what had happened that morning; there had to be some gossip. Leme knew what he had heard, and then seen.

His *pastel* arrived. He tore one in half and dripped hot sauce into the cheese that oozed from it. The crunch and grease went well with the beer. He ate two of the portion of six. Signalled to the counter attendant.

'*Pra viagem*,' he said, drawing a circle with his finger above and around the remaining four.

The guy raised his eyebrows and brought over a foil container and a plastic bag. Leme would put them in the fridge, and in a week or so, his maid would throw them out.

'Luis about ready yet?' Leme asked.

'I'll look.'

Leme nodded his thanks, sipped at his beer. The top part of the glass was so cold there was almost no taste.

Luis came out and leaned on the counter. 'Sr Mario,' he said to Leme. '*Como vai?*'

Leme smiled. 'Ah, *ta rolando, ne?* Can't complain, *entendeu?*'

'*Mais ou menos, ne?*' Luis smiled. '*Então, fala.* Got to get back to work, *sabe?*'

'Accident from earlier. Know anything about that?'

'Which one?'

Leme frowned. 'Eh?'

'There've been two recently. Car crash this morning, and a building collapsed few days ago. Which one do you mean?'

Leme paused. 'What building?'

'One of those old Singapore Project blocks down towards Real Parque. Bottom end of the *favela*. There was a partial collapse. Six died. Two children.'

'Right,' Leme said. '*Então?*'

'Bit of a stand off. Residents say the building was unsafe, that the security guards refused to let them get anyone in to examine the foundations or whatever. Militars turned up, apparently. Threatened them.'

'Why?'

'Fuck knows. Anyway, company's set to fix it up. They blamed the residents, undue pressure or something. I don't know.'

'Right.'

Luis looked at the clock behind him. 'We done?'

'Not quite.'

'Actually, it's the sort of thing …' Luis started and then paused.

'Yes?'

'Well. It's the sort of thing Dona Renata might have been involved in.'

Leme gave a tight smile. Made an appreciative face.

'They need some help,' Luis said. 'There's no one to look out for them. They're helpless; situation's hopeless. You should go down there. Take a look. My cousins live in the building.'

'They OK?'

'Yeah, you know. Safe. Bit fucked though. Nowhere to live now.'

Leme nodded. 'Probably not much I can do,' he said.

He watched Luis's expression change. He did owe him a favour, he realised that. And he didn't have much on. And Luis was right: it was exactly Renata's sort of thing. He raised his finger.

'I'll pop down there tomorrow,' he said. 'See if I can find anything out. Let you know.'

'Appreciate it. And if you're looking into the car crash, you'd probably end up there anyway.'

'What do you mean?' Leme asked.

Luis looked left and right and smiled. 'There's not much to know,' he said. 'The driver was some rich kid. But people are saying he came from the same site as the building that collapsed. He hung out there whenever he came to the *favela*. That SUV he crashed took off from the road just outside. Someone told me they'd seen him there before too – kid stuck out, drew attention.'

Leme had known of *traficantes* using abandoned or derelict sites to do drug deals before. That'd explain a lot, if that was why this playboy was in Paraisópolis.

OK, he thought, he would definitely go down to the site tomorrow. Well worth having a look.

'What do *you* think? He was buying?' Leme asked.

'I don't know, *cara*. Could be.'

Leme nodded. He wasn't going to get any more. He could come back.

'Cheers,' Leme said. He stood. They slapped hands. '*Vai com Deus, ne?*'

Luis grunted and went back into the kitchen, whistling.

Later, Leme sat on the balcony blowing smoke rings at the wooden-slatted ceiling above. He could hear children, smell onions frying: this was a family apartment block. '*Vem ca, filho,*' a woman called out.

He couldn't avoid it if he wanted to. And he couldn't move out. That was one thing Lisboa hadn't yet insisted on, Leme thought. He knew the idea alone would send Leme back months. There was something unbearable about parting with the things he and Renata had bought together, even when seeing them reminded him of arguments. 'Building a life together is about accepting the objects, the books, the furniture your partner brings with her,' Renata once said. 'It's not about feeling different or inadequate because they're not yours. Because you would never have thought to get them. They're all ours now, anyway.' Now they were all his.

He folded the cigarette in half and ash spilled. A dirtied white cloth covered the table. He tried to brush the ash off but only smudged it. He felt familiar guilt about his maid. He drained his whiskey and went inside for a refill. He looked down at his creased white shirt, yellow at the cuffs.

He went back outside. The children upstairs were still running around and the smell of food had thickened. He looked at his watch. *Porra.* He should eat something; the smell was making him salivate. The cheese *pastel* had congealed, cheap, *padaria*-hard. There was the food his maid had left him and he had eaten that for the last three days. He could order. It was too late to go downstairs to the restaurant, and besides, he didn't want to see any of his friends. By this time they'd be halfway drunk and shouting. Women walking past, shaking their heads at the vulgar jokes, the idiotic, half-arsed commentary on politics. On another night this was exactly what he might need, but not now. Christ, he thought, he was being ungrateful. My maid's food not good enough. I'm getting spoilt.

He went into the kitchen and pulled a can of tuna from a cupboard and skewered it with the rusty opener. He opened the fridge and took out a saucepan of congealing beans. Standing by the sink, he forked tuna and then beans into his mouth. He managed half a dozen mouthfuls before he spat hard, viscous beans back into the pan. He took the can and the saucepan to the bin and dropped them both into it.

He went back outside.

As he lit another cigarette, his phone sprang to life, buzzing across the table, light throbbing in time with the ringtone he couldn't seem to change. He let it ring for a moment, didn't look at the caller ID.

One thing that had never quite been extinguished was the tiny hope he had inside that when the phone rang it might be her.

It was Lisboa.

'*Fala*,' Leme said. He breathed smoke through his nose.

'*E aí meu.*' Lisboa's tone was upbeat, the afternoon's tension forgotten.

Lisboa barked something away from the phone. 'Hey, stop that! Leave your sister alone. Sorry, not you.'

Leme held the phone out in front of him and heard his friend shouting at his wife to keep the kids out of the living room. He was having an important conversation. Work. Leme could hear distant female cursing. He thought of an old joke: a man tells his wife he has invited a friend for dinner that evening. The wife is dismayed: such short notice! The house is a mess, I look awful and the kids are all over-excited. It'll be horrible for him. I thought he was your friend. Exactly, the husband says, he's thinking of getting married.

It'd been funny once, when he could adopt that put-upon persona of the stoic husband, the half-smile false, pretending he wasn't happy, when he was.

'So, tomorrow. What's the plan?' Lisboa asked.

Leme thought about it. 'Pick me up in the morning. Something for us to do.'

'What does that mean?'

'Favour for a mate.'

'*Ah é?* Who?'

'Guy I know. Used to work in my building.'

Lisboa grunted. Leme flicked ash on the floor. He wasn't going to tell Lisboa yet of his suspicions about Leonardo Alencar's death. There'd be time for that, once he'd found out a bit more.

'We're going to look at a collapsed tower block. In the *favela*.'

'Why?'

Leme sighed. 'Residents are having some problems. We're just going to pop by.'

Lisboa seemed happy with that. Eventually, he spoke. 'That fucker Lagnado isn't going to let us anywhere near anything interesting.' He paused. 'Mario? You still there?'

Leme smiled. 'I'm still here.'

'You don't sound convinced.'

Leme sensed Lisboa's physical bulk, at the end of the phone, straining to contain itself. He took a slug of whiskey and wiped his mouth.

'Well? Mario?'

'You're right,' he said. 'Though he wants us to help with the dentist thing now. You know, assistance. That's something.'

Lisboa snorted.

The fact is that Leme wasn't even sure they *were* being shunted aside. One day they're working a murder case; the next they're taken off it. In São Paulo, it was easier to investigate the wrong people than you'd think.

'Look,' Lisboa's voice softened, 'I'll be around more next week, I promise. It's just, you know, with the kids. It's been … difficult.'

'Don't worry about it. It's under control.'

'It's just … I know I'd appreciate your help if it were me.'

This, Leme recognised, was a compliment. *Então*.

Leme fiddled with the ashtray in front of him. He heard shouts floating up from the street. Young men going through their rituals: a steady beat from a car stereo, beeping horns, greeting newcomers; Renata had complained about it over the years. Now, Leme liked the feeling of movement it brought to the neighbourhood, even if admitting that felt like a small betrayal. He looked through the window at the pile of books she had separated for him to read. They were in the same order as on the morning she had left them. He pushed ash around the table with his finger, bent down and did the same on the floor.

'I –'

'Stay away from the *favela*, *certo*?' Lisboa said, suddenly. 'On your own, I mean. I know why you go there. Other people aren't so understanding. It's not healthy.'

Healthy: that word again.

Leme looked out across the balcony.

Clouds dipped between the tall buildings, lights from family apartments glowing like embers.

Electricity buzzed overhead, soft in the gloom.

'Just don't go back into Paraisópolis without me,' Lisboa said. 'I'll pick you up in the morning.'

Leme said nothing. There'd still be time to go in, if he wanted. It wasn't really a question of desire: he felt he *had* to go each day. As if by not going he was admitting that he would never find out what really happened to Renata.

The graffiti spelled it out: *São Paulo is run by cunts*. Two cleaners were scouring the wall, but making little headway. Leme smiled and crossed the road outside his building. He gave Lisboa an ironic salute. This morning, he felt lighter on his feet than usual.

Lisboa handed Leme a takeout coffee as he got into the car and Leme looked at it like it was some foreign object.

He turned it in his hands and examined it: a green logo on white. '*Que isso?*' he said.

Lisboa grunted something and pulled off on to Giovanni Gronchi, towards the *favela*.

'I mean,' Leme went on, 'this is what we drink now?'

Lisboa sighed, shoulders slumped. '*Porra*, Mario. It's too early. *Para de encher, eh?*'

Leme raised his eyebrows. 'Just making small talk.'

'Not like you.'

Leme grinned, thought that was probably right. There were mornings, moments really, of humour. *Alegría*, almost. A friend had once told him that the sadder he felt about something, the funnier he got. It didn't resonate with Leme, then. Now though, sometimes, a great shiver of pleasure zipped through him, like a reminder he was alive. He'd shake it off. Remember who he'd lost. What he'd lost.

There was plenty to distract him at the moment. Last night, after he spoke to Lisboa, he'd sat there thinking about the Gabriel murder again, and wound up calling his old friend Silva. Silva was a journalist. Leme had a rule that the one place he could never snoop was his own department. In situations where he needed a lead on what was going on inside the police, he'd sometimes bring Silva in to help. He was a resourceful fucker, Silva, enjoyed the challenge. Especially if it involved screwing over someone in authority.

'Tell me about this building,' Lisboa said.

'Part of a building on the edge of the *favela* collapsed few days ago,' Leme said. 'Six deaths. Two children.' Leme had done a bit of research online. 'Construction company is called Casa Nova,' he said. 'They blamed it on the *favelados* who'd moved across from the slum into the building. And then Casa Nova won the contract to fix it up. Nice one, *ne?* But the residents are blaming security.'

'No one'll back the *favelados*,' Lisboa said. 'This is a waste of time.'

But he didn't change his route or suggest anything different.

Lisboa rapped his fingers on the steering wheel. Leme stared into the glare of traffic at the top end of the *favela*, a snaking line of polished black and silver reflecting the sun. It was a shortcut to avoid the endless, shuffling queue on the main road Giovanni Gronchi – the most direct and busiest route to the centre – but the potholes slowed everyone down. That and the buses doing three-point turns in a space boxed in by *carrossos* laden with rubbish, boys rolling tyres down the hill, men unloading wooden cases of fruit and beer from rusty, double-parked vans. Beeping and shouting as more people joined the queue, with little regard to what was road and what was pavement. School children meandered right in the middle, slapping the bonnets of the better cars and waving into the darkened windows. Slum-safari, Leme thought. They do that in Rio, the cunts. This wasn't deep into Paraisópolis, but for some drivers, behind their bulletproof glass, it was intimidating enough.

And Leme felt intimidated.

This was Militar territory, *traficantes*.

Leme hadn't been there this morning. It didn't feel right, his routine altered. He felt slightly adrift, like an anchor in his day had been uprooted, was dragging along in the sand, and he was puzzled by how it had happened.

'They still going to stick a fucking great highway through this?'

Leme only half heard the question. They had shunted forward a dozen metres and were close now to where he sat each morning. Close to the accident. Close to both the accidents.

'What? Highway?'

'*Meu*, keep up.' Lisboa leaned out of his window. Waved his arm at a hapless man in vest and shorts who had spilled a carton of pineapples into the road and was gingerly trying to gather them up. '*Embora, cara!*' he shouted and edged up on to the kerb to pass.

They sat in silence for a few moments.

'Shouldn't do that,' Leme said.

'Why the fuck not?' Lisboa shook a cigarette free from the soft pack in his shirt pocket. Then shook his head. '*Puta*, Mario,' he said. He sucked his teeth as if there was no real way to end the sentiment.

'The Military operation's still going on here,' Leme said. 'No one wants to see police.'

Lisboa exhaled a cloud of smoke. He shrugged. '*Chega, ne?* You ever get tired of being right?'

Leme had friends in the Military Police who were involved in Operação Saturação and they had warned him to be careful in Paraisópolis. It was turning into a war. A hundred and forty deaths in six weeks over October and November. A mixture of Militars and *traficantes* and the odd innocent caught in the crossfire by a *bala perdida*. The idea was simple enough: saturate the place with cops with guns and clean out the dealers. It wouldn't last. The PCC gang – The First Capital Command – who controlled Paraisópolis wouldn't let it go on for too long and there would be an uneasy peace. Leme didn't envy the Military lot. In the Polícia Civil you were protected a little at least. Leme had only ever fired warning shots. If there was a serious problem, they sent in machine guns, not detectives in shirtsleeves.

But it was early morning and the Military presence was light.

At the bottom of the road where the bus queue was heaviest, Lisboa lurched right, seemed to aim the car with his own bulk down a slight hill and then he leaned back, accelerating up a much steeper one. They crawled up as the street narrowed around them. Washing sagged low in the breeze. Yellow and blue bags of rubbish sweating. The low hum of hijacked electricity. Kids poking their heads through glassless windows, tongues sticking out.

'*Filho da puta.*'

Leme turned to look where Lisboa pointed. A skinny man in rags lay curled up around two dogs as a group of boys jabbed him with a stick. He wasn't going anywhere. They could smell the Pinga from the car.

Leme shrugged. 'Dogs don't seem to mind.'

Lisboa laughed. 'Licking the sweat off him probably got them drunk.'

The boys were poking at the drunk's backside now, and recoiling with exaggerated holding of their noses. The drunk's trousers were slack, but heavy with something unpleasant. Leme watched, unmoved. He thought about the lowest moments, his own messy attempts at oblivion.

'Thing is,' he said, 'to get into that kind of state takes real will, *entendeu*, ambition.'

'Right. OK.'

'To live for nothing other than drink is a goal beyond most people,' he said. 'You need purpose, dedication, *sabe*, single-mindedness.' He looked at Lisboa. 'I never managed it.'

Lisboa smiled now. 'Work-shy, that's all,' he said.

Leme moved his gaze from the old drunk, who was scratching now, hands on his legs, to the dogs, the kids scattering, and let himself smile.

They reached the top of the hill and Lisboa stopped the car. He leaned forward, knocked on the windscreen. 'This must be the paradise part of Paraisópolis,' he said. 'Not a bad view, *ne?*'

They looked across the crater. Tall condominium towers flanked it on all sides. Leme wondered how the fuck they were going to build a main road through *this*. To the right the *favela* leaked down towards the river, a spreading brown stain. Beyond, a forest of buildings, light escaping through the gaps between them, rose up to Avenida Paulista in the centre of the city. When you're in it, Leme thought, it's just another place to live, the *favela*. You get used to it. That was what Renata had always said. It's no more or less real than anywhere else. Leme had never really believed this before. Sitting at the top of it, if he squinted it was like a vast field of maize.

'Ants,' he said.

'What? Fuck you on about?'

'We're all just ants, you know, when you think about it.'

Lisboa started the car. Shook his head. '*Porra*, Mario.'

'Perspective, that's all.'

The car came over the edge of the hill, skidding on the loose gravel, and arrowed down towards the collapsed building, which, from up there, looked to Leme like a sandcastle that had been kicked over by a bullying child.

The building was right at the edge of the *favela* and formed something like a barrier between it and the posh apartment blocks in Real Parque. Not a coincidence, Leme thought.

There was a lot of dust. Daubs of paint. Tape circled the collapsed building. A security guard dozed on a plastic chair in front of it.

As it was a *favela* project, there was no other security so they walked over to the guard. Lisboa kicked his foot and he snorted and grunted. He started and looked puzzled for a moment, smacked his lips thick with sleep, scratched a thatch of belly hair, and smiled, as if, in the great scheme of things, his confusion really didn't matter.

'Who are you?' he asked.

Lisboa forced a smile and showed him his badge.

'Oh, right.' The guard rubbed his eyes. 'Fuck.'

He patted the pockets of his suit, which hung off him despite his bulk. It was shiny and worn thin. Nasty shade of blue, Leme thought.

'You got a cigarette?' the guard asked.

Lisboa gave him one.

'Thanks.'

He smoked. Coughed and hacked. Spat a hunk on the floor. It was brown, muscular. Like it should still be on the inside. Leme raised his eyebrows.

'Sorry,' the guard said. '*Fazer o que, ne?*'

Lisboa forced another smile and nodded at the rubble. 'We need to ask some questions about the collapse,' he said.

'Nasty business.'

'Right.'

'What do you want to know? Not sure I can help much.'

The guard stretched. Leme looked up at the building. The walls were yellowing. Paint peeled from the frames in the windows. A plane crawled between the towers, disappeared for moment, then escaped the cover.

He looked puzzled again. 'Aren't you two detectives?'

Lisboa nodded. 'Why?'

The guard shrugged. 'No reason.' He paused and seemed to choose his words more carefully. 'Well, this is just an accident, *entendeu?*'

Lisboa glared at him. Leme noticed, but said nothing. The guard had it right though. They shouldn't be there. He wasn't to know though that this was all at Leme's instigation. Lisboa looked impatient.

'Why don't you just tell us what you know?' Lisboa suggested.

The guard shrugged. 'This is one of those Singapore Project buildings, right? Well, you know what that means, don't you?'

'You tell us, *porra*.'

'Well, put it this way, it's hardly a surprise it fucking fell down.'

'Oh yeah?' Lisboa, Leme noticed, was feigning indifference. An old trick of his.

'The materials are fucking awful.'

'And why's that?'

The guard laughed. 'Come on, everybody knows.'

Lisboa opened his arms. The guard continued. 'The contractors get state materials to build them, right? Well, they keep them for their own private, luxury developments and then buy the cheapest shit they can find for these buildings. That's why they look so fucking terrible, so ... cheap.' The guard spat again. Nodded at the buildings behind him. 'There was one I heard about where the concrete pillars supporting the fucking thing were hollow. They needed breezeblocks and it was more like fucking cardboard. I reckon that's what happened here.'

'Why?'

He looked around now, wary. 'No one gives a fuck, right? These are *favelados* we're talking about. The fuckers don't know how to live in these buildings. Goats in some apartments. Rubbish just chucked straight out the window.' He turned to look at the rubble behind him. Muttered, 'Good fucking riddance.'

Lisboa's look hardened. 'How long have you worked here?'

'Since the build started.' He raised his eyebrows. 'I'm a fucking expert, *cara*.'

They both knew about the Singapore Project. The principle of the thing seemed sound: tower blocks go up and the residents shift across and the slums are torn down. Better quality of life. Right. More significantly though, the city looks better to the middle-class voters who drive past the sites every day. 'It's an illusion of progress,' Renata had told him. 'Of safety. A right-wing political ploy to capture the upwardly mobile.' Leme knew what it was, but would never have articulated it in those terms. 'I don't want to be with one of those *men* who *teaches* me things,' she'd said, early in their relationship. 'It's so tiresome, being shepherded from car to restaurant to car again, *certo?* I think I'll be teaching you.' He smiled now at the memory.

'What about this business with the residents?' Leme asked. 'I hear they're being bullied.'

'Ah,' the guard said. 'They're just complaining as we won't let them back in until it's fixed up, *sabe?* What can we do?'

'And now they've got nowhere to go.'

'Not our problem. It's hardly fucking safe, is it?'

Leme nodded. 'Guess so,' he said.

He wasn't sure they'd achieve much more here without a warrant, and he'd need to figure out a few things before he tried to get one. He thought about Leonardo Alencar.

Lisboa looked twitchy.

'You work here nights?' Leme asked. 'Early mornings?'

'Depends,' the guard said.

'What about yesterday?'

The guard eyed him carefully. 'No,' he said, shaking his head.

'You hear of anyone ever coming here?'

'What do you mean?'

'Don't be naïve. *Traficantes*, you know, clients?'

The guard gave Leme a knowing smile. 'Nothing like that, *cara, sabe?* Not that I know about. Besides,' and he gave a little vicious smile again, 'Militars sorted it, apparently.'

Leme nodded. Militars.

They weren't far behind Leonardo when he drove past Leme.

And they had their weapons out, he was sure of that.

And a lot of them were dishonest as fuck.

But no one knew they were at the site this morning, so it was best not to raise any suspicions just yet.

He'd come back if he had to.

A movement caught Leme's eye and he turned. He nudged Lisboa.

Lisboa whistled. '*Puta que pariu*,' he said.

It was the drunk they had seen earlier that morning. He was staggering towards them.

'*Caralho*,' the guard said, standing. 'Him again?'

The drunk was waving at them and shouting, slurring really.

'What's he saying?' Lisboa asked the guard.

'Fuck knows. He's here most days. Always shouting about something. I ignore him. Chuck him out.'

Leme gestured to Lisboa. The drunk was waving at the building, at the rubble. His voice was a loose growl. He repeated the same word.

Leme turned to Lisboa. '*Podemos?* That what he's saying?'

Lisboa shrugged. Cocked an ear. 'Could be.'

They watched as the drunk careened towards them, windmilled his arms, collapsed in a heap.

Laughing. Growling.

'*Podemos*,' he said, again.

He giggled. He writhed around as if he couldn't control how funny he found the whole idea. He pointed at the two detectives and stopped laughing.

He shouted at them, eyes flashing. Shouted:

'*Podemos!*'

They drove in silence to the *delegacia*.

Leme sat at his desk. Scratched a groove on the desk with a bent paper clip. Lisboa had gone to pick up his kids. There was no need for him to stay and Leme wasn't going to complain. He wondered about this rumour that Leonardo had come from the building. Casa Nova. Never heard of it. He had a thought.

Any applications for building or construction work had to be notarised and filed at the public registry offices downtown with the company details provided to the public. It was a political move to give transparency and allay any fears of corruption or nepotism. Leme knew this as he had been on his condominium's planning committee when they decided to build an extension – a gym and squash courts – a few years before. He picked up the phone.

The switchboard connected him to the appropriate department. He ran the paper clip under his nails, picked out a thorn of dirt with it, flicked it on to the desk.

'*Pois não?*'

'Detective Leme from the Civil Police here,' he said. 'I need some information about a building project in Paraisópolis.'

'OK. Go on.'

'Company is called Casa Nova,' Leme said. 'Repair job. A building collapsed a couple of weeks ago.'

'What's the address?'

Leme gave it.

'Yeah, that's right,' the man said. 'Casa Nova. Application is pending. Some sort of administrative hold-up.'

'What's the expected confirmation date?'

'Couple weeks, I think.'

'What about Casa Nova? It an independent company?' Leme asked.

'Hang on.'

Leme was put on hold. An instrumental version of 'Chega de Saudade' played lightly in his ear. Interesting choice, he thought. He waited. The song ended abruptly.

'Casa Nova?' the guy asked.

'Yeah.'

'It's been around a while. Was one of the Singapore Project contractors. It's registered as part of a bigger umbrella company called Mendes Construction. That help?'

'What about Podemos? That mean anything to you?'

'Podemos? Hang on.'

More music. Leme leant back in his chair. He rubbed at his stubble. In the past it was these word association games that had led him down garden paths, wasted his time. Well, he thought, wasting his time is what he was being told to do.

'No record of Podemos,' the guy said. 'Sure you have the right name?'

'Think so, yes,' Leme said. He paused and made a decision. 'Thanks anyway,' he said, and hung up.

He moved the mouse on his desk and his computer screen lit up. He googled Mendes Construction. It looked a slick business, the site peppered with phrases like 'Global Reach' and 'Boutique Quality', 'Sustainable Resources' and 'Eco-Initiatives'.

The big project seemed to be one in the *centro*, a huge development in time for the World Cup. Leme called Lisboa.

'Pick me up in the morning,' he told him. 'We're going to have a look at another building site.'

'Sure,' Lisboa said, '*você que sabe.*'

Leme was grateful for once for Lisboa's unquestioning acceptance. He didn't really want to explain what he hoped to get out of this visit, but before getting involved, however indirectly, in a nasty little situation like this – the residents fucked over, the company made richer – he wanted to know a bit more about who was in charge. Silva might be able to help him, he realised.

He picked up the phone.

'*Quem fala?*' Silva said.

'You know who it fucking is,' Leme replied. 'You found anything out about my sidelining and the Gabriel murder yet?'

'Oh fuck off,' Silva said, which, Leme knew, was entirely in character, though not especially helpful.

He was the sort of investigative journalist who liked to show the police that he was the better detective. And it meant he was struggling a bit, which, Leme knew, meant he'd redouble his efforts. Silva didn't like being told he was incompetent, that there was anything beyond him, any elitist safe he couldn't crack.

'You think you can do any better, do it your fucking self,' Silva said.

'*Puta que pariu*,' Leme muttered. 'You know full well that the one place I can't do any investigating is in my own department. Do me the fucking favour, *caralho*.'

Silva laughed. '*Calma, bicho*,' he said. 'I'll call you when I know something.'

Tricky cunt, Leme mouthed into the phone.

'Wait,' Leme said, before Silva hung up. 'You know anything about Jorge Mendes? Owner and CEO of Mendes Construction.'

'I know who he is,' Silva said. 'He joined the state government years ago. Secretario de Obras. Ran the whole property bit in the whole fucking state. Some reward. When they dished out the rest of the contracts for the Singapore Project, he set up some kind of kickback scheme for the bids. Lot of offshore money, I hear.'

'How do you hear that?'

'I know a guy. Good with computers.'

This was Silva's stock answer, Leme knew. It didn't exactly fill him with confidence though, in a legal context.

'What's he like?' Leme asked.

'Guy's a fucking animal,' Silva said. 'Classic Paulistano politician. After he left politics, he handpicked his successor. He's got everyone he needs in his pocket and his best friend is Magalhães, the Delegado Geral of the Polícia Civil. Your boss. No one can touch him. He's running for Secretario again – just in time to green-light all his World Cup projects. Olympics, too. He's expanding into Rio, I've heard. And he'll do pretty much anything to make sure they happen.' He paused. 'Though I have heard Magalhães might be fucking his wife.'

'Charming,' Leme said.

'Well,' Silva said, an edgy leer in his voice, 'Mendes fucks us. Not a bad thing if someone's fucking him. Or his missus at least. Same difference, right?'

Leme sighed. 'Call me when you know something about the Gabriel murder.'

'Touchy prick,' Silva muttered before hanging up.

The whispering had changed. It was clearer now. A sort of low murmur, and though he wasn't always able to decipher the words, he recognised the voice. Renata. There were times when she interrupted him at the office or on the phone, and he had to pause, forgetting who he was speaking to, what the conversation was about. It was embarrassing. It hadn't happened with the same person more than once, except Lisboa, who took it for what it was: grief.

It was mid-morning when he left the condominium and walked stiffly to Lisboa's car. They didn't talk as they negotiated the city. At that hour there was no need to take the shortcut through the *favela*. Leme had been there first thing, watching, waiting, not sure for what or why but happy to have the routine. It felt like he was doing something at least, something for her.

Lisboa seemed tired and uncommunicative, and this suited Leme. He'd had a difficult night disturbed by mosquitoes, restless as his body tried, and failed, to process the whiskey he had drunk. He knew that alcohol was becoming a crutch, that he used it to deal with his anxiety. With his loneliness. With his grief. But it didn't excuse it. That he *knew* it didn't seemed to offer something like hope that it wouldn't last forever.

The sad thing, he thought, was that one day he might *not* need it. 'Grief is a bit like having your heart broken,' one of his drunken friends in the condominium had said to him not long ago. 'It gets better,' he'd said. 'We'll always get over a broken heart.'

'Tell me again why we're doing this?' Lisboa asked, as they crossed the river and headed up towards Avenida Paulista and the centre.

Leme didn't respond at first. He was mapping the city in his mind. So often, he thought, we gain our understanding of this place from the inside of a car. Here, as they approached Jardims, it was the imported dealerships that stood out, rows of Lamborghinis and Ferraris. Harley Davidsons. Toys, all of them. He wondered at the logic of a sports car in a city where on most days there were two hundred kilometres of congestion.

They were doing this, Leme thought, because they had to do something.

'This company Mendes Construction is developing something in the centre,' he said. 'You know, regeneration for the World Cup. That's where we're going.'

'I know *where* we're going, arsehole,' Lisboa said. 'But I don't know why.'

Leme sighed, smiled. 'Just to take a look. Nothing else to do, right? Mendes Construction owns Casa Nova. We're just having a look.'

The engine swelled as they pulled down Rua Augusta into the centre, Lisboa's face tight as glass. Leme looked dead ahead, willed his hangover to recede as the sun thickened.

Right after talking to Silva the night before, he'd turned the television on and there he was: Mendes and his lawyer on a news programme, talking about the project in the centre. All slick hair, fat knots in their silk ties. Mendes's face a vulgar, manicured mask, smooth lines, eyes empty.

'It's a new era,' he'd said, eyes fixed on the camera, the public, 'for our wonderful country. And this city is at the very forefront. This project is the future. For São Paulo, the past no longer exists.' He smiled, sneered. 'We *are* the future,' he said. He was nodding. 'And it's happening *now*.'

And that's why they were heading there this morning. Just to have a look. To see the scale of the project, see for themselves what had been sacrificed on the *favelados* in exchange for World Cup luxury. Leme doubted any of the pillars would collapse in this development.

They arrowed past the American bars and strip joints at the bottom of Rua Augusta and across the junctions manned by the hawkers selling umbrellas and candy and then passed the Terraço Italia and through Praça Princesa Isabel up to the Sala São Paulo – the venue of the one classical concert Leme had ever attended.

Groups of men and women moved quickly in twos and threes between the newspaper stands, thrusting fists into the paths of passers-by, clicking what was left of their teeth and muttering, yelling out some coded language of success and failure.

Palm trees drooped and sagged on the edge of the square, names and threats carved into the trunks, bent like hunchbacks.

Leme wound down his window and breathed in.

Exhaust fumes and rotten vegetables.

Paving stones were dank from urine.

The police presence was a little heavier than normal. Leme spotted the top of the Estação da Luz, its European towers rearing up above the Pinacoteca art gallery and gardens and was reminded that once, before the dealers and pimps and graffiti artists had moved in, this place really was the centre. Now, it was only that in name. Centre of what?

The *centro* had been the faux-European, urbane part of the city, but the elite quickly abandoned it in favour of high-rise modernity and fortress security. The decline was symptomatic of a bigger decline.

No, Leme thought, not a decline, a refusal: you can have this part, they'd decided. We'll just build a new city for ourselves.

Mendes was right: São Paulo has no past –

It's a mass of lives moving forward and another mass stagnating.

They could see dust rising in puffs like smoke rings in the next square, and, with it, keeping time, the sound of a faint pounding, chanting.

Traffic stalled, beeping and shouting, shouting and beeping.

The noise grew in volume and intensity.

'The fuck?' Lisboa looked across at Leme. 'You know something I don't?'

'I know a lot you don't.'

'About this, *porra*.'

Lisboa jammed the car into gear, squealed through the square, turned left and swerved into the lane closest to the site.

He pulled up on to the kerb and pointed at what they could both now see was clearly some sort of protest.

Whistles and drums. Flags. Banners.

Student types and troublemakers.

Just beyond, a twenty-foot fence ringed a space about a kilometre in diameter. Cranes poked their heads up above it, crunched and ground left right, up down in a dance.

'What, so this is a coincidence?' he asked. 'We come here when there's a fucking demo going on?' He clicked his teeth and muttered, '*Puta que pariu, eh*, Mario?'

Leme raised his eyebrows. 'Lucky, *ne?*' He smiled and slid out of the car. 'You coming?'

Leme strode towards the crowd. About a hundred, he thought.

Not a big deal and the security guards and police didn't look too bothered. He turned and saw Lisboa leaning against the car, lighting a cigarette, waving him on. Leme smiled.

A few young men had bandanas tied around their necks, but this didn't look like a group bent on violence.

They were singing a song: a number of politicians were being invited to take it up the arse.

A placard with a picture of Sepp Blatter on his knees in front of a laughing satanic figure, a map of Brazil and pictures of football stadiums smouldering behind his back.

A sign: R.I.P Jeitinho Brasileiro.

Leme smiled at this.

A few students and wasters singing amusing songs are going to end a system so endemic with corruption that it has its own nickname?

They were in the right place, at least. If anyone represented the *jeitinho*, the shortcuts and liberties taken by the rich, the politicians, it was Mendes.

Leme edged through the crowd, heading towards the entrance at the south-west corner of the site.

Young women with dreadlocks and bracelets danced, splashing water on each other, wide-eyed.

A megaphone cracked tinny slogans above their pumping fists.

The dust hung heavy in the heat, scratchy at the back of Leme's throat.

He spat.

A woman offered him her water bottle but he shook his head, moved away from her.

They were chanting something, more insistent now: *No World Cup without change*.

Then: *Não Vai Ter Copa*.

A banner read: *FUCK FIFA*.

A couple of Militars stood bored just behind a taped-off area by the entrance, hands on their hips, fingers tapping on their guns. Leme flashed his badge.

'Can I get through?'

'Why? Nothing to see.'

'I don't need a reason. This is enough.' Leme stuck his badge right in the face of the bigger of the Militars.

'You fucking lot,' the Militar hissed. 'Why you even asking, you arrogant cunt?'

Leme smiled. 'Courtesy. Exercise in diplomatic relations.'

The Militar shifted from foot to foot. He bristled and snarled something to his partner Leme didn't catch. Wouldn't be long, he thought, before some hapless student gets his head bashed in cos of this guy's boredom. A gang of young men in black heavy-metal T-shirts were getting closer to them, eyeing the Militars.

'So?' Leme addressed the other one, moving forward, an eye on the T-shirts. 'You going to call off your guard dog?'

'You fucking –'

But Leme was under the tape and through. The young men cheered and swarmed forward.

'Woof woof,' Leme shouted back.

Two large men in suits and sunglasses blocked the entrance, but Leme's badge bought him a little space and time.

Before they could muscle him away, a low, black Jaguar with tinted windows ghosted up an alley that was protected at the far end by more suits.

The men spoke into their headsets.

The car slowed and the back window came down just enough for Leme to sneak a look.

Mendes and a woman of a similar age.

The guards ushered the car past.

Leme turned and moved back towards the crowd, avoiding the looks of the Militars who were now bantering with the metal T-shirts. The sort of banter that ends abruptly.

The woman had looked unhappy. Something in the set of her expression. The way she gripped her handbag.

Fuck. Leme turned, but the car had been swallowed by the site, gates pulled across, and Leme was by now disappearing into the crowd, all hot, sour breath and hash.

That look, Leme realised, was grief.

Something he knew all about. But who was she?

Back in his office he googled the project, looked for news. Something about a potential partnership with another construction outfit. Articles in the two main city newspapers. He clicked on one of them. There was a photograph of a woman leaving an office. He zoomed in. It was definitely her, the woman he'd seen in Mendes's car. Her name was Aline Alencar. He googled her. She ran a private university, TAAP – the first woman to achieve such a position in the city. She was a noted philanthropist, ran a foundation, spearheaded a scholarship initiative at her university, helping kids from the *favela* get an education. Her husband, Milton, was in construction. Family a big deal.

Then he saw it, at the bottom of the biography. A biography that hadn't yet been updated: *Aline and Milton have one child, a son, Leonardo Alencar.*

Fuck, Leme thought. FUCK.

'Mario, this is stupid,' Lisboa said. 'Lagnado realises what you're thinking of doing, and there'll be more trouble, *sabe?* We'll have even less to do.'

Lisboa leaned back, spread against his chair. It creaked under his weight. 'It isn't an option,' he said. 'And besides, with the Military operation in the *favela*, it's dangerous.'

This Leme knew.

He said, 'I just want to know why Leonardo Alencar was in Paraisópolis, *entendeu?*'

'*Porra*, Mario,' Lisboa sighed.

'I spoke to the doctor who did the autopsy,' Leme said.

'Mario.'

'No drugs or alcohol in his system. He didn't go to pick up blow at the *boca de fumo*. That seems the only logical reason he'd be there.'

Lisboa crossed his arms. 'So there's nothing suspicious.'

'Which, in itself, is suspicious,' Leme said. 'Or strange, anyway.'

Lisboa raised his eyebrows. He whistled and shook his head. '*Puta que pariu, eh?*'

Leme continued. 'If he wasn't buying drugs, and he wasn't on some drunken mission, then why was he there? And why was he leaving in such a hurry? Sure, it was an accident, but it stands to reason something happened. He was driving like that to escape.'

'And?'

'It doesn't make sense, that's all.'

'What's this about, Mario? Why do you care?'

'I'm curious,' Leme said. 'You know why.'

'Ah. Not worth it. It was an accident. *Chega*. A coincidence.' Lisboa chose his words carefully. 'Accidents happen in Paraisópolis, he said. But they are exactly that – accidents.'

'There's something I haven't told you,' Leme said.

'*Ah, e?*'

'It wasn't an accident. At least, not entirely.'

'The fuck does that mean?'

'I saw his body,' Leme said. 'He'd been shot.'

'Jesus.' Lisboa shut the door. 'You're sure?'

Leme nodded.

'Fuck, Mario.' Lisboa shook his head. 'This is not something we can get involved in. It was an accident, that's what they're saying. You said yourself you spoke to the doctor. A gunshot wound is likely to make it into an autopsy.'

'Exactly.'

The silence sat heavy.

'I can't do this,' Lisboa said.

'And I've been back since,' Leme added. 'To Paraisópolis.'

'I know. And you're being stupid.'

Leme understood that Lisboa was trying to protect him. When he knew that he couldn't persuade Leme of something with reasoned argument, Lisboa became belligerent. There's no counter to that. Leme thought: he's making it clear he wants nothing to do with it.

'Remind me why you were there that morning?'

Leme glanced at Lisboa. This was another of his tactics. Make him feel bad. Show him that things can always get worse.

'Shortcut. Giovanni was stuck solid with traffic. I do it all the time.'

'But you were parked?'

'Pulled over for a smoke.'

'This has nothing to do with Renata,' Lisboa said, firmly. 'There's no such thing as redemption.'

Leme said nothing.

The two-tone ping of an arriving email echoed in the small space. Lisboa clicked at the mouse on the desk.

'Well, here's your answer.' He turned the screen so that Leme could read the message.

Leme looked at the message. They'd been copied in – it had gone out to all the detectives.

Re: Leonardo Alencar accident. No further investigation of the scene or surrounding locale required. Victim's car reviewed by forensics. Autopsy ruled death from irreparable internal damage caused by the collision.

A stripe of sunshine made the screen blink.

Dust drifted across it, a thin layer of passing cloud.

Ringing phones and the clunk and chatter of office machines punctuated the air-con growl.

Leme ran his finger across the splintered ridges of the desk.

He looked at his partner. Lisboa sat with a thin smile. This was the result he wanted. That he wanted it for Leme's own good helped little.

'I'll go to forensics tomorrow, look at the car,' Leme said. 'First thing.'

'Make sure that's the only place you fucking go,' Lisboa said. 'And don't let Lagnado know you've been. You're on your own, here, *certo?* Be discreet.'

Leme smiled. '*Calma*,' he said. 'I'm not stupid.'

He didn't like lying to his best friend.

He needed the anchor of being there each morning.

And the circumstances of Leonardo Alencar's death provided a good reason.

He probably should have kept them to himself though.

Leme glanced at his watch. 6.30. He had to get back soon. Lisboa was picking him up at 7, and he needed to pretend that he'd just got out of bed. Better he thinks I'm hungover than knows the truth, Leme thought. Besides, the streets in Paraisópolis were getting busier, and the kind of people Leme was looking out for heading home to sleep. He scratched at his chin, pulled at the stubble on his jaw. He'd lost weight in the months after Renata's death, but Lisboa was making sure, with a steady stream of meat-heavy lunches, that Leme was 'keeping himself healthy'. Leme knew what was going on – it gave Lisboa an excuse to eat as much as he could when out of the house. Certainly wasn't getting it at home.

Leme smiled at this thought, then saddened. What was it Lisboa's dad used to joke? I had to stop drinking and eating barbecue for two weeks to lose weight. And all I lost was a fortnight.

He pulled his cap up from his eyes and fingered the keys hanging limp from the ignition. He was in one of the condominium worker's cars, a rusting Beetle missing a wing mirror. He could see another three like it just down the street. He was careful to rotate the cars he used. He wasn't supposed to be there, and he doubted anyone would understand an explanation. He was, he realised, staking out an entire *favela*. This was police work reduced to the essentially hopeless: just being there, every day if possible, just in case.

He didn't even know what he was looking for.

He had one real friend in the Military Police. And he'd told him to stay away, that there was little or no chance of finding anything out, that she was dead and there was no way of knowing who'd fired the bullet, that it was a *bala perdida*, that it happened.

Leme knew all this, but he still came back every day he could.

Chega, he thought, realising it had been another waste of an hour. I'm off. But as he thought it, he stopped. It wasn't a waste if it gave him something, however little. And if it wasn't safe? Well, he was always careful.

Edgy as fuck though.

Civil Police not welcome here, by anyone: Militars or dealers.

A quick cigarette, he thought, and home. Loads of time.

He wound down the window and watched as the *favela* awoke. Metal grilles pulled up, goods stacked up on the street, blocking the kids who wandered noisily towards school. They weren't really going *to* school, Leme thought, but kind of not *not* going, in that disengaged Brazilian *jeito*. He checked himself. This was Renata's influence. He thought back to his own childhood, how he had escaped this life thanks to his father. 'I rescued your mother,' he'd always told Leme, 'gave her a life she wouldn't have had, *you* wouldn't have had.' And Leme had never been allowed to forget how close he had come to this *favela* half-life. How easily things can be so different. A decision here, a choice there. Renata never bought that. 'Free will doesn't exist, we're *programmed* to do what we do,' she'd always said. 'No such thing as choice. No point thinking about what might have been – what might have been is just what never was and never would be.' She'd palmed a book on to him. Freud's *The Ego and the Id*. It sat – quiet, seething – in the middle of the pile in the living room.

Leme flicked his cigarette clumsily and it slipped inside the window and smouldered down by the brake pedal.

Fuck.

He bent down and reached for it blindly.

Fuck.

He burnt his fingers but managed to grab it.

Time to go.

He turned to the window and started.

'*E aí, mano. Beleza?*'

A young man – a teenager – with tight dreadlocks leant in towards him. He wore a dirty T-shirt and baggy shorts hanging low.

'Want something, playboy?' He gestured at the quiet *favela* street behind. 'You follow me, *ne?* Sort you out. *E nois, truta.*' He smiled. His teeth were gold and they flashed in the sun.

Leme shook his head. 'You're OK.'

'*Ah, vai.* Don't be shy.' He gestured again. 'All good here. Whatever you need, *cara.*'

Leme tensed. '*Nada, valeu,*' he said. '*Nada.* Just leaving, *entendeu?*'

'*Então.*' The guy shrugged. 'You're the boss. *Você que sabe.*'

But he didn't move away, if anything got a little closer.

Leme gave him a tight smile. He felt the space of the *favela* close in on him. The strength in his legs leached out. He pointed at the case of beer he kept on the seat for exactly a situation like this. He ran his finger over it. 'Got what I need,' he said.

The guy nodded slowly. 'You came to the *favela* for that?' He raised his eyebrows. 'Like I said, *cara, você que sabe.*'

'*Isso,*' Leme said. He turned the key and the engine sputtered.

'You tell me you ever need anything, playboy.'

Leme nodded. '*Valeu,*' he said. 'Appreciate it.'

The engine juddered.

'Piece of shit car, *meu,*' the guy said. 'I know someone.' He jerked his thumb down the road. '*Vamos, eh*. Sort it out. *E nois, eh?*'

'You're alright.'

Leme looked down at the steering wheel. Come on, he thought. *Come on.*

He felt a hand on his shoulder. 'You not here for me, playboy, why you here?'

Leme said nothing.

'We seen you, motherfucker,' he spat. 'Stay away, *entendeu?*' He leant back, drew a line across his throat with his index finger. '*Entendeu?*' he said. He stepped away and lifted his T-shirt. A fat revolver glinted in the sun offset by the thin, silvery scars that criss-crossed his lean stomach. He backed away, nodding. '*Entendeu?*' he said again, and turned, sloped off down the street, laughing.

The engine caught and Leme manoeuvred the car in a tight turn and roared up a side street towards the main road.

His heart thumped, his head felt empty, hard; his mouth dry, metallic.

At the top of the road, a temporary Military Police post. Leme slowed as he passed. One of the Militars stepped into the road in front of him.

Now what?

He waited. The Militar swaggered around to his window, high boots and mirrored sunglasses, hands on his belt. Like a fucking parody, Leme thought.

'*Tudo bem?*' he said.

Leme nodded.

'Get the message?'

Leme's confusion must have been obvious.

'You think we don't know what these cunts get up to?' The Militar was laughing. 'Stay away,' he said. 'Fucking stay away. Too many questions, *entendeu?*'

Leme nodded again. He tried to see the ID number on the Militar's badge, but it was out of sight.

The Militar stepped back and ushered him on.

'Woof woof,' he said.

In his wing mirror, Leme watched him cross the road, slap hands with his partner.

He shivered, felt cold, lightheaded.

He was home in minutes and straight into the shower.

He scoured himself clean in scalding water and tried not to think about what had just happened.

Failed.

He'd never been to a car autopsy before. The fact alone was a distraction. As, of course, was the fact that he wasn't supposed to be there. He'd read the autopsy again to ensure he knew the official line; he wasn't about to reveal any of his own suspicions today.

The shell of the SUV sat in the middle of the cavernous space, surrounded by its own detritus. Stripped and taken apart, buckled doors and metallic sheets were dotted either side, as if the men looking at it were in the process of assembly and had laid the component parts in convenient spots. Leme was reminded of fathers helping sons with their go-karts. Of building flat-pack furniture. He stood at the entrance with his hands in his pockets waiting for one of the team to see him.

A short, balding guy in overalls approached, scratching his stubbly chin. He wiped his hand on his backside and offered it.

'You Leme?'

Leme nodded.

'*Então?*' The guy looked up at him. 'What are you looking for?'

Leme smiled. 'Not sure. What have you found?'

A wry chuckle. '*Nada.* It was an accident. Not much to find. We've stripped the car. There was nothing wrong with it. Brake fluid as it should be, considering. Engine, too.'

Leme pointed at the wreck. 'Shouldn't he have survived the impact, you know, with the bulletproof glass and chassis and whatnot?'

The guy nodded. 'Perhaps. These things are built to protect. But,' he paused, aware of the irony, 'it also makes it hard to get inside one of them without a key.'

They walked towards the vehicle. The guy continued. 'You can see here where they eventually were able to cut through and open it up.' He indicated a sharp edge with his finger, careful not to make any contact. 'This was done by a machine. This …' he pointed at another, more jagged line '… happened on impact. Look at the way it has folded in on itself. Part of the protection.'

'But he didn't survive, did he?'

The guy straightened and brought his hands out in front of him, about a foot apart. 'The car flipped over, right, in the middle of the

road? So the witnesses say. It may have hit something. Anything …
a brick, uneven surface … at the speed he was going – and we can
work that out from the damage – it would've taken very little. Then
it hit a lamp post and then the wall.' He brought Leme round to the
front of the car. 'That explains the nature of these dents. It's all pretty
obvious.' He pushed at an oily rag with his foot. 'Point is he wasn't
wearing a seat belt,' he said. 'We can tell. There's no damage at all
to the pre-tensioners. At that speed and with that impact, there'd be
something.'

Leme nodded. 'Fits in with the autopsy,' he said. 'No lesions
across the chest and shoulder.'

'Yeah, exactly. He would've been like a fish flapping in an empty
bucket, banging against the sides.'

'Nice image.'

'I like fishing.'

Leme arched an eyebrow. 'So what you've seen matches the
autopsy? Had they got in straight away, they may have saved him?'

'Yeah. Maybe. I mean it's hard to tell. This is interesting though.'

They moved around the car where the cracked windscreen lay on
its side.

'It didn't shatter, right? But look at this.' He pointed at the shape
and nature of the cracks, angling off like a spider's web. 'There's quite
a broad impact here on this side. The driver's side. Suggests he hit it –
first time at least – with his body, not his head. Can't be sure though.'

'Medics said something similar.'

'Yeah, well. So long as we're all on the same page, *ne?*'

'*É isso aí.*'

The guy scratched at his chin again. Leme knew the look well. He
wanted to know something, but wasn't sure how to ask. Inferiority
complex.

'Umm,' the guy said, embarrassed, 'why are you even here?'

Leme had learnt over the years not to answer that question
directly. More often than not, if it were asked at all, the person who
asked it would provide a far better answer himself. 'Why do you
think?' he said.

'It was an accident. We don't normally do this sort of thing for a
car crash.'

'No? So why did you?'

'Not normally. We're just doing what we're told. They want it confirmed the car was working as it should. Confirmation, I guess, that is *was* an accident. It is a bit odd, but you don't get anywhere asking too many questions, *sabe?*'

Leme smiled. He was aware that his presence here shouldn't be noted.

'And? What do you think?'

'Just making sure. That's all. Got to check everything, *ne?*'

'Suppose.'

'You're running tests on who else might have been in there recently?'

'Ready in a few days. Like I said, nothing suspicious.'

'Just a car crash then.'

'Looks that way.'

Leme took a last look at the car. He thought it looked like a broken toy tossed aside by a child. 'Thanks,' he said.

Both sets of forensics had come to the same conclusion: it was an accident that was caused by reckless driving and involved no other vehicles.

He started towards the door.

'Oi, Leme.' The guy called him back. He handed Leme a zip-lock bag. 'You might want this,' he said. 'Found in the glove compartment, which was crushed shut so we've only just recovered it. Admin. Car stereo instructions. Stuff like that. No use to us.'

Leme took it. 'Thanks. I'll log it, so don't worry about it.'

The guy shrugged. '*Você que sabe,*' he said.

'I'll be in touch if I have to,' Leme said.

Back in his own car, he put gloves on, opened the bag and flipped through the documents. Slipped in between the insurance details and a handwritten ledger receipt was a piece of paper with a mobile phone number written on it. Above the number was a word:

Podemos

Leme took a smaller plastic bag from his pocket, placed the scrap of paper inside and pocketed it.

He examined the receipt. A restaurant. He looked at the date: just over a year ago. Odd. Why would you keep a receipt for that long? He turned the paper over. There was nothing written on the reverse side. He looked back at the front. The restaurant name was familiar. He'd been there, he was sure. He looked at the address: Paraisópolis. *That's* why he knew the name. It was the restaurant Renata ate at every day. They had lunch there together a number of times. The owner was a friendly woman. He hadn't been back for a long time. Leonardo then, had been going into Paraisópolis for at least a year.

He kept the receipt. His curiosity twitched, hardened.

His car jerked forward on to Avenida Higienópolis, jammed its nose between two taxis. One of the drivers made a gesture. '*Porra, meu!*'

Leme waved it off. He edged around the other taxi and accelerated away as the lights changed into a dense cloud of exhaust that sat pregnant above the road.

'It's our cultural history,' Renata once said. 'Power struggle. We're conditioned to impose authority. If you're on a motorbike, and I'm in a car, well fuck you, I'm in charge.'

Leme chuckled.

'Same at work. If I'm a lawyer, but also something else, and you are just a lawyer, well fuck you, I'm going to show you I'm better than you. It's a sociological phenomenon. Look at our language, the way we talk to waiters: "Bring me this. Get me that." We're brought up on the imperative and that is a display of authority.'

Leme didn't doubt that.

'It's the heart of the Brazilian contradiction.'

'Oh yeah.' Leme always enjoyed her analysis, her theory.

'We're a hospitable, cooperative people,' she went on. 'We go out of our way to help, to be kind, to facilitate things for others, to enjoy life. In a social context. Any other though – like work, or in traffic – and we're animals, scrambling over and clawing at each other to get to the top.'

Leme smiled then, pained at the memory. Pulled away again, past the taxi.

He'd keep that paper to himself. *Podemos*, meaning 'We can'. The word ricocheted in his mind. But he couldn't place it. It was something Renata had said once. *Podemos.* We can. Something to do with work.

He shook his head.
He had to meet Silva.
He was, apparently, going to show him something.
Tell him exactly why he was being sidelined.
Before that, though, he'd pop back to the *favela*.
It'd only take a minute.

Leme sat in his car and watched the *favelados* milling about, calling out to each other, moving things back and forth. Wooden crates of booze, boxes of rice, greasy auto-parts. Banter and then dirty banknotes swapped, licked, counted and tucked into back pockets. He wore a baseball cap pulled low over his eyes and a tracksuit top zipped to his chin. He'd borrowed another old car from one of the *seguranças* in his condominium and traced the dust with his finger through the window. It was satisfyingly thick.

When Renata had worked here and he'd visited, he'd been treated with suspicion.

But, he'd reasoned, it was the middle of the day and the man he was going to talk to worked at the Giovanni end of the *favela*, the closest to the urban development of Morumbi, on the road even the middle classes would use as a shortcut to avoid the traffic. There weren't normally any Militars in this part; and he didn't want to find out how empty these threats were. Carlos had assured him that they were empty but he hadn't been able to tell him definitively which of them was collaborating with the PCC and the dealers in the *favela*.

In his wing mirror he watched a bus disgorge passengers, who skipped off into the warren, and then swallow up another queue of people. For a few moments now, the street would be at its quietest. Leme edged the car along the road and stopped in front of a tyre and auto-repair shop. He sat for a few moments.

It was important that the right man came to his window.

He spotted him. A heavyset man in work clothes stepped on to the street and up to the car. Dirty brown flesh matted with hair wobbled loosely as if straining to fit more snugly into the baggy overalls under which he wore nothing.

'*Puta que pariu,*' he swore, and not in greeting.

'Hello, mate. Long time.'

The man looked over each shoulder and up and down the street.

'You can't be here,' he said. 'If anyone knows I'm talking to you –'

'So, come a little closer. No one's watching.'

'Oh, and you've checked, have you? The great fucking detective. *Vai tomar no cú, eh*, Mario.'

'I'll be quick.'

'Too fucking right.'

Two boys pushed a cart laden with junk up the hill, swerving under the weight. Leme glanced in the mirror again. An old drunk weaved his way slowly down the road towards them. He recognised him from the collapsed building. Shouting *Podemos*.

'I need some information. About the playboy Leonardo Alencar who died here. In the accident.'

'And you think I have any?'

'I think you could ask.'

The man whistled. Shook his head. '*Não sei, viu, sabe?* Not worth it. Why would I care about that?'

'Use your charm. You're a persuasive man.'

'What do you want to know?'

The drunk was getting closer. He was muttering and staggering, laughing. Leme thought he could smell the urine and faeces, but it may have been the rubbish piled up on the other side of the road.

'I want to know why he was in here.'

'Isn't that a bit fucking obvious? Drugs.'

The drunk banged his hand on the back of the car. The man looked sharply to his right. 'Mario, *porra*,' he said. Then, to the drunk: '*Vai embora, porra. Tou trabalhando, meu.*'

'He wasn't using, and he wasn't drunk.'

'So ... I don't know ...'

The drunk was writing '*me limpa*' on the back windscreen of the car. Clean me.

'Mario, you have to leave. Now. This son of a bitch is drunk, but not stupid.'

Leme thought about this. 'Just ask around,' he said. 'You owe me.'

'OK, OK. Just piss off, will you?'

'Anything at all will help. Be casual. Second nature.'

The man guided the drunk away from the car. The drunk, eyes in an alcohol-droop, a leering mask, pointed his finger at Leme. 'Who's this motherfucker? Eh?'

'No one. A client.'

Leme smiled at the drunken man. Better to act natural. He waved and started the engine. He pulled out from the kerb and the drunk jumped back and raised his fist. Snarled: '*Babaca!* I know you!'

'You'll call,' he said as he drove away. That, he hoped, was the last visit for some time. His contact was a curious man, a gossip, a drinker, and Leme knew he'd not help himself. He'd hear something soon enough.

He drove up Giovanni towards his condominium and, on an impulse, stopped at a *padaria*.

He ordered a beer and a portion of cheese *pastel*. The beer was extremely cold and when he touched the bottle, it froze and slipped out in chunks into his glass.

Fuck.

He waved at the waiter who brought him another.

He broke the *pastel* into squares, thick with cheese, like lava.

He shook spicy sauce over the pieces and ate half of them.

He finished his beer and looked at the leftover food.

Threw a few notes on the table and went back to his car.

Leme sat in a *padaria* on Rua Gabriel Monteiro. The coffee was bitter and sweet. Filth. The old trick, he thought. Old burnt coffee beans mixed with sugar. Silva was late. A group of manual labourers sat over shots of cachaça. They looked up and clicked their teeth. '*Polícia. Ah. Se fodeu.*' Leme ignored their insults; envied, in fact, their fortifying drinks but he wouldn't have one. Exhaust fumes from trucks filled the air, complaining through gears on the busy road outside. He spotted Silva slouching across the road in a cheap, ill-fitting suit. Stood and left a generous tip.

'And you brought me here … why?'

'You're not a fucking teenager, Mario. Don't talk like one.'

Leme laughed. '*Sussa, meu. Sussa na buça.*'

This time Silva laughed. 'Cool in the cunt? Christ. God help us.'

'So,' Leme said. 'Explain.'

They stood in the shade under the awning of the Pão de Açucar supermarket on the opposite side of the street to a building site protected by high wooden boards on which pictures of the proposed development were printed. Curved, elegant towers; gleaming swimming pools, the sun glinting on the blue-white surfaces; narrow parades of trees; an impossibly good-looking family enjoying a barbecue; athletic men crouched and leaping in a glass-surround squash court. On the pavement in front of them, rich women dressed in tight jeans and heels hurried small children in school uniforms to the traffic lights. Botox and sunglasses.

'*Patrocinias.*' Silva nodded at a particularly imposing-looking woman. 'British school across the way.' He pointed. 'Fucking expensive.'

Leme ignored him. 'Not many condominiums as big as this in the centre of town,' he said.

'Breaking laws – well, *bending* laws, or creating new ones at least – to build it,' Silva replied.

'What do you mean?'

Silva waved his arms. 'This area's old school, right? Old money. All low-level housing. You're not supposed to build over a certain height to, I don't know, fucking retain the colonial character or something.'

Leme smirked.

Silva went on. 'The Jardims area is leafy, expensive, right? *Então*, Mendes made some shit up about how this new complex of his is eco-something and fits in with the philosophy of the neighbourhood. He's claiming that the building is going to actually *help* the environment. All sustainable energy resources and so on. It's all bullshit.'

'OK. Why did you bring me here?'

'You wanted to know why you've been sidelined, *ne?*'

Leme nodded.

'And where are we exactly?'

Leme looked up and down the road. 'I see,' he said. 'The building site. It used to be a row of houses, right? And in one of them that old guy was murdered – the Gabriel murder.' He pointed at the end of the site. 'The case I've been taken off. Houses have come down quick, *ne?* I didn't even know.'

Silva smiled. 'They didn't waste any time. Those two suspects you brought in. It's done.'

'And?'

'They didn't want any more questions asked.'

'Why not?'

'Something you don't know. That whole row of houses had been sold to Mendes but one. Old story. The guy who was killed was refusing to sell. Only one house, sure, but without it, no condo. Mendes needed that house.'

'Right.' Mendes, Leme thought. Right. He nodded to himself. What the fuck might that mean?

'The victim's son sold it on almost immediately after the old guy died. Like a day or two.'

'How do you know this?'

Silva winked. 'Public records. Property ownership. Difficult to hide that, as you know.'

Leme raised his eyebrows.

'Point is,' Silva said, 'for the building work to go ahead, there had to be a conviction. Can't knock down a murder scene, *sabe?* And they want it up for the World Cup, apparently. So Mendes applied some pressure on his friend Magalhães – your boss.'

'He's everyone's fucking boss.'

'You know what I mean. Chief of Police Magalhães,' he said,

mocking Leme, 'tells Lagnado, *your* boss, to get it resolved. So, he takes you off it. It's done. Two pieces-of-shit thieves confessed. Manslaughter. Lightish sentences. Robbery gone wrong. *Pronto.*'

Leme nodded. 'Makes sense. Maybe. How do you know?'

Silva tapped his forehead with his finger. 'You just have to ask the right people the right questions.'

'And who are the right people?'

'The archive guy at your office?'

'What about him? I've been denied access for a while.'

Silva winked. Rubbed a thumb and two fingers together.

Leme said, 'Really?'

Silva smiled. 'Case notes are signed off by Lagnado and countersigned by Magalhães. Rushed through.'

'That can happen. Rarely, true, but it can.'

Silva shrugged.

'Thing is,' Leme said, 'how can you prove Mendes put pressure?'

Silva pointed at the site. 'It's there to fucking see, isn't it?'

'Don't be a cunt.'

'Fine,' Silva slightly turned away from Leme. 'You're right. That's the problem. I can't yet. But I will.'

'Speculation, then.' Leme shook his head and breathed out hard. 'Wait. You said *manslaughter?*'

Silva lit a cigarette. 'Yeah. Accidental, you know, self-defence or some shit.'

Leme took a step forward, kicked a stone into the road. 'Manslaughter,' he said to himself. 'Fuck.' Then he turned to Silva. 'Why are you so excited about this?' he asked him.

'I like doing you favours.'

'Right.'

Silva smiled. 'Mendes. Fucker has a lot to answer for.'

'This a crusade, is it?' Leme joked.

Silva opened his arms. 'Why not?'

Leme smiled at Silva's shoddy bulk. 'You don't look much like Batman.'

'Ah, be nice. Neither do you.'

Leme looked at his watch. The traffic was thickening as rush hour kicked in. Cars rippling between two narrow lanes. He needed to get to the *delegacia*.

'So what's the next step?' he asked.

'Well,' Silva said, 'there is something …'

'Oh yeah?'

'There's a way I can get to one of them.'

Leme arrowed a suspicious look at him. 'OK. How?'

Silva tapped his nose with his forefinger. Flicked his cigarette into the road. 'You'll see,' he said. He took a step away. 'Keep in touch, yeah?'

Leme watched him amble awkwardly up the road.

Babaca, he thought, smiling.

Leme had never really been interested in politics. Although he was born during military dictatorship, he was a child during the transition and his life hadn't really been affected. His parents were stoic, unmoved by politics. He'd had a brief flirtation with counter-culture as a high school student, but it only really amounted to listening to Cazuza sing about how the country is like a brothel, everything engineered to make money. He liked the music and the sentiment – but that was it. But if this business with Mendes had anything to do with him being taken off the Gabriel murder, then he wanted to find out a little more about him.

Lisboa was nowhere to be found, the office bigger in his absence. The air-conditioning unit in the grey window thick with dust juddered into life, coughed and hacked for a minute or two and then gave up.

The newspaper lay open on his desk. A story about the Mensalão trial. Some speculation that the money was being hidden in property deals. This was the biggest political news for many years – and Leme knew next to nothing about it. He thought about what Silva had told him about Mendes. *Guy's a fucking animal. Everyone in his pocket.* He picked up the phone and called the paper's political correspondent, a guy Silva had introduced him to years ago and whom he'd done a favour for once before. It hadn't been a big thing – just some basic information on the structure of the Polícia Civil – but the guy had been grateful, impressed with Leme's attention to detail.

He answered on the third ring.

'*Quem fala?*'

'Oi Antonio. Mario Leme.'

'*E aí, cara. Beleza?*'

'You know,' Leme said, 'it's going.'

'What can I do for you? I assume this isn't a social call.'

Leme noted that he sounded friendly. 'I need some information. Not much. Just want to understand a couple of things.'

'What about?'

'Mensalão.'

'*Certo.* What do you want to know?'

'Probably easiest if I tell you what I already know.'

'Which is?'

'Fuck all.'

Antonio laughed. 'OK, simple version then.'

'Probably for the best.' Leme smiled. '*Valeu*,' he said.

'So, Mensalão, meaning large monthly payment, right? It's a neologism based on Mensalidade, in terms of monthly salary. I fucking hope this isn't new to you.'

Leme snorted.

'I'll take that as a no. It's pretty simple, really. Although the Workers' Party is in government, their power is based on a coalition, which can be fragile.'

'Between who?'

'A bunch of different groups, which, though varied, are ultimately left-leaning, *certo?*'

'Got it. Left-leaning coalition.'

'Thing is, although nominally connected to a party or faction, a lot of the politicos are basically self-serving and act purely out of self-interest, which means their allegiances can shift.' Antonio paused. 'Especially if they are influenced in the right way.'

Leme laughed. 'This sounds simpler than I thought,' he said. He picked at a piece of loose wallpaper and rubbed at it with his fingers. He watched it disintegrate.

'Yeah, I suppose so. Basically the accusation is that the government is paying for votes, to make sure certain legislation goes through. Paying for political support using public funds. That's why it's such a big deal. This is money that should go to the country. They've got some *politicos* – allegedly, *ta?* – on a monthly retainer. A large one. Mensalão.'

'So where are they with the case then?' Leme asked.

'It's going, *sabe?* There are likely to be convictions, but it's not clear what the sentences will be. Jail time or whatever.'

'What do you think?'

'I think that whatever happens when the trial is concluded, someone will make sure it is reopened and anyone convicted will appeal – and that'll tie everything up for a while. That fucking Judge Celso de Mello will make sure of that. He's been arguing that the right of appeal should remain in any case, whatever the public interest.'

'He's got a point.'

'Doesn't stop him being wrong.'

'What about the money?'

'What do you mean?'

'What happens to it? How do they clean it?'

'Like I said, a lot of it is public funds, *certo*? So it has to be accounted for. One trick I've heard about is investing it, creating a valid trail, though I'm not sure how that's possible. It's not like they can leave the country with the cash.'

'Investing in what? Like, property?'

'Could be. Depends on the scheme.'

'What do you mean?'

'Well, they'd need a guarantee of a return, otherwise what's the point?'

Leme thought about this.

Antonio broke the silence. 'I don't want to know why you're asking me all this, by the way.'

'I'm not going to tell you.'

'That enough?'

'Yeah, *valeu, eh cara*.'

'*De nada*. Call me you need anything else, *certo*?'

'*Certo. Até mais*.'

'*Ciao*.'

Leme placed the phone back carefully. Something flickered on the outer edges of his consciousness, like the beginnings of a migraine aura. He realised what it was. Renata. Her voice, whispering. It was like being tuned to half a dozen radio stations at the same time, though all of them speaking in the same voice.

He cradled his head in his hands, succumbed.

He leaned forward on to the desk.

His chest heaved, as if the life in it was escaping in panic, his heart swelling in despair.

He hoped Lisboa wouldn't come in.

Then, quickly, the blackness of sleep.

Saturday afternoon in the condominium bar. Antonia laughed. 'I'm glad you agreed to meet,' she said, touching his hand.

Leme forced himself to smile.

'You know, it'd be too easy for you to wallow.'

She blew smoke out of the corner of her mouth. This time, Leme's smile was involuntary.

His friend Nelson was sitting nearby, whispering loudly about a woman he'd met the night before. A *puta gostosa*, apparently, which, Leme realised, meant she was either very attractive, or a very attractive whore. He knew where he'd put his money. Knew where Nelson put his.

Antonia went on. 'I know Renata and I had drifted, but she was my friend. I see this as a favour to her. Get you out and about a bit, you know,' she paused, arched an eyebrow, 'show you … a good time.'

Leme fingered his glass of beer, let the drops of condensation moisten his fingertips. 'That sounds ominous,' he said.

'It doesn't have to.' Antonia smiled warmly, her default ironic expression dissolving as she did.

'Thank you, I suppose,' Leme said.

'It's just a drink. You're not cheating on her memory.' The ironic look returned. '*Yet.*'

Leme smiled again. Although they lived in the same condominium, he had rarely socialised with Antonia. They would occasionally exchange a few words by the pool, or she'd lean over him at the condominium bar; let the other men flirt with her. Well, flirt wasn't quite right. Insult her good taste and tell her they wanted to sleep with her was more like it. Leme had always been embarrassed. More than *she* seemed to be, at least.

Antonia was wrapped in what Leme thought looked like a bed sheet knotted loose around her neck. He could make out the line of her bikini beneath and her hair was damp and tied into a rough ponytail. Oval sunglasses dominated her face, accentuated her pursed lips and small sharp chin.

There were the usual Saturday noises: children splashing and shouting, flip-flops slapping, the whirr of the exercise machines in the gym, tennis balls being hit, the low growl and high-pitched laughter of the condominium's most notorious resident holding court by the pool, nailing cans of lager.

He hadn't done much socialising at all, beyond visiting Lisboa. Sitting in the bar with other men didn't count. That was a necessary chore rather than anything especially pleasurable. He was happy to drink on his own, but they always insisted on joining him. Part of grief is the illusion of solitude: the illusion, at least, that you don't want it.

Antonia breathed smoke at the table and folded her cigarette into the ashtray. Her legs were crossed elegantly and her chin high, arms like the hands of a clock, each limb positioned with the maximum economy, grace, really.

'You want to eat?' she asked.

'I could eat.'

Antonia turned her head slightly and one of the waiters materialised immediately. She ordered more drinks and some cheese *pastels*, a portion of fried cod, and a couple of meat *espetinhos*.

'Hungry?' Leme asked.

Antonia leaned forward, brought her hand to her throat, let it slide slightly down the sheet. 'Always,' she smiled.

'Bloody hell,' Leme said and she laughed.

They ate quickly, the fried food soaking up the beers and caipirinha leaving them bloated and satisfied. Leme watched as Antonia's eyes slid off the other residents as they wandered past or sat down or pursued their children, yelling at the babysitters to look sharp. The twenty-somethings clustered around the stone steps of the mini-amphitheatre, smoking and analysing the previous night's goings-on. Antonia nodded at them.

'They've got it all to look forward to,' she said.

'What's that, then?'

She gestured at him and then herself. 'This.'

'And what is *this*?' Leme asked.

'This,' she said, again narrowing the gap between them, 'is everything. The human condition, you know … life.'

'Very profound.'

She leant back, plucked another cigarette from her packet as if defusing a bomb, and winked. 'It's heavy. Let it sink in. You've got as much right to it as anyone else.'

Leme thought about this. He finished his beer. 'I better go,' he said. He signalled at the waiter and signed for the food and drinks.

'When we do this again,' Antonia smiled, 'I'm going to make you talk to me.'

Leme kissed her on both cheeks. '*Ciao*,' he said.

Back in his apartment, he thought that yes, the next time he probably *would* talk. Then he slept. That was always one way to pass the weekends. As he drifted off he thought that one day he might not even have to wake up.

Monday. Office. Leme drowned in paperwork.

Alvarenga came in. He told Leme about a case. A robbery. A shop on Rua dos Pinheiros. Sold clothes, accessories. Hippy stuff. The owner, a woman, was sitting in the back and saw three men in suits coming in on the CCTV cameras. She didn't like the way they looked and locked herself in the office. The door was forced. She was beaten about the head, tied up and doused in alcohol. They waved a cigarette lighter in front of her, demanding money. They took everything she had. A measly three hundred fucking reais. There was a lead. A map left on the floor showing details of the office and basement that only an employee would know. They were tracing everyone who worked for the woman. It was only a matter of time.

Leme shook his head, but he wasn't surprised. 'What about those dentists?' he asked. 'I'm supposed to be helping you.'

'Never had a chance,' Alvarenga said. 'Both died from the burn wounds.'

Leme grimaced.

'The surgery was targeted,' Alvarenga said, 'the equipment taken, all the money, and the two dentists tied up and then the place set on fire.'

'Second time in a month, right?' Leme asked.

'Bad time to be a dentist.'

'*Pois e.*'

'You can do something for me, though.'

'*Ah e?*'

'We think that a former employee might have been involved – again, you know how it goes – kid named Marcelo Manezes. Here.'

He gave Leme a piece of paper with his ID details.

'Get down to admin, will you, and get hold of his phone records.'

Leme nodded. 'No problem.'

'No rush,' Alvarenga said, and left.

Leme looked at the paper: a name, an address and an RGE number. He had a thought.

He left his office and crossed the open-plan area to a desk on the far side, tucked away behind a screen.

'*E ai,*' he said, smiling at Isabella, a young woman working what was basically an internship, organising files, making coffee, some secretarial work.

'*Oi*, Sr Leme,' she said.

'Mario, please,' he said. He smiled again, aware of an age difference, nervous. She was very beautiful and had something of a fierce reputation, quickly garnered. Didn't take any shit, he'd heard.

She smiled back.

'I think you can help me out,' he said.

'OK.' She looked up, keen to help.

'No big deal, but a young man died in car crash last week in Paraisópolis.'

'I remember,' she said. 'Leonardo Alencar.'

'That's right. I need his details, you know, address, ID number, that kind of thing. You'll have them, right?'

'Of course. Just give me a minute.'

She rifled through some papers in a filing tray on the desk. 'What do you need it for?' she asked.

He smiled again. 'Just checking something against another crime,' he replied. 'No need to mention it to anyone.'

She looked up again, sharply this time.

'*Relaxa*,' he said. 'This is routine. OK?'

'Here it is,' she said, and handed him a printout. He noted down the details.

'*Obrigado, valeu.*'

'*Prazer.*'

He handed back the printout and she tucked it back into the pile of papers.

'You enjoying it here?' he asked.

She shrugged. 'You know,' she said. 'The work is pretty dull. Admin removes the human element of what you do here. That make sense? A kid dies – I file away the details. It's a bit surreal. I used to work sorting files in a restaurant business.'

'Bit different,' Leme offered.

'Yeah.'

'I see what you mean though. That's very perceptive.'

She raised her eyebrows.

'And I don't mean that in a patronising way,' Leme said, quickly. He smiled again, felt his face flush.

'Don't worry, I know,' she said. 'You wouldn't be the first, though.'

'Huh,' he said. 'I'm sure. Thanks again.'

She gave a small, ironic bow. 'Between us,' she said, '*ne?*'

He nodded and left her to it.

He took the lift down to the admin department. Admin. That was a euphemism. What they did was poke around in people's lives. An IT guy had explained it to him once: all you need is the ID number and name and with the software they had you could pretty much hack anyone's phone. Not that they did, exactly, but it made tracking calls fairly straightforward, he'd said. Leme found him in a dark booth.

'Leme,' the guy said. '*Sumiu, eh?* Long time.'

Leme snorted. 'Picking something up for Vavá. Phone records for that dentist guy. Name's here.'

He handed over the paper.

'*Certo.* Give me an hour?'

'Sure,' Leme said. 'Do me a favour?'

The guy gave him a knowing look. 'One of those, is it?'

Leme handed him Leonardo Alencar's details. 'Same thing for this guy, *entendeu?*'

'*Claro, meu querido,*' he said.

'Calm down, dear,' Leme winked. '*Valeu, eh.*'

Just over an hour later Leme was studying the phone calls Leonardo Alencar made and received in the hours before his death. One number came up with significant frequency, not just that night, but on a repeated basis in the weeks before. Leme picked up his phone and dialled.

'*Quem fala?*' Leme said.

'*Não,*' a young man's voice said. 'I ask that. Who are you?'

Leme coughed. The voice was clipped and confident. Leonardo was rich, he knew, and this kid sounded it, too.

'Detective Mario Leme,' he said. '*Certo?*'

'Uh-huh,' the young man said. 'And?'

'I'll ask again: *quem fala?* I've got your number. So you know I can find out. This way's a lot easier.'

The guy exhaled. 'Alex,' he said. 'Alex Santos. Now you can tell me *why* you need to know.'

'I want to talk to you about Leonardo Alencar. I want to know why he was in the *favela*.'

There was a pause.

'You still there?' Leme asked.

'Why do you want to know that?'

'Long story. But it may be connected to something important.'

Another pause. Clicking of teeth.

'Alex?'

'There's a café, a Starbucks, *depressingly*, opposite Shopping Iguatemi. Can you meet me there in an hour?'

Leme said that he could.

He dropped Marcelo Manezes's phone records on Alvarenga's desk as he left.

Leme sat and listened as Alex spoke about his friend.

'Leo's mother runs the university where my father works,' he said. 'I haven't spoken to her since the funeral. Thank you, for everything, she'd said to me, but I didn't believe it. I watched her move away, comforted by my father. Leo's dad stood on his own. They've split up. I wanted to talk to him, but I didn't know what to say.'

Alex smiled.

Leme just stared. 'I want to know your version of what happened.'

There was a sharp light filtering in and Leme shaded his eyes from it. They were sitting in the window of the Starbucks, and Alex kept looking over Leme's shoulder, as if hoping there was something more interesting going on somewhere close by.

'They say he was still alive,' he said, 'despite the car flipping in the air and slamming into a wall that ran alongside the junction. I remember the roof, crushed like an empty Coke can.'

Leme made notes. 'Why were you *there*? You don't live nearby.'

Alex nodded. Leme thought that he must have known the question would come up. 'He phoned me,' Alex said. 'About an hour before it happened. Told me where he was.'

'Did he tell you why he was there?'

'No. He wasn't making much sense. We're friends. *Were* friends. Sorry. I'd do anything for him. No judgement.'

'What *exactly* did he say?'

'He told me he'd found who he was looking for and that he wanted me to meet him.'

'And who was this person?'

'That I don't know. He didn't say.'

'And why didn't you push him on it?'

'He was talking quickly, urgent, you know? Then he hung up.'

'And why didn't you do something about it?'

'Look, Leo had moments, projects, sort of when he would get involved in something. I thought this was one. No big deal, *sabe?*'

'So he was behaving normally in the few weeks before the accident?'

'I'd say he was, yes. We've known each other our whole lives. I could normally tell when something was serious and when something not.'

'And you didn't think it was anything serious that night, that morning?'

'No, I didn't. There's not much else I can say.'

Leme believed him. 'How do you feel now?' Leme asked.

'He was a friend. More than that: family. Have you ever let anyone down? When things can never be the same again as a result of what you've done? He was my best friend. That's why it's so difficult talking to you now.'

Leme shuffled in his seat. Alex smiled again. It was unnerving. Was it arrogance or nervousness?

Alex looked across the road and Leme followed his eyes to the Iguatemi shopping centre. It towered above Faria Lima, a citadel of chic. This was the new centre of the city, dripping with money. Women in heels, wearing too-tight jeans, tottered about outside carrying designer bags, climbing in and out of chauffeur-driven cars, on a luxury treadmill, consuming. How many of *them* are in mourning? Soon they'll be home at their jobs – telling their maids what to do.

A mobile phone with a voice-recording app sat on the table between them.

Leme said, 'It's natural to feel responsibility to your close friends. Guilt, even.'

'I don't feel guilt, I mean, I'm not guilty,' Alex said, 'but I do feel something.'

Leme looked hard at him. Didn't smile. 'Tell me about your relationship,' he said.

Alex nodded. 'You know, we did what all guys our age do.'

'You're what, thirty?' Leme asked. 'What do guys your age do?'

'Go to *baladas* where there are girls we're too old to date.'

'Charming.'

'But Leo wanted to change.'

'What do you mean?'

'He was having a crisis or something.'

Leme nodded. Alex was handsome, sure of himself. Muscles in his T-shirt. Diesel jeans. Very expensive if bought in São Paulo. But Alex looked like the kind of guy who made regular trips to Miami.

'Explain,' Leme said.

'We were at Leo's place with some girl who'd had a nose job. She was asleep on the sofa, snoring. I remember Leo said she sounded like a cat purring into a microphone. I said, that's what surgery and cocaine will do for you.'

Leme didn't react.

'We were drinking whiskeys,' Alex said. 'It was a little after 6 a.m., a Tuesday, I think. And Leo asked when was the last time either of us did something meaningful? I just thought it was a sketchy come-down. He was always like that, a worrying heartbeat, dizzy nausea, tricky panic, you know?'

'No,' Leme said.

'I remember I said, you're having an epiphany, and he got angry, told me he was being serious. I said, obviously. No such thing as a trivial epiphany.'

'Very clever,' Leme said.

Alex sneered. 'Fine. He just said he needed some direction and I told him we're doomed. Know the expression? *Pai rico, filho nobre, neto pobre.*'

Leme nodded. He did, and Alex seemed exactly to fit the stereotype: a wastrel from a successful family; his grandfather rich, his father a noble man, and he, the son, poor – morally, anyway.

'I thought that it was hard to take seriously someone dressed in Gucci loafers and an Armani shirt talking about bettering himself,' Alex said.

Leme raised his eyebrows. 'Go on.'

'We went to bed after that,' Alex said. 'Leo woke the girl and took her with him.'

A mischievous look crossed Alex's face and he leaned towards Leme and said quietly, holding his eye, 'I fucked her two years before, just legal. She snored then, too. Old habits. Sweet *buçeta* – wet enough she'd done it before, tight enough not too many times. Everyone knew. Not Leo though. I didn't tell him. Fact is her girl-friends seemed to get off on what I did to her. Certainly didn't stop any of them. Got to use the family name for something. Turns out I'm better when I fuck girls I don't actually *want* to fuck. Maybe that's why: I *fuck* them.'

Leme swallowed, breathed. 'Why did you tell me that?' he asked.

'You said you wanted to know about our relationship, about what guys our age do. It's a representative story.'

Leme thought that was probably about right. Looked out of the window. The cloud was thickening, swelling. It would be raining in an hour or less. Better get on.

'Though using the family name,' Alex said, 'had a lot to do with Leo getting himself killed, I reckon.'

Leme turned sharply. 'What the fuck do you mean by that?'

'Some girl in the *favela*. Ana de Moraes. Talk to her.'

'Who is she?'

'No fucking idea.'

Leme switched off the recording app. 'Don't go anywhere,' he said, and crossed to the other side of the café. He made a quick call to the office. Waited. A moment later, a text message appeared: Ana de Moraes from Paraisópolis – student at TAAP.

Paradise City.

A student at TAAP: had to be a scholarship-type situation.

Leme paused, breathed. It was likely Renata knew this girl, or knew of her, or her mother, or helped this girl.

He remembered what she said about girls and boys like this Ana.

They deserve more. We can help them have it. We can help them have what they deserve.

Leme went back to the table. Alex was leaning back, jabbering into his phone, laughing, rubbing his chin.

'She's a student at the university Leo's mum runs,' Leme said.

'Oh, fuck,' Alex said. 'I think I do know who she is then.'

Leme muscled Alex through the door and pulled him roughly down the street by the elbow.

'Where you parked?'

Alex nodded at the luxury shopping centre across the road.

Leme sneered. 'Of course you're parked there. Valet, I suppose?'

Alex smiled, shook Leme's hand off his arm. 'What's wrong with that?' he asked.

Leme shook his head. 'Doesn't matter anyway,' he said. 'You're coming with me. You can walk back.'

Alex tutted and sucked his teeth, waggled his finger. '*Mano*,' he said. 'Walk?'

'Take a fucking taxi if you don't like it. No choice, *querido*. You're coming with me.'

They turned down a side street. To their left was a private members' club and restaurant, an annexe of the Pinheiros Sports club.

'You a member here, then?' Leme asked.

Alex nodded.

'True what they say? Fifty grand just to get on the waiting list?'

Alex smiled. 'For the riff-raff, yeah,' he said. 'My grandfather's membership number? Two.'

Leme snorted with laughter. 'Get in the fucking car.'

He pulled open the passenger door and it creaked and swung awkwardly, rust showing round the edges.

'Nice wheels,' Alex muttered.

Leme glared at him.

The car started with a gulp and cough and shook itself into life. Leme wound down his window and the gasoline fumes felt like a sharp contrast to the palm-fringed, residential backstreet. Neither of them put on their seat belts.

Alex sat texting. Occasional snort of laughter. Leme thought about what he should say.

He pulled on to Rua Gabriel Monteiro and they lurched in traffic past Mendes's construction site.

'My old school that,' Alex said without looking up from his phone. 'British school?'

'Uh-huh. Piece of shit. Expensive though, so all the parents assume it's good.' He leaned back and yawned. 'That's the problem with the new members of my social class,' he said. 'Too many of them equate price with quality. No tradition of discernment, *sabe?*'

Leme couldn't help but laugh. 'You're quite something, you know?'

Alex looked at him and grinned. 'I know,' he said.

Leme made a decision. Turned right into the maze of Jardim Europa and pulled over in the first space he found, right in front of a private security booth in which an old man was napping. The houses sat large and airy around them and joggers and dog-walkers did circuits on the road.

'Thought you were taking me to the *delegacia*?' Alex said.

'Change of plan. You made me laugh, so I'm doing you a favour. We'll do this here. I just want you to answer a few questions, *certo?*'

'*Certissimo.*'

'Don't be a cunt – I said you made me laugh. Don't push it.'

'Sorry.'

'Better. Right. So this Ana studies at TAAP, which is run by Leonardo's mother, *ne*? She's from Paraisópolis. How do you know her? And put that fucking phone away.'

'I think, I *think*, Leo helped her get a scholarship to study there. He was helping his mother. Volunteering. Some do-good initiative she started when she took over the college.'

Right: scholarship.

'How do you know this?'

'I was there when Leo read her application. I skimmed the supporting statement. It said she wanted to study journalism, to report on street kids and educational opportunities or some such. I said it sounded like a lobbying tool. Told Leo I didn't realise the young were so politicised. I didn't see how a degree in journalism was going to help her. She'd earn more as a maid.'

The *cunt* – exactly the attitude Renata despised.

Leme breathed.

I should fill him in –

'You just said you *think* he helped her.'

'Well, we read the application, and then I met her at the university. So, there *appears* to be a connection.'

'You read the application?'

'Yes.'

'So you know it's her.'

'Yes, I guess so.'

'Then stop being a cunt.'

'Sorry. I can't help it.' Alex smiled.

Leme glared. Leme went on. 'How did you meet her?'

'How do you meet anyone?'

'You tell me.'

'I was fucking this English girl, Ellie. *Eleanor*. She's a journalist at *Time Out* São Paulo. Ana's doing an internship there, or something. Part of her degree.'

Internship: opportunity.

They deserve more.

'And what was her relationship with Leonardo?'

'You know. She's a good-looking girl, *sabe?* Bit of pro bono work, know what I mean?' He winked. 'Textbook, *entendeu?*'

Leme shook his head. 'So Leonardo was in Paraisópolis to see her?'

'*That* I don't know. He didn't say anything about her when he called me from Paraisópolis that morning.'

'And how did you meet this Ellie?'

'You want me to give you tips?'

Leme leaned across and smacked Alex hard across the face with his open palm.

And then he smacked him with the back of his hand.

And again.

Then Leme grabbed him by the neck.

'You don't know what you're talking about.'

He let him go. Alex's cheek purpled and he shook his head. Stuck his tongue out.

He leaned away from Leme, but looked him in the eye and said, 'So it *is* true what they say about the police.'

'Answer the question.'

Alex took a deep breath. 'I don't know how I met her. I just did. I woke up with her one morning and we went from there, *entendeu?* But she is Ana's best friend, as far as I can tell. In fact, I think Ana is *her* only friend.'

'Clearly you're not.'

Alex shrugged. 'She'll know more about Ana than I do. Interesting girl.' Alex regained his composure, curled his lip. 'When I was in bed with her, she told me I was being deferential when I fingered her. *Deferential?* The fuck? I told her it was a lost art, that most men my age thought it was childish. She asked me why I kept stroking her hair.'

'Why did you?'

'I always thought girls liked it. She told me showing approval of her hair was showing approval of a feminine accessory, or some shit. Didn't seem to mind my hand crammed up her cunt.' He paused. Winked. 'I'll give you her number.'

Leme checked himself, nodded and handed Alex a notepad and pen.

'There is something I do know, though,' Alex said.

Leme looked at him. He continued. 'Ana isn't just working at the magazine.'

'Go on.'

'Know that building site we just passed? Guy who owns it is Mendes. Ana works for him, too, though doing what, I don't know. Don't want to know, actually.'

Leme narrowed his eyes. 'What does that mean? What's that got to do with Leonardo being in the *favela*?'

'Talk to Ellie. She'll know. Oh and there's someone else. Name's Rafael Maura. He works for Mendes. He might know something about Ana. He and Leo used to be friends. He's seeing Leo's ex now. Dude's a piece of work, but he's a mate, so …'

'Write down his details,' Leme said. 'And here's my card. Here's a few, in fact. Pass them around Leo's friends. If anyone knows something you don't, I mean.'

Alex handed back the notepad.

Leme leant across him and opened the passenger door.

'Right, now fuck off. I'll be in touch.'

He called the English girl.

Leme arranged to meet Eleanor in a cheap *boteco* opposite the restaurant Consolado Mineiro in Pinheiros near where she lived. When he arrived, there were already two empty beer bottles baking on the rusting table and she was surveying the hippie market scene in Praça Benedito Calixto, hand above her eyes in the sun.

She could fucking talk.

No wonder she thought she was a writer. Her Portuguese was pretty good, though. The accent made it sound functional, like the words came out in their true purpose to literally *inform*, each chosen carefully, little fluency. He sipped his own beer. He had long understood that he now contextualised women within the frame that Renata had created, had left. The crackle of electricity raced along the power lines above the market. He'd just let her speak. And speak. She was like a fucking actress saying lines. And nailing beers, too. Leme could barely keep up.

'So, I met Ana in São Paulo,' she was saying. 'I wasn't prepared, *sabe?* I know that now. For her or the city.'

Leme nodded. Leme thought: *this Ana.*

'You know, from the air São Paulo goes on forever,' she went on. 'A fucking building site, dust and pollution above skyscrapers, flashing lights in the cloud, bridges that cross the stinking river. It's like futuristic but also sort of apocalyptic? I remember I struggled to collect my baggage, Paulistanos talking loudly to each other and into their phones. Artificial light.'

'Yeah,' Leme said. 'It can be hard.' He wondered how long he would be here.

'Look at this fucker,' she said, pointing across the street. 'He's selling what? A few piece of shit paintings and he's arguing over a couple of reais. *Babaca, eh?*'

Leme glanced to where she was pointing. It didn't look anything. The stalls were packed close together in the square, mainly *pastel* and *agua de coco*, beer and *espetinhos de carne*, the odd dreadlocked woman weaving bracelets; shirtless, dirty men kneeling in the dust making furniture from wooden pallets.

She was talking again. 'I wondered where I'd, like, fit in? Pink and pale, sweat patches under my arms. There were a couple of glances, head to thigh. Know what I mean? My skirt was too short for an airport.'

Leme carried on drinking.

He wasn't going back to work.

Might as well enjoy this.

'I started off in one of those serviced flats,' she said. 'The magazine had set it up but told me that I probably wouldn't be able to afford it for too long. That wasn't too encouraging. I moved out to a fifth-storey with dodgy plumbing and stains. My balcony was fucking tiny. When I first moved in I tried to sit out there in the evenings and read and drink, but I'd be forced inside by the fumes. And the noise. The fucking noise. I used to, like, lie awake until dawn, writhing around under the sheets. *Every fucking morning* I stood under the electric shower, terrified the water would react with the open wires, my head fuzzy from lack of sleep, and I thought: does no one go to bed in this city?'

Leme smiled. 'It's an adjustment, right? Why did you come?'

'I'd always wanted to become a journalist and my degree choice was supposed to set me up for it. This was the only job I could get. It's like feminism never happened, a clever girl said to me once as we smoked on our lunch break. I liked her. We promised we'd always be best friends. Until I met Ana, this was true.'

'Tell me about how you know her.'

'Ana's a student intern at the magazine. She reports directly to me. I remember the first day I saw her. She was standing in the corner of the office, head down, both hands holding her bag in front of her, like a piece of armour.'

They deserve more.

'And what do you do there?'

'Help with the listings, write reviews of some of the events, copy-edit the English of our Brazilian staff and do occasional interviews or features when they come up. I'd been, like, promised *a lot* more.' She made a face. 'Oh well.'

Leme waved for the waiter.

'Get the bill,' Eleanor said. 'Let's have a wander.'

Leme grimaced.

'Come on,' she said, dropping some notes on the table and pulling him from his seat. She marched him across the road, weaving between the cars, hot and glinting, inching up towards Avenida Paulista.

She kept up her narrative as they careened around the market square. 'On my first day at the office,' she said, 'my colleagues invited me out for a drink. We went to a local bar called Vaca Veia. Know it? Old cow, *ne?* They drip-fed me Caipirinha. There was a man outside the ladies toilets, handing me a shot. I staggered back to the flat with him and passed out in my clothes, threw up a few hours later. Fuck me. The hangover. My mouth tasted of limes and aftershave, my skin raw from stubble.'

'OK, Eleanor, slow down,' Leme said. He was getting a little tired of all this. She sounded like Alex. Must be pretty lonely, he thought. Be nice, eh. But he did want to find out if she knew anything about Ana working for Mendes. He said, 'What are you working on with her?'

'We're working on a piece about the construction magnate, Jorge Mendes. Know him?'

'Know of him,' Leme said.

'We went to meet him, actually.'

She stopped at a stall. Fingered a piece of cloth. 'This is nice,' she said. She looked at the small woman who stood politely behind the table. 'How much?' she asked.

'*Cinquenta.*'

'*Cinquenta? Ah, não.* Come on.' She tugged at Leme's sleeve.

He moved into step with her.

'Have you heard about this?' she said. 'These acid attacks happening around here. It's fucking terrifying! Thieves throw acid through windows – absolutely sickening, *appalling* – pull out the drivers and steal their cars. I heard stories of a couple of disfigured executives; saw photos, which made me *actually vomit*. I was in tears. They'll do anything; it's disgusting.'

'*Pois e,*' Leme said. 'So you went to meet Mendes.'

'Yeah. His press officer, Selina, was a complete bitch. Really security conscious, *sabe?* He's got this massive office. Two floor-to-ceiling windows that run its entire length. Walking down the middle towards a raised platform at the far end, windows either side, I felt dizzy. Mendes stood at the far window looking out. I saw the river, the city racetrack. There was a young guy hunched over some papers at a big table. We sat down facing him. He looked up, did a double-take when he saw Ana. He looked at her for a long time. Ana smiled at him and I told her to take out her notebook.'

'Why did you arrange to meet him?' Leme asked.

'We were looking at Mendes's whole career, but he only wanted to talk about the *centro* project, you know, this development for the *Copa*. At the end, I went over to his desk. Ana stayed and talked to Rafael, the young man. Rafael Maura. Bit of a smarmy wanker is this Rafael. Always playing with his hair, moulding it into a greasy little Mohawk. Smelled of cheap aftershave. Well, not cheap, but over-powering, you know *vulgar*. Cheap French, *entendeu?*' She laughed. 'Anyway,' she went on, 'I heard Rafael say, I'm sure I know you from somewhere. I heard them laugh, but by then I was too far away to hear anything else. When I looked back a few moments later, Ana was taking photos with her phone. They laughed again. Rafael was pointing at a painting on the wall I recognised. Modern, trendy, name like Militias. Artist Priscilla Something. I watched Ana line it up and tap away several times, Rafael at her side, leaning a little closer than I'd have liked. She took loads of photos. When I asked her about it later, she said she liked art, that's all.'

They deserve more.

'What happened then?'

'We went back to the office, and listened to what Mendes had said. Ana looked disgusted. That guy, Rafael, told me that this is just the start, she said. A charm offensive. I was like, why? She said that the guy has a dodgy past. Whatever. I thought they all did. Then she showed me the photo again. I remember she said, *bonito, ne?* This painting. And it is, actually. She sent it to me.'

This Ana. The thought made him smile.

They stopped at a bench and Eleanor sat down.

'Too hot,' she said. 'To be drinking, you know?'

She rubbed sweat with a tissue from around her neck and bare shoulders, lifting her ponytail.

Leme smiled. 'I've heard that Ana might be working for this Mendes guy.'

'*Ta louco?*' Eleanor said. 'No way. What? That's ridiculous. She's sweet, but she's not stupid. Where did you hear that?'

Relief. If this Ana were anything like he imagined, no way she'd work for Mendes.

'Rumours, that's all.'

A look crossed Eleanor's face, slowly, as if she were just then realising something important: curiosity, concern, then suspicion.

'Why do you want to know all this, anyway?' she asked.

Leme weighed the question. He watched her face crease in the sunlight, eyes hidden behind sunglasses but with an obvious squint of anxiety. Her arms were white with patches of red from the sun and where she had scratched at mosquito bites. She tapped her feet double the speed of the music that drifted through the market.

'A young man, Leonardo Alencar,' he said, 'died in Paraisópolis not long ago. I think he knew Ana. Do you know him?'

Voices and laughter pierced the low hum of traffic. The sun dipped behind a cloud and Leme felt the pressure in the air. It would rain in a few hours. He wanted to be home before it did. He looked at Eleanor, who was studying a group of men sitting around a table eating rice and beans from plastic containers.

'Oh,' Eleanor said. 'Yes, you know, a *bit*. Well, you might want to talk to her about that.' She sat up stiffly. 'I better go. That OK? I live just over there.' She pointed at a fairly miserable-looking building and stood.

'Hang on,' Leme said. 'Sit.' She sat back down, tossed her ponytail. 'When did you last see him?' he asked.

'Oh, I'm not sure. Couple weeks, you know, *maybe*.'

'And what was he like? Did he seem normal? Or nervous? Anything like that?'

'Look, I didn't know him that well. I think he was pretty keen on Ana. We used to have drinks occasionally. That's pretty much it.'

Leme nodded. 'So there was nothing about him that was different or unusual when you last saw him?'

'You know?' she said. 'I'm not sure I can help.'

Leme nodded.

'You can go,' he said.

He watched her wind her way across the square.

The men called to her to join them, but she didn't.

Leme went back to the *lanchonete* to talk to Luis, let him know what happened.

Well, let him know he'd been to the site of the collapsed building.

That there wasn't much he could do just now.

'I'll keep my eyes open, though,' he said. 'If anything comes up ... *entendeu?*'

Luis nodded. If he was disappointed, he didn't show it. Not the kind of man, anyhow. Fact was he'd turned Leme on to the building in the first place: there wasn't much Leme could tell him, as he didn't quite know where it fit in yet, if it even did.

Leme started his car. It was parked off Avenida Giovanni Gronchi and he had to cross against the traffic to turn left towards home. It was always a fucking pain getting across Giovanni like this. Not for the first time, Leme marvelled at the way Brazilian drivers went bumper to bumper, every inch of tarmac claimed as their own, the road *dominated*.

He sat as the car did its little dance, nosing out into the road, retreating when no one stopped, rocking on its heels, sighing. As he sat there, impatient, Leme noticed two Militars on motorbikes slip out from the restaurant lot and into the road. One held the traffic and the other went slightly ahead. They waved Leme into the gap and he nudged the car across the road and turned left. Did they know who he was? It was possible they were part of Carlos's lot; he couldn't recognise them with their helmets and aviator sunglasses.

Leme hefted the car up the hill, crunching through gears, but the motorbike in front was idling, and bang in front of Leme's car. The one behind was tight against Leme's tail so there was no way for him to change lanes. His chest started to tighten. It was still light, seven o'clock, and the traffic was heavy; there shouldn't be anything to worry about.

They approached the T-junction where the steep road that ran alongside the *favela* met Giovanni. This was a difficult junction. The traffic lights changed far too quickly, only allowing a few cars to pass each time in whichever direction. It was a notorious spot for accidents as, fed up with the indecision of others, some drivers simply accelerated around waiting cars straight into a blind spot.

Leme was four cars back now as he sat waiting at the lights. The motorbikes continued to pin him in. He wasn't sure what to do. There wasn't much he could do. He was in his car. There were hundreds of people around. He didn't even know who these Militars were. It would be fine. Breathe, he told himself, and he'd get away from them as soon as he could. Wave thanks. Get home.

The lights changed.

The first three cars got across easily.

The first motorbike edged into the road.

Leme knew he couldn't wait: the motorbike behind was pushing against the boot of his car and there was a tailback to the stadium, almost a mile further down the road.

He edged into the junction.

The first motorbike stopped.

Leme tried to turn left, then right, but cars passed either side, up from the *favela* road to his left, past him down Giovanni to his right.

The lights changed and cars swarmed around him again.

He wound up his window.

The two motorbikes pulled away, leaving Leme in the middle of the junction, boxed in from all sides.

Beeping and shouting, shouting and beeping.

'*Caralho, porra!*'

'*Vai tomar uma, eh!*'

Leme looked around him. There was nothing to do but sit it out and take the abuse.

A different, civilian motorbike roared past, banging on his window.

Another accelerated down the driver's side and kicked Leme's wing mirror clean off.

Beeping and shouting, shouting and beeping.

People on the pavements were laughing and pointing.

A truck staggered up the hill from the *favela*, five men covered in dust sitting in the back, exposed to the heat.

They spat on the roof of Leme's car.

He looked further down the road.

The two Militars had stopped at the side of the road, on the right, their bikes pointed out into it, lights flashing, helmets off.

The lights changed again and Leme was able to shunt in front of the first car that came up the hill, which gave him the space to move down the road.

As he passed the Militars, he wound down his window.

They leaned towards him, bowed ironically.

It was the same two from the other morning.

Leme was home in five minutes.

He pulled a beer from the fridge and sat outside.

Lit a cigarette.

He hoped the Militars had seen him by chance in the *lanchonete* and taken the opportunity to fuck with him a little.

Anything else would be a lot more worrying.

The next morning, Leme met Ana at the campus café. Two-birds situation. He also planned to ask Aline Alencar what she had been doing at the construction site in the *centro*.

He saw her approach from the other side of the room. She attracted a lot of glances from young men and women alike. Leme wondered if it were her beauty or her skin colour. Not too many *negras* at this college, scholarship programme or not.

They sat apart from the bustle and clink of trays, cutlery and glasses. Leme had his notepad open but had decided against recording the conversation so as not to draw attention to them. He thought he owed her that. Hard enough being an outsider without the sort of prejudice and suspicion talking to a detective would bring.

'I wonder which comedian named the *favela* Paradise City,' he said.

She smiled. 'My mother used to joke: France has Paris. Brazil, Paraisópolis.' She raised her eyebrows.

'Some flash fucker told me there is a bar in Paris called Favela Chic,' Leme said. 'Hypocrites and wankers the world over. You got out though.'

She laughed. 'Sort of. Going back is never easy, because you realise that you've never really left. Even when it all looks so different. So *shabby*.'

She was dressed down – jeans and a faded black tank top. A uniform. *Uniform.* That was a good word for São Paulo, Leme thought. On the way over he'd watched the cars creep forwards on Faria Lima, engines throbbing in the midday sun – the city a blank canvas of automobiles, dead slow. They're all going somewhere, but not quickly: darkened windows in black sedans, white taxis jabbering a conversation with their horns, rusty Beetles filled with brown faces panting from the windows like dogs.

In the tunnel underneath the river the cool was brief; the signs telling him to turn off his engine when the traffic is stalled ignored – like everything else – and the fumes hanging low.

He'd exited the tunnel.

Tree roots lifted paving stones.

Motoqueiros rode figures of eight in between the lanes, honking.

Leme agreed. '*Exactamente*,' he said.

'Funny thing about us,' she said, 'this way we talk, agree. I only noticed it when I first spoke to my English language teacher – part of my course. The English have their own little conversational tics, I suppose. His agreement always seems genuine, like he considers what you say and makes a decision to agree with you, *entendeu?* In Portuguese, it's instinctive. We're always asking: understand? It's about the language, not what the words mean.'

'That the sort of thing you learn here?' Leme asked.

'That's the sort of thing you learn anywhere.'

Leme was warming to her. She reminded him a little of Renata. Not physically, but her poise, slight distance, sense of humour. He wondered what she was protecting.

'I'm one of the lucky ones,' she continued. 'That's what my mother tells me, at least. I'm so blessed, she says, that she thanks God every day. Maybe that's why I keep away.'

'She's right,' Leme said.

'She's always so grateful. Her faith means she has to be. Thing is, if you're told you're lucky too often, then a part of you will think you don't deserve whatever it is you've had the luck to get, blessed or not, *entendeu?*'

'Looks like you've achieved a lot.'

'I'm just another *morena* in dirty jeans.'

Leme smiled. Ana was tapping her fingers along to the music.

'You like this?' Leme asked, nodding at the ceiling.

'Yeah,' she said, smiling. 'BNegão. Know it?'

Leme laughed. 'You'd be surprised.'

'This song is funny though, right? There's a line, goes something like: I've got lots of ideas but nothing in my pocket.' She smiled and looked around the canteen. 'Irony, right?' She laughed.

Leme laughed with her. 'This guy's not a lot younger than me,' he said. 'Real name is Bernard.' She made a face. 'I'm not that *careta, sabe?*' he said.

Ana shrugged, amused.

They sat in silence for a moment, listened to the song.

'Tell me about your home,' Leme said.

'This about Professora Aline's son? Leo?'

'Yes.' Leme watched her eyes widen sharply and her mouth set in a tense line.

'When they first built the condominiums around the *favela*, the view brought the price down a little,' she said. 'But now, the demand means there's no issue, *entendeu?* I study economics too, right? And that price relationship never worked the other way round: the value of our homes isn't affected by the new surrounding wealth. When I pointed this out to my mother, she said, "Is that what they're teaching you? How to disrespect?"'

Leme smiled. She answered his questions like Renata: anecdote, irony, *point*.

'What do you want to know?'

'What's it like there?'

'Close to my mother's house,' she said, 'along Rua Iriri, blue, green and white plastic bags line the street, sun-baked leftovers turning to shit. Telegraph wires criss-cross overhead. Barred windows and rusty gates painted orange and yellow and green: bright, optimistic, *entendeu?* Cars in bits, white as bone. Kids throw stones at them and laugh.' She paused. 'That's what it's like.'

Leme nodded. 'What does your mother do?'

'She's a dressmaker, a *costureira*, and teaches it at the Mosteiro in the *favela*. What she does is provide a means to earn a living, a trade. With hard work and faith, she says, you can make a life from this skill.'

'Sounds about right,' Leme said.

Ana shook her head. 'That was something we disagreed on,' she said. 'After my first classes on ethical capitalist models, I said, "But they're only going to be exploited. None of them will ever have the resources to set up on their own. It's a form of slavery."' Ana touched her cheek. 'She slapped me for that.'

'I'm not surprised,' Leme said, smiling.

'I'm all she's got left,' Ana said, 'and she seems to want to keep me out, which suits me, actually.'

Leme raised an eyebrow. 'What about this police occupation? Operação Saturação. That made much of a difference to life there?'

'I've heard about this,' she said. 'There's supposed to be over five hundred police knocking about in the *favela* now. I heard they've already killed the big boss men in Paraisópolis, Piauí and Robinho.'

Leme shrugged. 'A lot of people have died,' he said.

'When I go back to visit, I don't care about any of that,' Ana said. 'My mother folds me into her and it smells like home. And when I leave, she presses money into my hand – money I don't need, money that she can't afford to give me, and money, for exactly those reasons, I have to accept, *entendeu?* On the walls in her house the plaster is ridged and swollen, right? And the cloth that shields her bed from the rest of the room is threadbare and miserly. And she's a *costureira*. Makes no sense to me.'

'Tell me about the scholarship,' Leme said.

'I applied and got it.'

'With Leo Alencar's help.'

Leme watched her expression change, soften, drop, like the life was being drained from her face.

He changed tack. 'And what does the scholarship cover exactly?'

She breathed hard and smiled. 'Tuition fees. Some living support.' She paused. 'Not much.'

'So you work?'

'Yes.'

'With this English journalist, Ellie?'

'Yes.'

'Tell me about her.'

'You know, a *gringa, ne?*' She laughed. 'Chipped and discoloured nails, *entendeu?*'

Leme was confused. 'She's your friend though, right?'

'Those white thighs are just right for some Brasileiros,' she said.

Leme repeated his question.

'*Olha*,' she said, 'Ellie is my friend and colleague and she is clever and sweet, but she's calculating when it comes to men, that's all. Brazilian men, anyway.'

'And what does she think of you?'

'She thinks she's my boss and I play along. It's one advantage of being an underprivileged *neguinha*. If I play dumb, everyone thinks it is because of my *favela*-naivety.'

'And what are you working on at the moment?'

'A story about the regeneration of the city centre by Mendes Construction,' she said.

'Right.' Leme thought about what Alex had told him, what Ellie, it appeared, didn't know. But he didn't want to ask the question – he was afraid of what the answer might be.

He took a deep breath. 'I've heard you do some work for that company,' he said. 'For Mendes.'

She shook her head. 'No. And I wouldn't want to. My first term at university? Away from the *favela* for the first time? That showed me how this city works. Professora Aline taught me. The elite group aim to improve the city without surrendering their grip, right? And the question, the thread that ran through all her lectures? *Who makes the decisions?* According to her, the nature of the political system prevents anything other than a conservative government. Of course, everyone in the class except me directly benefits from this system. But you know, it's nice she thinks it.'

'What's your point?' Leme asked.

'My point? I wouldn't *want* to work for a man like that, *entendeu?* From what I've seen of him, he's a *malandro* and *ladrão.*'

'How do you know?'

'The article we're doing. We've been to his offices, visited the sites, talked to people. We're just trying to figure out how to present it without getting sued, *entendeu?* We're going to visit a site in São Bernardo dos Campos, you know in the south of the city? Something interesting there, apparently. A new project. It's a model, you know, for a thing he wants to do for the Olympics in Rio? Not enough to own most of this city, apparently.'

Leme nodded. Sighed. 'Be careful,' he said. Then realised the futility of it. She was, he realised, very like Renata. And it hurt.

'Ah,' she said. '*Relaxa.* It's going to be a good piece.'

Leme didn't doubt that.

'There's another line in that song,' she said, 'BNegão? Something about advice after the fact, you know, that it's not much fucking good, *entendeu?*'

He smiled, but it didn't feel right.

He waved her off.

As he watched her go, he realised that he should have pushed her further on her relationship with Leo.

And this question of whether she worked for Mendes.

There'd be time for both.

Leme's instinct told him that Ana was a smart girl.

And not one to do the wrong thing.

Leme had a bit of time before he was due to meet Aline Alencar and decided to pop off campus for a smoke. As he exited the main gates, the security guards eyed him with hostility. He smiled. 'Back soon,' he said, and winked. 'We'll see,' one of them said.

He stood in the shade of a tree. Gaggles of high-spirited kids sauntered past, flirting and laughing. Seeing groups of students always made Leme reflect on his own decision, nearly twenty years ago, not to go to university. All that promise. All those acres of exposed flesh. No thoughts of anything beyond what might be happening later that night. For most of this lot, anyway. Private universities dominated the city: they were places to hang out. Public universities were places to go on strike. He wondered at the logic of this.

He lit a cigarette and leant back against the tree. Cars shuffled up through Itaim towards the centre of town. A taxi driver swore at a *motoqueiro* who clipped his wing mirror as he zipped past. The bike stopped and caused another jam as he turned left into the traffic to remonstrate. Leme looked down the road. There were no other motorbikes about. If there had been, they would have joined in and God help the *taxista*. They exchanged insults, threw their arms up at each other, threatened violence. Other drivers, stuck now in a lengthening tailback, added to the conversation. Engines simmering in the heat. A haze of smoke thickened above the road from the cheap VWs that burped black fumes from their exhausts. The *motoqueiro* thought better of his row and put his helmet back on, pointedly slowly. The cars filtered along in his wake.

Leme looked back at the security hut by the main gate. Two Militar motorbikes had arrived, their lights flashing silently. He could see one of the Militars talking to the guards. The other stood by the bikes, his hand resting on his gun. Leme moved slightly behind the tree.

He lit another cigarette. He'd have to wait this out, be late for Aline Alencar if necessary.

The Militar slapped hands with the security guard and ambled back to his partner. They exchanged a few words and pointed up the street to where Leme was standing. He tensed. Decided to step out from behind the tree.

The two Militars nodded when they saw him and spoke quickly into their radios. Leme took his phone from his pocket and flicked through the contact list to his friend Carlos's number, his one trust-worthy contact in the Military Police. If it came to it, he'd call him. He always answered when Leme called.

The Militars walked towards Leme, looking over their shoulders. A couple of pedestrians, seeing the Militars, crossed the road and walked hurriedly away.

Leme brought his phone to his ear and pretended to make a call. He turned circles as he spoke, head down. He felt the Militars approach. He looked up and they were either side of him, hands on hips. He feigned surprise. 'I'll call you back,' he said into his phone.

'*Pois não?*' Leme asked with a smile.

'Woof woof,' the taller of the Militars said.

'Slow down,' Leme said. 'Don't be a cunt, eh?'

The Militar laughed. 'We should stop meeting like this. People will start talking. Anyway, what are you doing here?'

'Signing up for evening classes. You?'

'We heard there might be someone bothering the students,' he said. 'When we saw you, we assumed it was you.'

'*Então.*'

The Militar nodded at the gate. 'You planning on going back inside?' he asked.

'*Claro*,' Leme said. 'My first class in a bit.'

The Militar nodded. 'One thing to bump into you here,' he said. 'Bit different in the *favela*, *entendeu?* Lot quieter in there, *sabe?*'

He smiled and touched his neck, then his gun.

'I thought I told you to slow down,' Leme said, pushing past.

The other Militar blocked his way.

Leme held his phone up so that they could see the screen: Carlos's full name in bold type.

'I was just having a chat with your superior,' Leme said. 'He asked who you were.'

The Militars swapped a look. 'What did you say?'

'A couple of mouthy no-mark cunts, that's all,' he said. 'Fucking dry lunches, the pair of them. You, *entendeu?*' He smiled. 'Just that,' he added, and walked towards the gate.

He didn't look back.

'You better hope you don't see us in Paraisópolis,' the Militar called after him.

The security guard waved Leme back on to campus. He'd speak to Carlos when he could. For now though, he had to think up a plausible excuse for meeting with Aline Alencar.

'When I was appointed to lead it, the university was in a mess,' Aline Alencar told Leme as they sat in her office.

She looked through him.

She looked through him with her tired eyes, her tired, grey eyes.

Leme admired her. He wasn't as composed in the throes of his own grief. Women, he'd once decided, are colder than men. But it was *there*, the grief.

'I was the first female vice-chancellor of this university,' she said. 'First one in São Paulo.'

'That doesn't surprise me.'

Her lips thinned. Her grey, cracked lips thinned.

'Oh, I see.'

'You're an impressive woman.'

Leme opened his palms and gestured vaguely at the street.

'You mean that as a compliment?'

He smiled and nodded. 'Don't be defensive.'

'You're right, I shouldn't be.' Her face woke, hardened into a steely mask. 'But you shouldn't be telling me what to *be*, detective. It's a difficult time,' she said. 'You should know that.'

Leme nodded – contrite. 'Just need to establish a few things. Routine.'

'I'm not sure I understand why you're here exactly. Leo died in an accident.' She looked more carefully at Leme. 'What is it that you're investigating?'

Leme gave her a tight, sympathetic smile. It slid off her. He wanted to tell her what he knew about Leo's death, but couldn't implicate himself just yet. He had to get her to trust him. He wanted to tell her about Renata, too, but felt duplicitous, as if earning her confidence to aid his own investigation.

He didn't like that idea at all, true or not.

'In any accident,' he said, 'it's important to establish that it was exactly that: an accident. And, insensitive or not, it's useful for us to know a bit about Leo.'

'I don't understand that,' she said.

Leme decided to tell her something. 'I want to know why Leo was in the *favela* that morning.'

'I'm not sure I understand why.'

Her fingers rapped the table. Her grey, cracked fingers rapped the table.

Leme looked at her. She was confused, blank. Grieving. 'It's something we need to do. Routine. That's all. I'm checking a few things about Leonardo's background. I apologise if it's insensitive.'

'OK,' she said. She shrugged. It occurred to Leme that there were much bigger things going on for her than this minor irritation.

Her face slipped into a distracted mask: valium-glazed.

Her limbs, underwater-slow, going through the motions.

She shook herself back into the room.

'What do you want to know?' she asked.

'Tell me about what you do here. Let's start with that.'

'Before the university, I worked in finance,' she said. 'I was successful, and that's why the university asked me to teach there.'

'And why did you accept?'

'Everyone wants to study economics, these days. Venture capitalism. Ethical business, you know?'

'Tell me about the scholarship scheme and your son's involvement,' Leme said.

Aline breathed. She spoke as if to the press, autopilot, running through a prepared statement. 'The idea was simple enough,' she said. 'We were to offer scholarships to deserving, under-privileged kids from Paraisópolis. These scholarships were to be underpinned by university funds, but we also invited outside investment, including money from the foundation set up by my husband Milton. These were to run concurrently – and this included combined publicity – with the capital investment and marketing expertise others and I were putting into a young entrepreneur scheme for start-up businesses. I asked Leo to be involved.'

'How?'

'To look through applications and pass on any that were worth pursuing.'

'Very noble,' Leme said.

'My name.'

'Eh?'

'Noble – it's what my name, *Aline*, means.'

She gripped the table, her knuckles white.

Her white knuckles tightened.

Leme raised his eyebrows.

'I wanted to give him something to do that would make him feel valuable,' she explained. 'Sometimes I felt that growing up rich was a hindrance to him. It had never been my experience, but Leo had drifted from school to university to unemployment with none of the fear of failure that might motivate less fortunate young men.'

Her voice cracked. Her thin, grey voice cracked.

And she steadied herself.

Leme looked out of the window. Outside, the air throbbed. Something hung from a tree, a piece of fabric or a ripped plastic bag, and, in the heat, it contracted like a muscle. He touched the desk with his thumb.

Felt his heart beat. Stop. Beat.

'And he agreed to do it?' he asked.

'Yes. The day I asked him, we went out for lunch. He said yes. And that's when I bumped into Jorge Mendes and all this started.'

'All what started?'

'The problems.'

She stared at Leme, eyes empty.

Her grey eyes, empty.

'Explain,' he said.

'My husband Milton never liked him,' she said. 'But Mendes knew some contact with Milton would be useful to him. So he came to me.'

'Why?'

'Mendes was focusing on construction. Still is. Milton's influential. Jorge said to me, "There's something we need to discuss at some point. Now's not the time." I felt my body harden, I remember. "One of your investments," he said, "a venture capital thing." He told me he might be of some use. I remember I didn't like his tone. It was threatening.'

'So what happened?'

'We had lunch the next day. He's always looking to see what he can get out of people. His trick? He seems to be giving you his undivided attention but he's really got an eye over your shoulder for someone who offers more. He's a weasel, really,' she spat. 'Rodent-faced. Feral.'

Leme gave her a look: OK, *chega*, it said. Get to the point.

It sparked something. Aline glared. 'This is relevant,' she said. 'You got somewhere you need to be?'

Chastened, Leme shook his head. Why did he feel that? He shifted in his seat. Felt his back bead with sweat.

'So,' she said, 'one of the handouts I give to first-year business students leads with the Henry Ford quotation.' She made quote signs with her fingers, '"You can't build a reputation on what you're going to do." But, I'd argue, you can project the appearance of someone who gets things done. The reputation will take care of itself. These were business principles; morally speaking, reputation-wise, Mendes was already suspect.'

'So you were suspicious?'

'Absolutely,' she said. 'And I had no idea what he wanted. I mean, we'd been sponsoring young entrepreneurs. Start-up capital for promising businesses based on some ethical premise or other. Helping a company that designs, markets and sells reusable bags for supermarket shopping, for example. I didn't see how this would be of interest to him.'

'But it was,' Leme said.

'Yes. My name, you see.'

'Noble.'

She nodded.

Her grey face cracked.

'Exactly,' she said. 'He told me there was a project and that the administrators had a couple of conditions that he needed to fulfil.'

'The regeneration project in the *centro*?'

'How did you know?'

'I saw you there. Couple days ago.'

She raised her hands questioningly. Her grey hands shook.

'I wasn't looking for you,' Leme said. 'Coincidence.'

She didn't look convinced, but went on. 'Mendes told me that there'd be a lot of potential for the projects that I'm mentoring and I realised he wanted something from me to guarantee that potential.'

'What does that mean?'

'His projects get credibility if my name is attached to them. They *will* happen if my foundation is involved because all of the people he needs to green-light them respect me. That simple.'

Leme nodded. 'I think I can guess where this is going,' he said.

Aline looked pained. 'It's, nominally at least, state- and city-run,' she said. 'But with my name and the foundation attached there are fewer questions about his integrity.'

'Your name that big a deal?' Leme asked.

She narrowed her eyes.

She narrowed her grey, tired, cracked eyes.

'Having my public backing would give the project integrity, in terms of my history as a businesswoman, the work of our foundation and my position at the university,' she said.

'That seems like an awful lot to stake on a man like Mendes,' Leme said.

'I asked him how he got the backing to lead it. But I knew the answer.'

Leme smiled. Nodded. 'Politics,' he said, rubbing his thumb and fingers together.

She glared. 'I told him I didn't think we were ready for such a big project.'

'And were you?' Leme asked.

She sighed again. Her face creased into a frown then softened, as if she had made a decision. She nodded, gently – confirming it to herself. She spoke quickly. 'He told me that when I attach my name to it, the information he had about my private life would disappear and that the opportunities and so on would remain. The university authorities wouldn't be notified. My reputation would be fine.'

'Your private life –'

'Is private.'

'Well, that depends,' Leme said.

Aline stood, leaned over the desk, looked down on him. 'I had no choice, *certo?* I reasoned that the project was a good one and that I'd have some influence over Mendes. My reputation was based on cleaning up the mess after the Singapore Project. Bailing them out financially and rescuing the buildings. But,' she shrugged, 'I may have made a mistake this time, which is why I'm glad you came to see me. So I can help put it right.'

Her voice cracked.

Her thin, grey voice cracked.

Her grey, tired eyes fell.

'I want to help put it right,' she said.

She sank back down into her chair – heavy and exhausted.

Her eyes hollowed.

Her grey, tired eyes hollowed.

Leme nodded – he believed her.

Put what right though? And where did Leonardo fit in? And why was he sure that it was connected somehow to Renata?

That word again: *Podemos*, echoing.

It was time to speak to Mendes.

Next day. Lunchtime.

Leme sat in his car on Rua Leopoldo in Itaim. Aline Alencar had given him the address of Mendes's office. It was an impressive building, curved glass thrusting out above the road. Nice area. Quiet street just off the bustle of Faria Lima heading down towards Juscelino Kubitschek. Lot of offices here. Handsome young men and women in suits and skirts flirting over lunch. Lot of juice bars and fancy cafés. There was an abandoned public tennis club, the space no doubt about to be developed into another office block or a condominium. Shame, Leme thought. Then again, it may well have been public, but the hourly rate for a court was more than the minimum weekly wage. He'd played there, badly, a couple of times. Definitely not worth it. Still, rather the illusion of space and opportunity in the city than another building, he thought.

Aline had told him that Mendes liked to get out at lunchtime. Drive around. How she knew he wasn't sure, but he trusted her and while involved in his project seemed keenly aware that she needed to act as a balance to Mendes's excesses. In Leme's experience, people cooperated with him for one of two reasons: guilt or fear. With Aline, he believed it was guilt. She was too important to fear anything, really.

Mendes drove a Jaguar, apparently. Well, was driven in one. Leme was a little way from the entrance/exit to the building's car park and he smoked two cigarettes. People never asked what you were doing if you were smoking, he'd learned. That's the whole point, he thought: what you're doing is, you're smoking.

A dark blue Jaguar ghosted out on to the road and Leme waited a moment and followed. They looped round the block and then back up the parallel road to Faria Lima and turned left. The Jaguar switched lanes and accelerated and Leme, dawdling as a mass of workers streamed across the road just before the lights changed, was left behind. He kept his eyes on the Jaguar, watched it switch back to the left lane. It stopped at the next set of traffic lights and Leme was able to catch up, just three cars behind. The Jaguar's windows were dark and he had no idea if Mendes was even inside. They crossed the road leading up into town from Cidade Jardim Bridge, passed Clube Pinheiros and then turned left into the entrance of Shopping Iguatemi. Leme followed, winding upwards through the narrow twists into the car park, tyres letting out squeals on the tighter bends. Mendes's car pulled into the valet parking section.

What a surprise.

Leme turned right, keeping the Jaguar in his rear-view mirror.

Leme pulled into an empty bay.

And there was Mendes getting out of his car, a large man in a suit with him. They headed to the lift. Pushed a button and went inside.

Leme stood in front of the lift and watched the numbers go down. The lift stopped on the lower first floor. He called another and followed. He came out of his own lift in time to see Mendes stroll into an expensive sushi restaurant. Pretending to examine clothes in a shop across the corridor, Leme watched him take a seat on his own. Next to the sushi restaurant was an old-style *boteco* serving *chopp* and sandwiches. Leme took a seat at the bar. There was a mirror behind the bar, the angle of which enabled him to keep an eye on the entrance to the sushi restaurant. He ordered a beer and threw down some change.

He sipped at the beer. The barman tried to make small talk, but Leme waved him away, pulled out his notebook and studied its empty pages. He finished his beer, ordered another one and paid. How long did it take to eat sushi? He wanted to get Mendes in a place where he couldn't make a scene, a shop perhaps, or in the food court.

'*Mais um?*' the barman asked.

Leme shook his head.

'Something to eat?'

He clicked his teeth, waggled his finger, said nothing.

'Liquid lunch,' the barman said. 'Lucky you.'

Leme snorted.

He caught sight of movement in the mirror. A dark suit turned towards him. Mendes. He let him pass the *boteco*, thanked the barman and followed.

Mendes's shoes clicked as he walked. He was speaking on his phone. Sounded like a personal call, though Leme couldn't be sure. His wife, perhaps. Talking about their plans for the evening. What they would have for dinner. Discussing their days. Some update on work they were doing on the house.

All foreign to Leme now. A memory.

The large man in the suit then came round the corner and walked with Mendes. They exchanged a few words. Mendes laughed. The large man looked happy. They turned into a jewellery shop. No good. There were security guards inside and out. Leme crossed the hall and stood outside an electronics store, watched a cartoon on an enormous flat-screen television. There was a video camera trained on the hallway in the store window and a screen showing who walked past. Leme kept an eye on it. Mendes left the jeweller's carrying a small bag, which he handed to the large man. They headed towards the main concourse and Leme followed.

Mendes was back on his phone. This time business, Leme thought. At one point he stopped, turned a circle, making a point. Leme walked straight past him, smelled his aftershave, the gel in his hair, felt the crisp lines in his white shirt, the flash of cufflinks. He stopped again outside another shop and let Mendes pass him. This was an opportunity, while he was on his phone, but the large man was close and something stopped Leme from approaching. He didn't know what. Bodyguards were no issue to him. But the very manner in which Mendes moved suggested authority, entitlement. It was unsettling. Fuck, Leme realised, he was intimidated. And this angered him.

They turned another corner, a sports shop on one side, a music store on the other. The main shopping area opened out. Leme quickened his step.

Now.

Then, the noise of a crowd. Other shoppers stopped, looked up. Mendes, too. Hung up his phone.

The noise got louder. Singing and chanting, chanting and singing: teenage voices.

A lot of them.

Then, older voices swearing and shouting, shouting and swearing.

More chanting and Leme sensed movement. A swarm of around fifty youths ran up the ramp towards them. Black, mixed-race kids dressed in shorts and T-shirts. Boys and girls. Music blasting from a stereo. Singing and laughing, laughing and singing. Fuck, Leme thought, a *rolezinho*.

They moved as one and terrified shoppers jumped into stores whose employees quickly slammed and locked the doors. Leme wasn't worried. This *rolezinho* fad wasn't dangerous. He knew that. He stood, amused. The kids were making a point. They didn't belong in this posh shopping mall. Their point: why the fuck not? The mall security pursued them. Hopeless. The kids were running laps around the corridors, screeching in delight. Beer cans and food wrappers left in their wake staining the pristine floors.

Leme lost sight of Mendes for a moment. Then he saw him. Bundled by the large man into the sports shop. Doors locked. His bodyguard directed him to the back of the store. Leme waited.

And waited.

After a while the kids cleared off out the main entrance: triumphant singing. The sports shop opened its doors and Leme went inside. No one in there, save the employees.

He waved one of them over.

'That guy came in. One with the bodyguard. Where'd he go?'

The girl wore a tracksuit. Her dreadlocked hair smelt of coconut. Her skin glowed dark. She shrugged. '*Sei lá*,' she said. 'I didn't see them.'

Leme grabbed another, asked the same question. The guy shook his head and said nothing.

He went to the back of the store by the checkout desks. There was a locked door with a sign on it: Staff Only.

'Where does this go?' he asked a girl at the till.

'Staff exit,' she said. 'Service lift is at the bottom, *sabe?*'

'What's the combination?'

She shrugged. 'Manager lets us out one by one. Don't trust us, you see, to get back in, *sabe?* We weren't working here we'd be with them.' She jerked her thumb where the *rolezinho* kids had been.

'Where's the manager?' Leme demanded.

She shook her head slowly, dramatically. '*Já foi embora*. Went with those two guys. Sorry.'

Leme smiled a rueful smile. His heart thumped. Two beers on an empty stomach not normally an issue, but the adrenalin had got to him.

'Hey man,' the girl said, 'you OK?'

Leme steadied himself on the counter.

Nodded.

'I'll get you some water,' she said.

He nodded again. A blackness surged up from his stomach, he saw lights. Closed his eyes. Gripped the counter. His heart thumped. Slowed. Settled. He opened his eyes to see the employees gathered around him.

He waved them away. Stumbled back through the door.

What a fuck-up.

He had to clear his head.

He was meeting Antonia later that afternoon.

And in the evening, he was going into the *favela*.

'See, that wasn't too hard now, was it?'

Leme didn't really want to answer that. If Antonia had understood how reluctant he'd been to go to bed with her, she may not have been especially flattered that he had now done so. Not that it was an act of charity on his part. More like on hers. Willing volunteer. Giving something back to the community to atone for her sins as a corporate finance lackey.

They both smoked cigarettes, propped up in her bed. This was one cliché he hadn't lived for a long time. Renata was never impressed with his smoking in the bedroom despite her commitment to it generally.

'How long's it been anyway?' Antonia exhaled and turned to him at the same time, her arm bent at the elbow into a question mark, her cigarette like the pointers Leme imagined her using in presentations.

Leme shrugged.

'No!' she said. 'That long? I mean it's what, nearly a year?'

Leme nodded. 'More,' he said, quietly.

He was comforted by her lack of tact, her inability to dwell on it. For Antonia, it had happened, and now she would be a part of his rehabilitation.

'I'm curious,' she said, 'when did you know that you were in love with her?'

Leme sighed. 'Immediately.'

'Really? Love at first sight? You'll have to do better than that.'

'Uh-huh. It was physical. A realisation. A kind of sharp pang in my chest and then a settling. I just understood, immediately, that this was the woman I would be with.'

Antonia clucked her tongue, eyed him with ironic appreciation. 'Dark horse,' she said.

'Wasn't easy,' Leme carried on, in spite of himself. He shifted the pillows behind him to see her better. 'She was living with someone else. She told me it was over, but still. It's hard. Lonely, you know?'

'Not really.'

Leme smiled. 'I was lonely. Weekends especially. Everything you do is a reminder that she isn't there. Fucking heartbreaking, actually.'

Antonia reached over. Placed her hand on his neck. She had known Renata at college. They'd been friends, but drifted when it was clear that their career paths were taking very different directions. Antonia, Leme knew, had resented Renata's righteousness. Renata had resented Antonia's lack of it.

'But she did leave him,' she said.

Leme nodded. 'Not before I almost ruined it.'

Leme lit another cigarette. He felt her foot pass up and down his calf. It felt nice, and he was surprised. Antonia shrugged. 'Oh?'

'We're not all as lucky as you. She said I was the kindest person she'd ever met. Well, I fucked that up for a while.'

Antonia laughed. 'Oh dear.' She pouted and thought about this. Said, 'How funny.'

'Not really.'

'Worked out though, didn't it?'

'I sent her something, you know, when I knew. A sort of answer to a question.'

'What question?'

'Why do you love me?'

Antonia laughed loud and long. 'You soppy bastard.'

Leme smiled. 'That's what she called me.'

She laughed again. 'Didn't know you had it in you.'

She wormed her hand under the covers. Leme felt its warmth between his legs.

'Women, eh?' she said.

He laughed, relaxed. He'd been tense, swollen with anxiety, guilt. And now it had dissipated. He laughed again, at himself. All I needed was to get laid, he thought. No, that wasn't true: it was this, the easy intimacy of the aftermath, that he was enjoying. And it wasn't just in the last year that he hadn't felt it. He'd missed it in the six months or so before Renata died.

But the creeping knowledge didn't quite go away and inside he was half-tight with anticipation: later, he'd be in Paraisópolis again.

'This is going to be a standard night for us. Which means we don't know what's going to happen, *entendeu?*'

Leme nodded. His friend Carlos twisted his head and looked Leme in the eye. 'We do it differently in the Military to the way you lot do,' he said. 'You know that, right? Or you think you do. Now you'll see. You sit tight at the back there in the middle. And watch. Nothing else. *Certo?*'

Leme suppressed a chuckle. Carlos was an old mate but he had the same superiority as the other Militars Leme had met. We're fighting a war, they always say. Sure, but you're not actually fucking soldiers. It had taken Leme some time to persuade Carlos to do this. Carlos hadn't wanted to indulge him. 'There's no point seeing where it happened,' he'd said. 'What are you going to achieve?'

But Leme was convinced it would help, offer something. If he could see the scene at the time the accident happened, perhaps he could better understand why Renata had been taken away from him.

He knew it was very unlikely that he would, but he couldn't turn down the opportunity.

Carlos was in the passenger seat, an automatic weapon hanging from his hand out of the window. The driver was a gnarly man of about Leme's age, and the two in the back that flanked him were younger – new recruits. Both had weapons pointed out of the window.

They went into the *favela* via the temporary Military Police post that Leme had passed the other morning. He didn't recognise either of the two officers standing by motorbikes, red lights flashing.

Carlos nodded at them. 'Good lads, those two,' he said.

Leme gave a tight smile. Thought about the others he'd met.

Carlos went on. 'We'll be passing through where … well, where it happened. I thought, you know, it might be … well. *Entendeu?*'

Leme leant forward and touched Carlos on the shoulder. Their hands met briefly.

The *favela* at night was a different place.

They drove slowly down a tiny, poorly lit street with a shop-front bar, mosquitoes buzzing around naked bulbs, crates of empty bottles of beer stacked up in the street.

A couple of sullen-looking men sat at rusting, beer-brand tables, not talking, raising their bottles and glasses of *cachaça* to the owner.

They turned away from the police vehicle.

In the dark, each house looked different, but the same, Leme thought. The same rough brick and corrugated iron, the same painted-on house number, the same noises echoing out from the hollow walls, the same thick smells hanging in the heat like clouds.

In the wires strung criss-crossed above the car, there was a low, constant crackle of electricity, straining to carry the current around the labyrinth.

'So what we're doing, basically, is looking for *traficantes*,' Carlos was saying. 'We tour the *bocas de fumo* where they mainly sell to the middle classes, and we make ourselves known in the busier parts round the bars. That way they come out to us, or skulk away. Either is a victory.'

Right, Leme thought.

'They come out there's a good chance a couple will be dealt with, *entendeu?* They don't, then we're fucking with their trade and there's a chance one of the bosses will get impatient and get rid of one himself. Either way, *sabe?*'

Leme was beginning to think it wasn't such a good idea coming along. But he'd insisted. He'd wanted a feel for what had actually happened the night that Renata was killed. He knew that he would never *know*. But to feel something of the situation was almost a relief, though he didn't know why.

'They try some shit, I'm telling you,' Carlos went on. 'You're not going to believe this. Couple weeks ago a young guy is selling in the entrance down by that furniture place on the road to Shopping Morumbi, *sabe?* He was carrying a bundle, couldn't tell what. Three of us chased him. We managed to spread out and trap him. We pulled him back towards the entrance, where the car was. On the way, we passed this girl carrying a baby wrapped in a blanket. A fucking bundle, right? The two of them exchanged a look, just for a moment, but I spotted it and told everyone to stop. The girl smiled at me. I knew where he was keeping the drugs.'

'Right,' Leme said, 'in the baby's diaper or clothes. Sick, right?'

One of the younger guys muttered, 'Yeah, we wish, *sabe?*'

'No,' Carlos said. 'Stuff wasn't in the diaper or the fucking clothes. The stuff was *in the baby*.'

'What do you mean?'

'The baby was fucking dead. It was a dead baby. There were stitches up its back. The guy wasn't selling from it: he was *importing* it. There was shitloads in there. In the fucking skull even.'

Leme wanted to vomit. 'How did you –?' He wasn't sure how to end the question. Wasn't sure he wanted to know the answer.

'You really want to know? At first I thought it was like a doll, but there was something about the skin, so we took it in. Doctor, forensics did the rest. *That*, I'm grateful for. Know where they learnt this shit? Mexico. Fucking spics. Here, they bring them into the city on the buses like that. I heard they lift the dead babies from hospitals, but could as easily get them undeclared in *favela*s all over the place. Who fucking knows. Worst thing I've ever seen.'

Leme nodded. It was the worst thing he'd ever *heard*.

He drifted. Tried to process this. It didn't seem possible that anyone would go to those lengths. For what? For money. To survive? Renata always had such faith in the dignity of so many of the *favelados*, all those men and women she helped. The one per cent that ran the place certainly made up for it. He could see why the Militars thought they were at war, why this Operação Saturação was taking place. It didn't feel like an initiative brought on by the World Cup – this wasn't regeneration. This was a straight fight with the PCC gang for control. The PCC wouldn't give that up too easily. It wasn't even pacification. That's what they were doing in Rio but there was a very clear reason for it: the *favela*s were in the way, the residents cleared out to make space for the visitors, for the development of areas around the new stadium, same thing for the fucking Olympics. To keep these visitors safe from violent crime. Who was more important? Rich people visiting Brazil for a month or less, or Brazilians? It was becoming very clear, very quickly.

They sat: quiet. The two younger Militars had their eyes and guns trained on the street. The red-blue flash punctuated the silence. In the dark, down the back alleys, *favelados* slipped in and out of shadows like ghosts. Leme didn't know who they were looking for. What they would look like. Young men, he supposed. But they all looked the same. Vests and shorts, flip-flops and baseball caps. Which was honest, which was not? Complicated. Easy to mistake a kid who gets up at five to travel three hours to a shitty job for one swaggering about with a mouthful of crack. Collateral damage when they shoot the wrong one, *bala perdida* or not.

Then Leme realised where they were.

Another squad car was parked at the top end of the junction. Two Militars stood behind the open doors, guns pointed at the ground. Fingers close to the triggers. The siren flashed, silently. They parked next to the other car and the two younger Militars adopted the same position as their colleagues. They nodded at each other, exchanged a couple of words, looked tense, alert.

'You stay in here,' Carlos told Leme, and slid out the door.

He spoke to the more senior-looking officer by the other car. He nodded. He shrugged. He pointed across the road at the bar in which road workers dressed in orange drank beer and scowled. Maids and nannies dressed in white scurried past, hunched and tired, carrying string bags of rice and beans, no doubt heading home from their employers in one of the condominiums up the hill.

A man limped along, robotic in the way he engineered his crippled leg, both feet bent inwards, a hard expression set on his face.

But Leme only took all this in in flashes, impressions. The image registered then was gone. He was staring at Renata's office. Boarded up now. A little way down from the bar. He was staring at the window where she would sit and watch the movement below. His eyes turned to the tiny restaurant where she got her lunch every day. He saw her stepping across the road, smiling at the woman behind the counter, tipping her, taking her food gratefully. He realised where he was. He was staring at the spot where she had been killed.

He looked to his left. The Militar had moved away from the door and was doing something in the back of the car. Leme heard clicks and shunts. He lifted himself up off the seat and pushed feet-first through the open door. Without looking, he crossed the road towards the bar. The workers eyed him suspiciously. Muttered. Leme heard nothing. A car beeped angrily, just missing him.

As he passed the bar, he ran his hand over one of the plastic tables.

It wobbled and a bottle of beer teetered and fell, rolled off the table and smashed.

'*Ai, porra!*' the drinker shouted at him. '*Que isso, eh meu?*'

Leme looked straight through him. Examined the bottle on the ground, foamy liquid running slowly to the kerb. Bent down and touched it with his palm. Brought it to his nose, dabbed at it with his tongue.

'*Puta que pariu*,' the drinker said, shaking his head. '*Que isso, porra?*'

Shouting from across the road.

Leme moved slowly to the door to Renata's office. He turned to face the Militars. He took a step towards the place he knew Renata parked her car. He looked down. A drain. He looked up. The junction opened up in front of him. Here he could see each of the five roads that led to it. He was exposed. And it was the Militars who stood opposite where he was standing.

They were all he could see –

Then Carlos was dragging Leme back across the road through a small crowd of men demanding to know what the fuck was this guy's problem. Leme was jostled, felt hands on him, in his pockets, he shrugged at them helplessly, like a child who didn't want to be fed, pushing away from the spoon. Carlos was swearing, elbowing his way through. There was a cry and a man fell. More shouting. A blow to the back of Leme's head. He reached his hand to where it had landed. He snapped back into focus and saw that the Militars by the cars had their weapons raised. The lights in the bar were off. Carlos pushed him forward, turned to the crowd and raised his own weapon. Hands were raised. Cars stopped.

The men stepped back, mouthing defiantly, clicking their teeth, waggling their fingers. Snapping their wrists. '*Calma, meu!*' they said. '*Puta, e nada, Policial.*' They spat. '*Nossa, eh? Esse filho da puta.*' Sneered. '*Babaca.*'

Carlos strong-armed Leme the remaining few metres to the car and bundled him inside on to the back seat. The other Militars stepped forward, their weapons pointed at the crowd, which was dispersing down the alleyways. A few men stood in the darkness and taunted. Threats. Fingers across their throats, hands cocked like guns.

'What the fuck, Mario?' He stared at him, hard. Gripped his face. 'Mario, this has to stop. It's over.'

Leme's face was a blank mask. Carlos slapped him lightly.

'Mario, are you hearing me? This is not acceptable. You have to let it go. You have to let *her* go.'

Leme shook as though physically dismissing the idea. Felt his eyes twitch.

Carlos jumped out of the back, slammed the door and got into the driver's seat. He barked some instructions at the others and pulled away. As they accelerated up the hill to Avenida Giovanni Gronchi, Leme sensed the scene retreat from him, soften.

Sitting outside Leme's condominium, they smoked.

'What happened?' Carlos asked.

Leme shook his head. 'I didn't realise we were going there. I didn't know. I'm sorry. I thought I could handle it.'

Carlos put his hand on Leme's neck. '*Cara*, don't worry about it. It happened.'

'And there's more,' Leme said. 'When I was standing outside her office all I could see were you guys. You were opposite. They were opposite.'

'Listen to me,' Carlos said. 'Where she was, it could only have been a *traficante*. Our guys were not shooting across the street. They were aiming at the entrances to the junction.'

'You weren't there, you said. How do you know?'

'I saw the report.'

'And what does that guarantee?'

'My guys are good guys. I trust them. So should you.'

'But they're not *all* good guys. How can you be sure which is which, eh? How can you fucking know? I've been fucking threatened, basically. For what? It doesn't make sense.'

Carlos said nothing.

'I'm sorry,' Leme said.

Carlos nodded. 'Leave it with me.'

'What do you mean?'

Carlos gave a tight smile. 'Just leave it with me.'

They finished smoking. Carlos led Leme inside where Antonia was waiting.

She took his hand.

Leme waited across the road, half-hidden around the corner, behind the plastic sheet of a bar, protecting customers from the wind and the threat of rain. He drank two *chopps* and picked at a portion of cheese *pastels*, doused in *molho da pimenta*. He looked again at the address that Eleanor had given him: he was definitely in the right place.

After an hour, he saw Alex – dressed smartly in shirt and trousers, removing his sunglasses for a moment, looking right and left – and Ana leave the building. She walked a little unsteadily: none of the confidence he'd felt when he met her – none of that Renata-poise, his recognition of it, the consequent, instinctive desire to protect her. Alex steered her with his hand at the small of her back. Leme followed at a distance.

They worked their way up Brigadeiro towards Avenida Paulista. She stumbled along, tripping slightly, struggling to keep up with Alex. The evening thronged with commuters. The air hummed with the sounds of traffic and snatches of music from the *botecos*, workers sitting upright on hard stools at the bars. The light was fading fast under the thickening cloud.

They turned left on to Alameda Santos, away from the exhaust and noise. Leme paused behind the trees that lined the street, letting them get further from him, but keeping them in view. Ana looked lost, harassed, confused: far from the young woman he'd met not long before, someone assured, distant, wry even. He watched as they entered on the ground level of a tall building that he knew housed the famous View Bar on its top floor. And a hotel beneath.

He smiled at the security guard and receptionist and took the lift.

He edged between tables and out on to the deck area. The bar was well named. The buildings of Jardims below, concrete rectangles of all sizes, joined by thin corridors of space, windows lit in irregular patterns. To the south, the communications tower glowed purple, pink, orange, green.

He dithered, pretended he was looking for a table. He felt strangers' eyes on him. Suspicion. No, apprehension.

Where *were* they?

He walked over to the edge of the outside area, casual, leaned back against a protective piece of glass, an eye on the inside. The city stretched out in front of him. Sunset drenched. Yellows and reds flickered, turning salmon-pink. A fat, pregnant hue, conceived where pollution unloads its seed into the thick atmosphere that threatens to break above his city. It never does.

It hovers, vast and carnal.

Ominous. Quite beautiful too, though, he thought.

A seething need to dump some writhing, living, destructive spawn down amongst its masses.

The tower blocks, the cityscape, teetered down towards Faria Lima, Pinheiros, Itaim.

Like a swaying, upright Morse code message of privilege.

Dark dots, glowing dashes where windows filled with light.

Two words visible: Intercontinental Hotel.

Leme had stayed there, once, with Renata. A sort of holiday, a mere one-hour drive in rush hour traffic from their home. Sanitised, air-con heavy. Good fuck pad, though, he smiled. They should have gone to the swank Astúrias Motel in Pinheiros. Swimming pool, jacuzzi, sauna, wet room shower to finish. He'd pin her against the headboard and try to sort of inhabit her. Bite at her neck, feel her turn to kiss him, feel her *want* him, feel her want him want *her*.

That, and the coursing electric current when they came –

This flashed through Leme in a heartbeat. Grief had that effect now. A whole lifetime distilled into a quick memory, a place. Just needed a jog, and there it was.

Not something you can ever forget, or would want to.

Then, he caught sight of movement inside and turned. It was them. Alex was introducing Ana to an older man. She curtsied and kissed him, his hand lingering on her shoulder and back. She smiled and giggled – slow, dopey – her eyes glazed, uncomprehending. They made to leave.

Leme slipped back inside as they disappeared into the lift. He watched the numbers change. It stopped at the eighteenth floor.

'What's on that level?' he asked the operator.

'Hotel.' She gave him a sardonic look. 'Very expensive,' she said. Meaning, you can't afford it, *querido*.

Leme nodded.

He went down to the seventeenth and then hefted up the stairs to the floor above. He was just in time to see the older man ushering Ana into a room. Alex had his back to Leme, talking on his phone.

Leme stood still.

He backed to the edge of the staircase.

He listened to Alex's back and forth.

Easy, day-to-day, routine-type bullshit chat.

Pussy and football, middle class, *mano bobagem*.

He should try and get into that room.

Then, Alex's tone changed.

He heard the slap of hands, the slap of backs.

He sneaked a look.

A uniform: Militar.

Fuck.

He turned and went back down the stairs.

Nerve lost. Fuck.

FUCK.

He hesitated as he approached the exit. Alex. Ana. A Militar. An older man. What could he have done with his nerve held? Nothing. Yes, nothing.

Again, the Militars unbalancing him, undoing him.

He breathed.

As he walked back through Jardims to where he had left his car, he rationalised his decision further. It was the right thing to do. Play a longer game. Too often in the past, acting on an impulse had been the wrong thing to do. He couldn't blunder in.

And for what? There was a uniform. No choice, *mesmo*.

He was sure this time he'd done the right thing, for now.

For her.

He sat at the wheel, his head spinning. Her voice, *Renata*, whispering.

That moment in the bar, that memory.

Always with him.

'*E aí? Que, que isso?*'

Sunday morning and Lisboa stood in front of Leme's building with his arms spread in a gesture of amused defensiveness, as if to say 'and you expected what exactly?'

'The state of you. The state of us.' Leme stepped through the entrance. He sneered and shook his head. 'This is what, an intervention?'

Lisboa laughed. 'Trust me. You'll enjoy it.'

Leme looked him up and down. He was packed tight into the tracksuit. Flesh bulged in unseemly pockets. The trousers formed a triangle on the hips and then tapered alarmingly down to the ankles. The zip-up top strained, rode up revealing a copse of dark hair.

Lisboa noticed Leme's stare. 'Like you're some sort of athlete?'

Leme indicated the cigarette.

'Oh, *bonito*, Mario. Let's go, eh?'

Leme nodded at the condominium *porteiro* and they crossed the road to Lisboa's car. Leme was in a tracksuit, too. Less garish than Lisboa's. Looked like it had shrunk a little since its last outing, though.

Sunday morning. No anchor. Easiest option was to sleep until lunch and then drink in the bar by the pool downstairs with other men. Shouting and drinking, drinking and shouting. Forced laughter. Sunglasses over tired eyes. Wives drifting by with their children. Pool-chatter. Then it empties into a lunch-silence. Collapse into the sauna in the dark. Bed by nine. Flushed and dehydrated, shivering.

Skin scrubbed red.

Not this Sunday.

It was Lisboa's wife's idea, apparently. 'Said I need it.' He'd patted his belly, ruefully. 'So, she wants me out the house? Least you can do is come with me.'

They took a shortcut, turning left from the condominium and again down beyond the high gates and barbed wire that fenced the residents inside their green, barbecue area, past a half-finished building that had visibly rotted since Leme last drove by. No more money and the investors bailed. Cheaper for the construction company to leave it standing, rank, and stick a couple of rabid dogs behind the gates to deter anyone who wanted to help themselves to the materials. Little point now. Cracked, mouldy and grey-brown. Even the abandoned buildings were fearful of crime.

The outskirts of Paraisópolis threaded along a slow-moving, dirty stream that sagged, heavy with the weight of the slum, below them to their left. Brown faces poked between gaps in the wood. A woman, bent under a basket, limped down the road on to the dirt track ahead of them.

'Lock your door,' Leme instructed.

Lisboa looked at him: 'What? *Fala sério.*'

'New trick,' Leme said. 'She drops her basket in front of the car and we get jumped.' He pointed at the thick shrubbery either side of the track. 'Had people playing dead, getting cars to stop.'

Lisboa whistled and accelerated past the woman, giving her a wide berth. They bore left and turned away from the shacks and piles of rubbish that marked the edge of the *favela* and rejoined the asphalt road. Opened their windows. Swung past the German International School. Down to the Marginal and back up and into Parque Burle Marx.

They strode up the footpaths, winding their way to the top. It was cool, damp, dark. The sun a distant eye, winking above the river, its light intercepted and filtered by the trees. Power-walkers and runners skipped figures of eight around them. Lapped them, Leme thought. It's still the city. There's a limit to how much of this there is. Unlike the sprawl of concrete and brick that inched ever outwards, redefining the boundary between city and state, there is a limit to greenery. To how many trees we can have in one place. This is no forest. It's a reproduction. And these runners are passing again and again. Like a pebbled, wooded treadmill.

'OK. I'm doing it.' Leme lit a cigarette. Lisboa reached out and leant against a tree.

'This the top, then?' Leme asked.

'Might as well be. Can see the house through there.' He pointed over Leme's shoulder.

'What house?'

Lisboa held his hand up. Caught his breath. 'Unfinished,' he said. 'Built for a rich business fucker and his Austrian princess wife or something in the forties. They split up.'

Leme raised his eyebrows. It was a dilapidated colonial mansion. Gaping rectangles waiting to be filled with glass. Threadbare slatted roofs. Blue wooden shutters hanging splintered like loose teeth. They stood at the fountain – a pastel-coloured, modernist block of concrete, Leme imagined Renata passing judgement – gulping at beers bought from a vendor with a gaffer-taped cooler. Looked down over the patch of grass. Leme watched the Marginal go through its Sunday half-life. The pace, the rhythm, almost lazy. He didn't drive on Sundays. It reminded him how bad it was driving during the week. The senseless weight of traffic. Where are they all going?

Eighteen million people in between places all at once.

Lisboa cracked a second can. Nodded at the couples lounging below them. 'No dogs. No games. No kids, mostly.'

'Yeah, no life.'

'It's why people come here. It's for adults.'

'It's fake.'

Lisboa grinned. 'Try and tell me you're not enjoying yourself.'

Leme tipped his beer. 'I am now.'

'There's music.'

'I don't like music.'

Lisboa spluttered. 'Now you don't like music.'

'Well, I don't listen to it. Is that the same thing?'

'It's like saying you don't like food.'

'I don't like food, either.'

Lisboa shook his head. Jabbed a finger into Leme's chest. '*Cara*, I don't like you.' He laughed.

Leme bent and splashed water on to his face. 'Music loses its meaning when you're not in love. Music's all about being in love.'

Lisboa placed his hand on Leme's shoulder. Leme turned away from him slightly and coughed. He gave a rueful smile. 'Those two seem to understand it.' He pointed at a couple sprawled, legs twined in some yogic embrace. Lycra and lips.

'*É isso aí, garoto!*' Lisboa raised his drink, cheerleading.

Leme turned back to him. 'Silva says he can get to one of the convicted. Find out what really happened with this Gabriel murder.'

Lisboa groaned. 'This again? Jesus.'

'It's important.'

'No, Mario, it's not. They won't let us. *Ta viagando, meu.*'

'I'm not giving up yet.'

Lisboa stayed silent, steamed.

'Christ, do you think I want this?' he said. 'Look, I'll say this now. I'll always be here, always be your friend. But I can't do this with you. Not properly. You know, the family ...'

'I know,' Leme said, gripped his friend by the arm. 'But you should understand why I need to do this.'

'Go on.'

'We've been taken off the Gabriel case, right?'

'Right.'

'We don't know why, but we do know that the victim's house was bought by Mendes immediately after his death. And we also know that there is something off with the confessions, but that we can't do anything about it.'

'OK. What's your point?'

'The building that collapsed is connected to Mendes. One of his smaller sister companies is doing the refit.'

Lisboa sighed. 'Fuck's sake.'

'Leonardo Alencar dies in the *favela*.'

'Which has got to do with what? *This* is why I'm fucking worried about you. You're obsessed. Not seeing straight. It's toxic.'

Leme smiled. 'It's a hunch. He'd been going in there for a while, *sabe?* He was shot. It was not an accident. So, why is everyone claiming that it was?'

Lisboa conceded this with a shrug. 'Is it worth it?' he asked.

'His girlfriend is from there, and she may have been working with Mendes.'

Lisboa looked across the park. He examined his can of lager. He raised his eyebrows. 'How many calories do you reckon we burnt off on that walk?'

Leme snorted, spat beer on to the grass. 'Calories? The fuck?'

Lisboa looked rueful. 'Yeah, I know. I'm supposed to keep track or something.'

Leme looked at his friend. Knocked his beer can with his own. 'I know.' He smiled. 'Now take me home and we'll have a proper drink.'

'Yeah. *Embora*.' Lisboa wrapped his arm around Leme's shoulders as they moved towards the *estacionamento*. 'We've earned it, *ne?*'

Leme looked back through notes for a kidnapping case.

A woman grabbed from her car, hidden away in a *favela*.

A woman taken out once a day to withdraw the maximum five hundred reais from her bank account.

After a week, a woman was released, hysterical and bedraggled, had hardly eaten, hardly drank.

No family, no boyfriend; it took two days for her absence from work to be noticed.

Four days until a friend reported her missing.

The city connected all the victims, swallowed up the unsolved cases.

Leme leaned back and swivelled in his chair, pressed his nose against the window.

He drew a single line in the grimy dust with his finger.

'Knock, knock,' said a voice in English.

Leme turned.

Eleanor gave him a silly smile.

'What are you doing here?' he asked.

'You gave me your card.'

'Social call then, is it?'

She sat down and rifled through an oversized handbag that spilled papers. Dropped make-up. Her purse. Painted nails chipped.

'Where is it?' she said. 'Ah. Here.' She pulled out a folded newspaper. 'These stories really true?' she asked. 'They're disgusting. And terrifying. They scare me.'

'Which stories?' Leme asked.

'These attacks.' She pointed at a photo and article. 'Car jacking executives and throwing acid in their faces. How? I mean, how can anyone *do* that?'

She looked hard at Leme, lips pursed. Eyes unblinking.

'What are you doing here, Eleanor?' Leme repeated.

'Why do I need a reason? I'm a journalist.'

Leme smiled. Gestured at his desk. 'And I'm busy.'

Eleanor bristled. 'OK. Fine. *Chega*. No need to be rude.'

Leme raised his eyebrows. Alex was right: she was an interesting girl.

'I'm worried,' she said.

'What about?' Leme was actually, if he was honest, pleased for the distraction.

'My friend Ana. You spoke to her.'

'I remember. What about her?'

'I can't find her.' Leme's stomach dropped. 'I don't know where she is.'

'OK.' Leme paused. He leant forward. His heart jumped. His head light. His chest tight. 'What do you mean by that?'

'I … normally see her after university. Most days. She hasn't been around.'

'Did you arrange to meet her?'

'Not … exactly.'

'Right.'

'We meet most days. There's no *need* to make an arrangement. It's a girl thing.'

Leme raised his eyebrows – angry. His head light. His chest tight. 'Have you been to her house?'

'Yes.'

'And she's not there?'

'That's what I'm trying to tell you. I don't know where she is.'

Leme nodded. 'How long has it been?'

'I think four days.'

'You *think*?'

'Ah. You know.'

'So you're here to report her missing?' Leme felt panic.

His head light. His chest tight.

Powerless.

'Yes. Why not.'

Leme thought about when he had followed her to that hotel. How he had felt. Eleanor was certainly a little chaotic, unreliable, but she was her friend.

'I'll need to take a statement,' Leme said. 'And I'll look into it.'

Eleanor smiled. 'Thought you would,' she said. Her eyes gleamed. She collected herself. He gave her a pen, some paper.

'I'll take you somewhere quiet,' he said. Here was a new case. An actual case. One he could pursue in the open.

Missing person cases had spiked by over thirty per cent. Over four thousand in the last year alone. It wasn't an exceptional thing. That is, Leme reflected, if the person is not well connected. And Ana de Moraes was not well connected.

There were two obvious starting points: the internship at the magazine and the university. The university authorities did not seem overly bothered by her absence, as it happened fairly regularly: a student loses interest or motivation and disappears for a while before turning up again with an excuse – family problems was apparently the most common – and a desire to continue their studies.

With no reports of foul play, they would wait it out until she came back. Normally, they said, this would happen within a few months.

It hadn't been this long.

But Leme had managed to get an address for the girl out of the university administration office: different from the one Eleanor had given him. It was an apartment in a reasonable neighbourhood in Pinheiros. The block was unassuming with few of the amenities of the more expensive buildings. It was situated just off Rua dos Pinheiros, close enough for the traffic noise and pollution to drift up and make it that little less desirable.

Across the road was the building site for the new metro station.

Drills hammered in metronomic bursts, puncturing the constant, low moan of passing cars.

Leme sat in a *boteco* opposite the building for a coffee and a think. He picked at a pastry, gave up and lit a cigarette. The waiter came out and glared: Leme was sitting under the awning and with the new law on smoking this was illegal.

He ignored the waiter.

He looked up at the block. The faded red concrete was darkened in patches by what looked like smoke damage, years of road pollution. Balconies jutted out like drawers pulled from a dresser, some with washing lines strung across them, others with tall plants, several with cheap-looking patio furniture, most protected by a tight net to stop children from falling. High up, a man in shorts and no top leaned out and smoked. He flicked his cigarette. Turned away not checking where it landed. Leme saw it smoulder on the pavement and then go out. He threw a couple of reais on the table and crossed the road.

As he walked he decided how to approach the *porteiro*. Doormen were not well paid as a rule, but they retained a sense of loyalty to their residents and generally seemed to protect their privacy above and beyond what their pay scale might suggest. Leme had had trouble before extracting simple information from crotchety, unsympathetic condominium security men. He'd had to resort to threats more than once and this didn't square well. In his own building, the *seguranças* were well remunerated and were friendly and helpful to residents and suspicious and thorough when dealing with outsiders. This was, Leme thought, probably the safest and best route in Morumbi. He wondered what sort of man sat in the booth overlooking the street. Whether he would even get to see him face to face.

Leme buzzed and leaned into the intercom.

'Apartment 603.'

'And you are?'

'Mario Leme. From the university.'

'I'll call up.'

Through the speaker, Leme could hear the ringing that he was sure would go unanswered. The gate was firmly shut and behind it was a second gate that would not be opened until the first was closed behind him. If he even got that far. Standard security measure.

'There's no answer. Want to leave a message?'

Leme paused. 'Can I give you something to give to her?'

'What is it?'

'A note.'

'I'll come round.'

The door to the booth opened and a squat man appeared dressed in an ill-fitting black suit. Leme scribbled his name and number on a page of his notebook, tore it out, folded it and wrote Ana de Moraes on the front.

The *porteiro* exited from a side door and approached Leme. He did not look friendly. Leme waited for him to get closer and held the paper at a slight distance.

'You seen her recently?' he asked.

The *porteiro* shook his head. 'She comes and goes. I work days. I don't see many people after the early morning.'

'But you'd know if they weren't spending much time at home.'

'I might. It's not my business.'

He moved towards Leme and extended his hand for the note.

Leme took a step back.

'You have any idea if she ever has any visitors? Friends? That sort of thing.'

'Who did you say you are again?'

'From her university. We need to get some important information to her. It's proving difficult.'

'I'll pass on the message. I can't do anything else. She in trouble?'

'Nothing like that. Administrative stuff, you know how it is.'

The man raised his eyebrows and shrugged. 'Not really.'

Leme nodded slowly. He waved the piece of paper. 'You'll guarantee she gets this?'

'Sure.' He gave Leme an ironic look. 'It's the most important part of my job here. You can relax.' He paused and sighed. 'I'm an expert.'

Leme glanced inside. As rudimentary as the building was, getting in undetected would be extremely difficult and he couldn't afford to do anything that wasn't strictly legal. Technically, he hadn't lied to the *porteiro*, and he could always come back. If he showed his badge or explained the real reason he was there, it might make things harder the next time.

'OK. Thanks.'

He handed over the note. The *porteiro* looked at it.

'You sure you've got the right apartment?'

Leme opened his notebook and double-checked the address he'd been given. 603.

'I'm sure.'

'No one of this name lives there.'

'Really? You sure?'

'Like I said,' he drew out the words condescendingly, 'I'm an expert.'

'There's no Ana de Moraes in 603?'

'There's no Ana de Moraes in the building at all. Maybe you've got the wrong condominium.'

Leme had watched as the university administrative assistant had looked up the address on her database. It was the right one, he was sure.

'Well who does live in 603?'

The man smiled. 'I can't tell you that.'

'But it's a woman? You said *she* came and went.'

'People come and go. You lose track.'

Leme's stare hardened. 'I thought you were an expert.'

The man bristled. '603. Been passed around. Last few months ... I don't know, it's basically been empty.'

'Whose name is the apartment registered in?'

'I'm just the doorman. Expert or not.'

Leme smirked. 'Is there an admin department here?'

The man gestured at the building. 'What does it look like?'

'What if someone wasn't paying their rent or condominium charge? Who'd take care of that?'

'It's managed by the realtor. An agency.'

'You know the name?'

'Apartments are sold and let by Casa Pinheiros, based close by. The place was built by Mendes Construction. That's all I know.'

Mendes. Leme smiled. 'Of course.'

'Can I get back to my job now?'

Leme nodded. 'If anyone shows up at 603, call me.' He pointed at the paper. 'Number's on there.'

'Sure.'

'Thanks.'

Leme watched him unlock the side door and go back in. He heard music spring to life from inside the booth. His phone buzzed in his pocket. He looked at the screen. Lisboa. He let it ring. He'd call him once he'd paid this agency a visit.

Somebody had made a mistake. University records must be riddled with them, students changing address, forgetting to update their files: at that age it was unlikely they saw the consequences of their casualness.

Leme went back to the *boteco*, ordered another coffee and tapped the agency name into the search engine on his phone.

This time, in a rare moment of hunger, he ate the snack that he ordered.

'This Mensalão trial,' Lisboa said, 'could change everything.'

Leme moved away from the smoke spilling out from the barbe-cue. Rubbed his eyes. A group of women sat at the wooden table closest to the back door. Children circled like pigeons, swooping in groups of two or three to scavenge for their mother's attention.

The wind changed direction and Leme waved the smoke from his face.

'But that fucker Mendes is a clever bastard. No way to know if he were really involved. Here.'

Lisboa poured beer from a can into Leme's glass. He raised it in thanks. He felt the alcohol's reassuring grip on his stomach, tighten-ing against hunger. The sausages that Lisboa had prepared sat in a fat bunch of fingers on the table next to the grill, pink and swollen with gristle. Leme remembered the gourmet, spicy chorizo he had brought and thought about going to fetch it from the fridge. He lit a cigarette.

Leme glanced over at the other men. They were tossing a tennis ball about with their kids, pulling at cocktails, sending the ball further away each time the child got in the way of their conversation. Every time they wanted to swear or swap some story they didn't want Mummy to find out about. The women leaned close around the table, picking at cold cuts, in a conspiratorial huddle. Leme had known these people half his life. Having children hadn't changed them. It was something else. The children had amplified their personalities. They were the same people, just more so. If they were lively and fun before, they were still fun, and now they had new, amusing stories to tell. If they were annoying, they were still annoying, and now had child-related things to complain about. If they were flat, cautious before, well, now at least they had something of value, something that justified this caution. Following your child around so he doesn't bump his head is one way to raise him. How many of these children will rebel against this lifestyle? Leme wondered. Relative privilege can do strange things to a child. What would the city offer these kids when they grew up? Not for the first time, that he and Renata had none stung.

'Having children is something to do,' she'd once said. 'We'll get there.' Leme watched his friends with their kids. Renata had pointed out the generational change. 'When we were growing up,' she'd said, 'our parents never gave us a choice. They told us what we were going to do. Here, eat this. Then we're going for a walk. Then this, then that. Nowadays it's all about the child. Would you like some breakfast? Would you like a drink? To play? It's not fair. They're two-year olds. They don't know what they want.' Leme laughed now at the memory.

Lisboa poured them both more beer. Leme saw he was loose with alcohol. Probably got an early start. The host's prerogative.

'I heard from Silva,' he said. 'He's covering the trial in Brasilia.'

'*Ah, é?*' Lisboa arched an eyebrow.

'Yeah. He sent me an email. A joke. "The difference between the government in England and the government in Brazil is just a matter of changing a couple of letters."'

Leme watched as Lisboa's expression softened in anticipation. 'And?'

'Over there, the government is *parlamentar*. By parliament, democratic.'

'Right …' Lisboa's smile broadened, the sausage he was turning forgotten and crisping too quickly.

'While over here, its *pra lamentar*. Pitiful.'

Lisboa laughed. 'That Silva …' He shook his head, not quite sure, Leme thought, how to finish that sentiment. As if Silva were beyond the simple definition he'd attach to most people. Dismissing them in a phrase or word. Banker. Lawyer. Mother. Cop.

Leme was pleased with this response. He didn't want to ruin a Saturday afternoon on politics.

Lisboa looked around him and seeing no one young or female said: 'I know a joke.' He gestured for Leme to move closer. 'A German, an Englishman and a Portuguese are arguing over whose wife is the stupidest. The English says, "It's mine. She bought a fancy new bike, really expensive, and doesn't even know how to ride." The German says, "That's nothing, mine built a swimming pool in the garden and she doesn't even know how to swim." The Portuguese laughed. "You two have no idea. My wife is going to spend Carnival in Salvador, bought a huge box of condoms, and she doesn't even have a dick!"'

The two of them laughed and then faded into silence. Lisboa poured a little beer on to the cooking sausages and they popped and sizzled. Stuck a knife in one. It opened into a fleshy gash.

'Nearly there.'

He dropped a sausage on to the chopping board and cut it expertly into half a dozen pieces. 'This'll be for us,' he said, looking over Leme's shoulder and seeing no one approach.

They chewed, their mouths flapping like fish, trying to cool the meat down. Lisboa thrust his chin towards the far end of the garden and they turned so their backs were to the others.

'Give me a cigarette.'

Leme lit two.

'It's just easier, like this, *sabe?*'

Leme shrugged.

Lisboa sucked on his cigarette hungrily. 'What else?'

'I went to the girl's flat. Ana. I told you I'm looking into it.'

'And?'

'She wasn't there.'

'Well, I thought we'd established that.'

'Not what I mean. She was never there. According to the *porteiro*.'

'Fuck.'

'So I went to the realtor. The agency that owns and manages the place.'

'What did they say?'

'Never heard of her.'

'Here, quick, take this.' Lisboa handed Leme the cigarette. '*Oi amor, que foi?*' He bent down and wiped a smear of mud from his daughter's forehead.

'I ... I ... I was playing, and then the ball came and I ... I ...'

Lisboa straightened. 'Did someone throw the ball at you?'

'No. Yes. I. It came and I fell.'

'Who threw it?'

'I fell.'

Leme looked over at the other kids. They were oblivious. No idea they were being ratted out. Which, Leme thought, meant they probably hadn't done anything wrong.

The girl smiled. 'I want to play more.'

Lisboa stroked her head. He looked at Leme. 'No damage. *Vai, amor*. Off you go.' She ran off.

'So who owns it?'

Leme was caught off guard. Not because of the question – he knew the answer to that – but because he was still not accustomed to the way in which parents were able to move so quickly and seamlessly between talking to adults and their children, often changing their voices from one sentence to the next. Baby talk. Politics. Negotiating a mouthful of food. Praising the arse of the host's twenty-year-old niece.

'Well?'

'It's registered in a company name. They own it.'

'Which company?'

'It's an odd name.'

'Mario.'

'Podemos.'

'Which we've heard before. The word, I mean. That drunk. Never heard of the company.'

'Not surprising. I couldn't find a single record of it anywhere.'

'What did the agency say about that?'

'Nothing. They don't know that I know.'

'Eh?'

'They wouldn't tell me. So I had one of Silva's computer guys get into their records. Told you he could be useful.'

'What's in the records?'

'Nothing.'

'What do you mean?'

'This company owns it. But they have, apparently, nothing to do with it. All run through the agency.'

'What about the documents that show they own it?'

'The guy wasn't sure about that. He reckoned it was a part of the deal when the property was developed. Given away, basically.'

Lisboa nodded. 'OK, that can happen. We need to know who built it then.'

Leme popped another piece of sausage. Smiled. 'We already do.'

Lisboa narrowed his eyes. Let out a single bark of laughter. 'Fuck. No. Really?'

'*Isso.*'

Leme raised his glass and watched the foam race to the top as it was poured.

'Mendes,' they said together, laughing.

They drank. 'Well, Silva,' Lisboa conceded, 'is going to fucking love this.'

Leme ducked his head, kicked downward, arms straight by his side. His lungs filled. He opened his eyes and the lights in the pool traced uneven patterns around him. He kicked again and then righted himself, inches above the bottom. His pale body was a half-moon suspended in the dark. The cold water beat against the rush of that afternoon's alcohol, the beer, the Pinga shots burning his throat but calming his stomach. Now he felt that churning emptiness at the end of a long day topped off with the sour aftertaste of charred flesh. He opened his mouth and let the water in.

Blew it out. Let it in.

He broke the surface like waking from a bad dream. Underwater, he was cushioned against the Saturday evening in his condominium. Now, the water lapping at his mouth, he heard the familiar noises: men talking loudly outside the bar; children racing on roller skates, their maids shouting for them to slow down; teenagers sneaking cigarettes just above, enjoying the faux intimacy of the dark, that cloak of anonymity.

He lay back in the water. The tops of the buildings were dotted with lights that looked like colourful stars from down there. He drifted to the side and stayed there, a boat swaying on its mooring.

He closed his eyes.

The water churned as the women swam circles in formation, Leme surrounded. Ghost-white swimming costumes against tanned skin. Leme reached his hands to touch but couldn't. Their faces blank and wobbly, eyes wide, whispering as they got close.

Renata's voice.

She grabbed his arm, shook him.

'*Porra, Meu. Que isso?*'

A boy was pulling Leme's head towards the side.

'You OK?'

Leme spat water and rubbed his face.

'I'm fine. Really. Just relaxing. Sorry. Thanks.'

'*Caralho.*'

The boy sucked his teeth and slouched back to his friends.

'*Nossa.* That old fucker. Next time, eh.'

The girls he was with squealed. 'I can't believe, we like, almost had to totally save some guy's life?'

Leme smiled. He climbed out and towelled himself, nodding at the group. His rescuer tut-tutted, dismissed him with a wave of his hand.

'What am I, like, this fucking guardian angel? *Sabe?*'

The girls squealed again at this.

Leme wrapped the towel around his shoulders and lay back on a sun lounger. The darkness ringed the tower blocks, throbbed between them. His mind buzzed and his ears rang with booze and cold.

The next thing he knew, the *segurança* was tidying away the chairs and he was shivering.

'Sr Mario,' the guy said, nodding. They didn't judge.

Leme pulled on his clothes.

Back in his apartment, he curled up under the blankets on his bed. Sleep offered something that he could still take.

This morning, Leme woke fresh. He'd left the curtains open in his bedroom and the light cut through the dust that floated above his bed. In moments he was in the shower, playing in his head the sounds his wife would make as he scrubbed and cleaned. Today though, it was reassuring: he sensed something like solidarity or support. He dressed quickly.

In the kitchen, his maid whistled and hummed as she washed up.

'Sr Mario,' she said. 'Eat something. Here.'

She handed him a cup of coffee and placed fruit and bread on the table. He took the cup, drained it and shook his head.

'No time.' He turned and sensed her disapproval. Pocketed a banana. 'Thanks – kind of you.'

'*De nada*,' she said.

He left.

Sitting in the traffic on Giovanni Gronchi, he read again the address that Alex had given him. Rafael Maura, who worked for Mendes and was now seeing Leonardo's ex-girlfriend, apparently. It wouldn't do, he thought, to approach this Maura kid openly: he'd be straight on to Alex. Best do it this way. Even scare him a little. Maybe.

Rafael crossed the road, jabbering into his cell phone, nodding in agreement. The gate of the condominium slammed behind him. Tall building. Tucked in a quiet street a few blocks from Ibirapuera. View of the lake, probably.

'*Isso, e isso ai.*' I told him that. You're right, no. Yes. *Claro.* Fuck that shit, *sabe?*

Leme watched him approach: white shirt, dark tie, slim black trousers, shiny, alligator shoes. Ray Bans. Hair in a ridiculous little Mohawk, stiff and crunchy with gel, just like Eleanor had said. A leather bag slung across his shoulder, the smile-scowl of entitlement. Leme nosed his car forward.

'I can't – like – you know – keep bailing this fucker out. *Sabe?* I've got my own shit to take care of, *mano*. I said, Alex, don't even step to me, *entendeu?* Said to him: *nem vem, cara.* Always the fucking same with the motherfucker. I'm supposed to put that on hold? For this ... *babaca?*'

He slapped the roof of an SUV and jumped in the back. Leme pulled in behind.

Through the tinted back window, Leme could make out Rafael's outline. One arm stretched out across the seat, the other bent to his ear. The SUV moved through the shadows of the thick greenery of Curitiba, and then accelerated into Pedro Cabral. Leme had to drive fast to keep up. The driver was hammering it, despite the traffic, weaving in and out, shouting and beeping, beeping and shouting. They skirted the edge of the park, and then moved right across the lanes in front of the Monumento às Bandeiras, cutting up the cars waiting patiently for the lights to change, and jammed to a sudden halt. A chorus of horns. Leme examined the monument. It rose up away from him, some kind of progress. Order. *Portugueses, negros, mamelucos e índios.* Blocks of granite, unmoving.

They arced around the statue and hit Brigadeiro, speeding down towards Itaim. They turned right against the flow, but were down the road so fast it didn't matter. Leme edged round more slowly. Careful of the cars in the street outside the one- and two-storey houses, roofed in orange. Across São Gabriel and into Itaim, past burger restaurants, serviced flats and office blocks. A low city hum, ruptured by sirens. At the corner of Floriano and Bandeira Paulista the SUV jumped the kerb and stopped. The back door swung open and Rafael got out, greeting a group of young men dressed in the same office uniform who sat outside a pavement café. They slapped hands, bumped fists. Leme pulled over and walked towards the SUV. He leaned into the driver's window.

'I should have stopped you for reckless driving,' he said.

The heavyset man in the front seat turned, lowered his sunglasses. 'Who the fuck are you?'

Leme smiled. 'Someone who needs to talk to your boss.'

'I don't think so,' the driver said, opening his door.

Leme placed his hand on it, pushed it shut. 'In private.' He pulled his badge and the man sat back.

'Who did you say you were again?'

Rafael watched his friends leaving the café and Leme sized him up.

'Just answer the question.'

He sucked air through his teeth. 'Alex is a friend. But mother-fucker did some wrong shit, that's all. End of. Not my business, *sabe?*'

'What does that mean?'

'His boys. They'll tell you.'

'I thought you were *his boys.*'

'*Nem fodendo.* Dude's a piece of work. We were at school. What can you do?'

Rafael pulled a cigarette from a soft pack. 'Want one?'

Leme nodded. They lit up. A waiter approached shaking his head and pointed at the awning above them.

'Mate,' he said, looking at Rafael, 'you know the law. Got to stand over there.' He gestured at the pavement with his jaw.

'It's not a problem,' Leme said. The waiter turned to face him. Gave him a sour look.

'Erm, hello? It. Is. A problem? My manager's staring. Come on, man. *Para de encher, eh?*'

Leme pushed his badge across the table. 'Tell your manager not to worry.'

The waiter thought for a moment, then shrugged. '*Você que sabe.*'

Rafael curved an eyebrow. Smiled. 'You do that a lot, do you?'

Leme met his look. The truth was that he didn't normally take advantage. He paid for his coffee, his lunch – he didn't have to. Something about this kid had got his shackles up and the waiter bore the brunt. Leme ignored the question.

'What about Leonardo? How well did you know him?'

'You know. Enough.'

'What does that mean?'

Rafael sucked on his cigarette and blew smoke from the side of his mouth. Grimaced towards his driver. Flicked the still-burning Marlboro into the road. It traced a shallow curve as it fell. Leme watched the tip detach from the butt in the air and float down like a smouldering flower petal.

Rafael put his sunglasses back on. 'We were at school. Since we were three years old. Our families know each other decades, or some-thing. Dude had issues with that. With me. Well, recently. We were pretty tight when we were teenagers. But, you know, it happens.'

'What happened recently?'

'It's complicated.'

'That normally means it isn't.'

Rafael raised his eyebrows. 'You're like, what, a philosopher?'

'*Chega, cara.* What was so complicated?'

'Ah, you know. What it always is.' His lips twisted into a meaty knot. 'Pussy.'

'Charming.'

'Ah, *vai*, it is what it is.'

Leme considered the boy. All appetite; no need to think about what happens as a result.

'What do you know about Podemos?' Leme asked.

Rafael looked straight through him. 'Eh? Never heard of it.'

Leme smiled and leaned back. 'Maybe you're not as smart as you think.'

'Like I said.'

'Maybe, *ne?*' Leme smiled again.

'*Olha*, I need to get to work. You know, work?'

'I know. What do you do again?'

'Construction.'

'Sure.' Leme ran his tongue over his teeth. 'It's what every young man should be doing. Right? Building the future.'

Rafael shook his head, whistled. Muttered: '*Caralho.* São Paulo *is* the future, remember?'

'Interesting perspective.'

'*Sei lá.*'

Leme took a card from his wallet. 'Call this. You may want to.'

'This like a formal interview? Or are you just fucking with me?'

'Where you work,' Leme said, 'you may need my card, that's all.'

'OK, guy. *Você que sabe, ne?* We done?'

'We're done.'

Rafael pushed his chair back, gestured at the table. 'You'll get these.'

Leme nodded. 'You know, Rafael, keep your name away from this Podemos, *certo?* Tell Mendes you want nothing to do with it.'

He pushed his sunglasses down his nose. 'I would but he's my boss? *E ele que manda.*'

'It's him, is it? This company?'

'Like I told you, I've never heard of it.'

Leme watched him saunter, loose-limbed, over to the car.

The driver opened the back door for him.

Rafael was on his phone in moments and the car pulled away sharply before the door was even slammed shut.

Leme threw some notes on the table.

Leme decided to go back to Ana's apartment and this time he wasn't going to fuck around. He'd been to the university administration office and they were no help. No one could find the original application folder or a home address. 'If she was a scholarship girl,' the harassed, tight-mouthed lady had said, 'she may never have given us one.' Leme raised his eyebrows. The secretary tilted her head and clucked. 'Don't be naïve. Where do you think they come from? It can be embarrassing.'

Leme slapped the desk, looked her in the eye. 'This girl is missing. Shouldn't you be more worried?'

Another thin smile. 'Happens all the time. She'll turn up.' She glanced either side of her, gave Leme a prim, disapproving look. 'Who knows what these kids get up to, *sabe?*'

It was true. Leme certainly didn't. He'd sat in a bar across from the campus after that and watched. It looked like fun. Beers and cigarettes and laughter. Young, tanned flesh, the promise of something. He'd asked a couple of groups of students about Ana, but no one could help. He began to feel conspicuous and paid his bill. As he was leaving the bar, a girl called after him. 'I don't know her,' she'd said, 'personally? But I saw her sometimes, here. With older people? Not like you though. Younger than that.' Leme smiled. 'Oh, sorry, I'm, like, *tipo*, awful with ages? I don't know if she had any friends, who are, *tipo*, you know, students.'

Leme nodded. Gave her his card. 'Thanks. If you hear anything …'

The girl looked at the card. Flicked her hair. Brought her hand to her mouth. 'Oh, shit. What's happened?'

Leme smiled. 'Nothing. Routine thing. Just need to contact her.'

The girl gave him a disbelieving smile. He didn't care. He'd thanked her again and left.

At the apartment building, Leme flashed his badge at the *porteiro*. 'You again. I didn't think you were from the university.'

He buzzed him in.

'I need to see the apartment.'

The *porteiro* nodded and led him inside.

They took the lift in gruff silence, shoulder to shoulder. Leme stepped out first then let the *porteiro* pass. He nudged the light on and examined a large bunch of keys. The corridor was damp, the light a faint yellow moon.

Leme poked at a line of flowering mould with his toe.

'Nice.'

The other man shrugged and found the key. '*Isso*,' he said and waved it in the air.

He thrust it into the lock and wriggled it around until the door gave with a click.

Light filled the hallway. Leme pushed at the door slowly. There was a strong smell he thought he recognised, like perfume but floral and misty. The apartment was whitewashed. A clean wooden floor. Leme realised why he knew the smell: his own flat – an expensive floor cleaner. The only one his maid would use: it scrubs away any problem, she'd say.

Leme took in the emptiness of the room as if in a museum.

'What the fuck?' the *porteiro* said. 'There's nothing in here.'

It was a studio space and the bathroom door was open. Leme reached it in three steps. He checked quickly behind the door. Nothing. Even the shower had been dismantled. Then he spotted it. Stuck to the mirror circled by a heart drawn in lipstick was a business card, blank but for a printed phone number.

He keyed in the number. 'Don't touch anything,' he called out.

Three rings. He tapped his foot.

'*Oi, quem fala?*' A brisk, dismissive voice.

'I'm looking for something.'

'Oh yeah? Aren't we all?' A barked laugh.

'Services.'

'Anyone in mind?'

'Ana, preferably.'

'Ah.' The voice dropped. 'Difficult, I'm afraid. Has to be someone else.'

'Pity. When's she back?'

Leme heard the guy take a breath.

'She doesn't work any more. Look, mate, I'm kind of busy? Call me back if you change your mind.'

Leme hung up. Turned his phone over in his hand. He had heard the voice before, the clipped arrogance, the rising intonation. It was Alex, Leonardo's friend. He'd seen them together in the hotel. But now Alex was saying that they weren't working together any more. And she was missing.

He made another call, to the office.

'You can go now,' he said to the *porteiro*. 'My colleagues will arrive soon. I'll wait for them here.'

The courier brought the papers in a pink envelope. Leme opened them in front of him and out fell a red, cardboard heart. Silva had a sense of humour, Leme thought. Then realised it was likely one of his little schemes. Guy thinks he's a fucking spy. The courier made a face, winked. Leme smiled and slammed the door. The courier yelped.

He sat out on his balcony, drinking. After more than an hour in traffic on the way home his legs were stiff and his neck ached.

He turned to the file. Anonymous testimony. New transcript of one of the Gabriel killers. Silva said so, at least, but Leme wasn't sure.

'It's him, trust me,' Silva had said earlier that afternoon.

'But who made the recording?'

'Don't worry about it. I told you I could get to him.'

Leme breathed out. 'Francisco, this is no fucking use if you can't corroborate it,' he said.

'I can. It's from a family member, OK? That's all I'll tell you for now. It's the first bit and there *will* be more.'

Leme was tiring of this. But he didn't argue.

He examined the transcript. In it the killer claimed the two of them were given orders and paid. No actual mention of a robbery. Doesn't say who paid them. But Mendes buys the property just days after the old guy's death. *Entao*.

Leme lit a cigarette. Blew smoke down at the papers in front of him. A word jumped out:

Manslaughter.

They were convicted of manslaughter. The guy was killed by accident. Self-defence. Collateral damage, no intent.

Leme half-smiled. Of course, he thought, if they could prove they were paid, then it's no longer manslaughter.

Pre-meditated.

Conspiracy meant a new crime. New case. Leme jabbed at his mobile phone. Silva. He was looking forward to pointing this out. A neat role reversal.

Silva was supposed to be the clever one.

'You know, I'm kind of getting used to you in my bed.'

Leme smiled. 'That doesn't sound like a compliment,' he said.

Antonia laughed. 'You know what I mean, silly.'

Her breath was sweet with wine.

'Don't worry,' she went on, her finger boring its way into his chest, 'I won't get too used to it.'

Leme said nothing. The truth was, *he* was getting used to it.

'This is what it is, *ne?*' she said.

'Uh-huh,' Leme said, still smiling. 'Not that I know what that means.'

'Don't over-think it, *querido*. Believe it or not, it's an escape for me, too.'

It was Saturday afternoon and the sounds of children playing by the pool drifted up to her open window, as well as Leme's friends' drunken and belligerent bellowing.

He turned to her, nodded at the window. 'They never fucking shut up, do they?' he said.

'Join them if you like.'

Leme couldn't figure her tone. And he realised that though he hoped she wasn't being difficult, he also realised that he didn't really know her at all.

He said, 'If they knew where I was, they'd never forgive me for abandoning you to have a drink with them.'

Antonia wrinkled her nose, pushed a leg between his. 'Now that *does* sound like a compliment.'

They kissed. Leme hadn't realised he missed this, hadn't understood that the joy of burying himself in someone else's smell and skin would ever be pleasurable again.

After a while they stopped kissing and Antonia got up, wrapped a towel around her and left the room. Leme lay back. He wondered what Lisboa would make of all this. Be right behind me, he thought. '*Tem que comer, cara*,' he'd say. 'All good.' Thinking about what other people would think meant he didn't have to think about it himself. He wasn't sure what that meant.

She came back in carrying a bottle of white wine in some sort of case, which, he assumed, kept it chilled. Very her, he thought. The flat was full of gadgets, things.

'Top-up?'

He nodded.

She held the towel around her with one hand as she poured with the other, placed the wine on the bedside table and let the towel drop. She took a sip and wriggled back into bed.

'Anything you want to do tonight?' she asked.

'Haven't thought that far ahead.'

'I'm not doing anything – well, there's a *thing*, but there's always a thing.'

'I wouldn't know.'

They drank in silence, listened to the splashing and shouting from downstairs. Weekends. Some people never left the condominium at the weekend, he thought, and he knew why. It was a cocoon, São Paulo distant, unreal for a couple of days. A relief.

'I was worried about you the other night,' she said.

'Oh yeah?'

'I phoned. We spoke for a while and then you just disappeared. Mid-sentence.'

He'd forgotten. 'I did. I'm sorry.'

'What happened?'

He took a deep breath. He hadn't told anyone about this, apart from Lisboa.

'Something that happens to me, you know, occasionally.'

She raised an eyebrow.

He went on. 'Like an episode,' he said. He wasn't sure he should be telling her. It didn't feel appropriate, or something. Yet, who else could he tell? He didn't want to lie. He put his glass down and turned to her. 'I get these sorts of episodes,' he said. 'It's like I can hear her voice, though I don't know what she is saying.'

'Renata?'

'Of course,' he said, then immediately regretted being terse. 'Sorry. I mean – you know.'

She touched his arm. 'I do.'

'It's overwhelming,' he said. 'When it happens, I feel faint, light-headed. Sometimes I black out.'

'And that's what happened?'

'Yes.'

She touched him again. Kissed his shoulder. 'I'm glad you told me,' she said. 'It was strange.'

He smiled, wanted to lighten the mood. 'Don't tell me you're insecure.'

She punched him lightly. 'Of course not, silly.' Her look hardened. 'Not my style.'

They kissed again, quickly.

'It's good that you told me,' she said. 'I think I understand.'

Leme sighed. 'I'm not sure I do,' he said. 'Thing is ... no, it's silly.'

'Go on.'

'Thing is, while they're difficult, uncomfortable, scary, and, you know, could even be dangerous if they happen at the wrong moment, I don't want them to stop.'

She nodded. Pointed at his glass. 'Have a drink,' she said. 'They will stop, one day. Until they do though, know that I get it, *entendeu?*'

Leme breathed out. It felt like the first breath he'd taken in a long time. 'Thanks,' he said. 'You're lovely.'

'I told you not to get soppy with me, detective.'

He laughed. 'Why don't I cook us dinner?' he said.

She kissed his forehead. 'OK. Or at least you can *try*.'

Leme wandered into the kitchen, a towel around his waist. He picked at an olive, opened the fridge. He scratched his stomach. Pulled a beer and snapped off the top.

Then his phone beeped, buzzed across the counter. A message from Carlos: **Call me. Now. We've found him.**

Leme stood apart, fists clenched – scoped the scene. Carlos conducted three of his Military Police goons. In the middle of them, on his knees was a kid with gold teeth and dreadlocks, gasping, his head inside a plastic bag.

Leme had seen him before.

That morning in the *favela*, leaning into his car. Threatening him. Showing him his gun.

They were in an empty house at the highest point in Paraisópolis, raised up from the ground.

Bricks and dust.

Gaps for windows but no glass.

A dirty blanket on the floor.

A broken wooden chair.

The room: a touch bigger than Leme's office at the Polícia Civil.

'Get up.' Carlos nodded at one of the Militars, a huge guy with broad shoulders and a blank look in his eye. He dragged the kid to his feet.

Blood-black puddles. The Militar pulled the kid's head out of the bag as though taking a piece of meat for the barbecue. The kid breathed heavily through his bleeding mouth, nose broken. Blood stuck like a spreading tattoo to his cheeks and forehead. His arms and knees were dirty and Leme guessed from the state of his T-shirt and shorts that he had been dragged up the hill. Perhaps even behind the vehicle that was parked outside.

'Tell him what you told us,' Carlos instructed the kid, pointing at Leme.

The kid's eyes rolled up. The big Militar struck him across the face with the back of his hand. The kid groaned. The Militar wiped his bloodied hand on his trousers. The kid said nothing. His legs buckled.

'We've found him,' Carlos had told Leme earlier that day on the phone. 'I'll pick you up at midnight. Don't tell anyone. Got that? *Anyone.*'

'How?' Leme asked. 'Why now?'

'He'd been away a while. Came back not long ago. A *traficante.*'

'How do you know it's him?'

'We know. He was there. One of our guys ID'd him. Dreadlocks and gold teeth. Young. We picked up a kid last week who ratted him out. Said Gold Teeth was back and trying to muscle in. We found him pretty quick. And like I said, one of our guys saw him that night. He was younger, but it was him. He had the automatic weapon. He was closest. We know.'

'OK,' Leme said.

He'd sat in his living room in the dark steadily working his way through a bottle of Scotch. He felt nothing. He'd been waiting for this, but now the moment was here, he didn't know why.

They'd driven in silence through the *favela* to the house. Inside, the kid was tied to a chair, a young Militar standing over him. They'd gone to work immediately, knocking him about between them like a football, breaking the chair over his back, using the legs to beat him senseless. The sounds of ribs cracking, low thumps like pounding meat with a rolling pin as his stomach and back blackened with bruises. He'd passed out. They stuck his head into a bucket of freezing water then beat him all over again. When he still hadn't spoken the plastic bag came out and his head went in it. His neck strained upwards and his mouth flapped at the plastic like a fish out of water seeking air. The bag filled slowly with blood. Each time they pulled it off, more dripped into the dust. Leme had bent down to touch it. The big Militar jammed a chair leg in his mouth and levered it hard into his face and outwards again. He prised his front gold teeth out and they dropped in a bloody, shiny clump. Leme shuddered.

'Tell him.'

The kid shook his head. It rolled around on his neck as if detached. The plastic bag again. Then the bucket. Then they forced him on to the floor on his front and pulled down his shorts and underwear. The big Militar looked at Carlos. Carlos nodded. He gripped the roughest chair leg and thrust it between the kid's buttocks. Pushed down hard. The kid let out a scream, a ghostly wail of anguish and incomprehension. No one to hear it though. They were too deep inside the *favela*. The Militar stopped and pulled him again to his feet. The kid's genitals hung limp between his legs. The Militar tapped them lightly with the chair leg and then drove it hard between them. Another gasp and scream and the kid flopped faint to the floor.

'*Chega,*' Carlos said. They threw the remaining water over him. And again pulled him to his feet.

'Tell. Him.'

'*Foi eu que matou ela,*' he said, spitting, drooling blood and teeth with each word, his limbs limp, lisping through the blood in his mouth.

'Again.'

'*Foi eu. Foi eu que matou ela.*'

The words echoed in Leme's head: *It was me. It was me who killed her.*

'Who?'

'*Aquela mulher.* The lawyer. *Foi eu.*'

His wife, the lawyer. It was me.

Renata. Leme's wife. He clenched and re-clenched his fists.

'You're sure?'

'*Certeza.*'

Carlos looked at Leme. Leme nodded.

The plastic bag went back on and the youngest and smallest Militar held it tight round the kid's neck. The others then attacked him again with the chair legs. The young Militar couldn't hold on and the kid slid through his arms to the ground. They set upon him with their feet then, kicking and stamping.

Leme took a step forward. Stopped. Stepped back.

Stepped forward.

His mind blank.

This kid killed Renata. This kid took her life.

Now he knew.

Leme stamped. They all did. And then the kid's body seemed heavier, as if there was no more punishment it could take.

Carlos stepped into the middle. '*Acabou.* It's over,' he said.

Back in his apartment, Leme examined his shoes. They were scuffed, dusty, ridged with black blood. He poured the last of the whiskey into his glass and sank it.

Now he knew.

He owed Carlos something; he understood that.

But he wasn't grateful.

It wasn't worth it.

When he woke the next morning, everything had changed.

PART TWO

What is the city but the people?

Coriolanus, *William Shakespeare*

Who owns you? No one, São Paulo

You wake –
You lurch –
You retch –
You vomit.
You drink –
You lurch –
You retch –
You vomit.
You shake. Your head light. Your chest tight.
What have you done? What have you done? What have you done?
Fuck. Fuck. Fuck. Fuck. Fuck.
You shake. Your head light. Your chest tight.
Your shoes scuffed, ridged with black blood.
Renata. Renata. Renata.
Your head light. Your chest tight.
In the night time, the skies grey, your soul black –
Ridged with black blood.
In the night time, you see a dead man's glinting, empty mouth –
Gold.
You're as bad as they are. Renata. You're as bad as they are. Renata. You're
as bad as they are. Renata –
What have you done?
Foi eu que matou ela. Foi eu que matou. Foi –
In the pit of your stomach: black bile, your soul black.
In the night time –
You lurch –
You vomit.
You –
Then, morning.
You are what you are –
You can do what you can do.
For her.

It still surprised Leme, after all this time and after everything that had happened. His professional life was defined by certain persistence and belief and the outsider assumption that enabled insight. He was dogged in pursuit, not without flair exactly, but aware of the qualities of patience and insistence.

In his love life, there had been little difference. As a teenager there were the obligatory crushes, some of which were fulfilled and others not. He was neither markedly successful nor unsuccessful and attracted little attention amongst friends as a result. He'd guessed romantic involvement would continue this way, and in his twenties it more or less did. There were several semi-serious girlfriends who all eventually tired of his unpredictable routine and failure to ask them to move in with him. It was simply something that never occurred to him. There was no conscious decision to live alone or remain a bachelor. He didn't fear commitment, at least he didn't think he did – it was never really put to the test, and he was not a womaniser or a man who needed the freedom to go out drinking and whoring with his friends.

Hindsight cleared it all up for him – he'd never been in love. We don't act impulsively if we're not in love, he understood. We don't change our lives – we don't even alter our lives.

And not to take the risk is the biggest risk of all.

And Leme understood all this the moment he met Renata.

It was immediate. Something stirred inside him when he first laid eyes on her and made him determined to speak to her. And it was just that: determination. Sleeping with her was the last thing on his mind – oh, it was there, it was just that passion was one of a number of feelings, all of which energised him, animated him, shaped him into a person he actually liked.

'I'm a lawyer,' she'd said and Leme remembered feeling a little let down. Lisboa had introduced them as they mingled in his garden before a weekend dinner. 'I work in the *favela*. Paraisópolis.'

Straight away, Leme felt something like vindication.

'So, pro bono?' he'd asked, not entirely sure what the phrase meant, but aware it had something to do with helping the less fortunate.

She'd laughed. 'Sort of. I do actually earn some money. I am lucky though. My partner works in the private sector, so we get by.'

'Your business partner?'

She'd laughed again. 'No, my ... well ... boyfriend, I suppose.' I *suppose*.

My boyfriend. Two stinging wounds. Leme felt his insides empty, all excitement and optimism drained away and he was faint and lightheaded, as if from a physical blow. He recovered himself, took a long pull on his beer and realised he was being silly. *I suppose*. What did that mean?

'I live nearby,' he'd said, 'if you ever fancy a drink?'

'That might be nice.'

Might?

'Here's my number.' He gave her a card.

'Ah, of course. You're the famous Detective Leme.' He felt his chest swell in nervous anticipation. 'Lisboa has told me a lot about you.' She offered her own card. 'We should definitely meet. I want to pick your brain. I'll be away for the next month, but get in touch mid-January. We can grab a drink.'

They had more than one drink the first time they met in a bar in Morumbi. They went outside for a cigarette and Leme was sure the evening was coming to an end.

'Well, we could get the bill, or ... have one more? *Saideira?*'

'I probably should get home.' She looked at him, her arms crossed, cigarette to the left of her mouth. 'But I want another one.' Leme smiled. 'You have to stop being such good company,' she said. 'Bad, bad influence.'

He'd never been called that before.

She had said something: that emotionally things were simple, practically not. So there was some hope.

The next time, as he watched her approach, noted the fresh make-up and smile of recognition when she saw him, the way she greeted him from across the room, he knew that something was going to happen.

They kissed, that was all, but it was enough.

'My situation is complicated,' she wrote in an email, 'and the last thing I want to do is hurt you. Maybe this is bad timing. I want to wait until everything is resolved, but I can't imagine not seeing you.'

'Bad timing is an excuse,' he replied.

'It's not an excuse,' she wrote.

That had hurt, felt demeaning.

He struggled to sit still. Restless, his feelings veered from optimism to despair. He thought about her constantly: always, always, always. It was new.

'There's not a moment when I'm not thinking about you,' he told her.

They saw each other. Spent a week together when she took time off. Afternoons in bed, bars, and shared pizza. He told her he loved her. She said she had felt it the first moment she laid eyes on him, that her stomach had dropped and settled and a physical understanding had dawned on her: this is the man I will marry. This is the father of my children. This man is the rest of my life. But at the end of each day, she went home. To him.

He believed she would leave him. But she didn't.

He sent her messages in the knowledge that he was trying to elicit certain responses. But she never responded in the way he hoped. And then when he wasn't expecting it, she'd write something truly disarming. It was all so hopeless. And yet he couldn't stop.

Months passed. They continued to spend time together, walking, talking, drinking. She told him she didn't love the man she lived with. Felt trapped, she said.

'So leave him,' Leme said. 'Live with me.'

'I want to, silly,' she replied. 'You know that I love you.'

'That's enough,' Leme said. 'The rest is details.'

And she held him and they kissed.

But even as he said it he feared it wasn't enough, that he was wrong.

He became demanding, confused. Tried to tell himself it wasn't his fault, that the situation was making things impossible. But he didn't know if he was asking too much, or if she had promised too much.

She stopped answering his messages, left his calls unreturned. He began to feel stupid. He wondered what he had done wrong other than try to be honest, try to be understanding.

All he had done was fall in love with her and believe in her.

'I can't do this any more,' she wrote in an email. 'I need space.'

He didn't understand. 'Space? You're living with someone you don't love. What about everything you have ever said to me?'

She ignored his questions. Told him she loved him.

It felt cruel, or confused – he wasn't sure. Perhaps, when it came down to it, she simply didn't love him enough?

He didn't know what to do, and so left it, left her, walked away. It was harder than he'd imagined, mainly, he realised, because he had never thought that he would walk away.

But confusion settles, wounds heal; he would give it time.

And then, when he felt he had accepted what had happened, she called him. She had decided to leave her partner but had needed to make the decision without feeling that Leme was an undue influence. She had needed the time to do it. Her partner had been suspicious and she needed him to know that it was more than just an affair, that there were deeper, more final problems.

Just like that. An analysis and a decision.

Very her, he thought, smiling at her terminology. Undue influence. That was what he had been.

Later, she'd tell him that the practicalities had become overwhelming, that ending a chapter of her life had been harder and taken more time than she'd envisaged.

He told her he understood.

She wanted to take things slowly, but she wanted to see him.

He had to hold back but agreed it was what he wanted, too. And it was. All he'd ever wanted was to be with her.

And from that lunch, for the eight years they were together until she died, they did everything that a couple can. Almost everything.

And when Leme reflected on it, as he did every day, that frenzied early period, when all his prevailing sense of caution evaporated, still amazed him. That he was capable of it. But, of course, it was all because of her. She brought out something in him he hadn't known existed.

He'd been like a magpie, engaging totally with the world, collecting things to share with her. Every little shiny nugget in his life had a new purpose: to make her smile. To make her love him more. Grief, he had begun to realise, was a consequence of love, a counterpoint: the world was empty now, of things to collect.

Nature is precise, forensic in its examination, its balance.

Step by step, Leme thought. Acclimatise. He slammed the door and beeped the alarm. He had found a parking space on Rua Costa Rica, just a block or two from the church. A very different Sunday morning from the one he'd spent with Lisboa.

He'd chosen this church, as it was unlikely anyone he knew would be there. This was not a local parish, but a picture-book setting for rich weddings. The Sunday morning mass was public and visited as an attraction as much as for spiritual guidance, he'd been told when making discreet enquiries at work. He stepped on to Rua Colômbia and immediately spotted the domed towers that shot up at the sides of the building, the spikes like a cardinal's hat. The cross in the centre, a defiant, upright, middle finger to non-believers. He'd driven past countless times, never noticed the colour. Faded pastel, urine-grey. He smiled at his inappropriateness.

Leme paused at the little side street that led to the entrance. He studied the Eastern curves, suggestive of some exotic, incense-heavy ceremony. The circle of palm trees, an odd tropical backdrop. This is what missionary work must have looked like, Leme thought. Foreign belief. Spiritual colonialism. We're what, Roman Catholics? This was an easier empire to hold on to.

On the steps, serious-looking men in shirts greeted each other with vigorous handshakes and backslapping. Mothers shooed children inside. Leme was late, but he wasn't the only one.

He stepped into the gloom and waited for his eyes to get accustomed to the dark. There were clusters of visitors at the fringes, quietly considering the artefacts and murals. The first dozen or so of the pews thronged with kneeling or hunchbacked worshippers, whispering back the priest's incantations. You don't have to be alone, his neighbour had told him. But what if that is exactly what you are supposed to be?

A sign instructed: Respect the prayers of the faithful. What about the unfaithful? Leme looked around. They have prayers, too.

Leme began a slow half-circle at the back of the church, heels clicking on the stone. He paused in time with the priest and the congregation, stopped still, head bowed. He'd read somewhere recently that if we appear to do or feel something, it is, from the outside, the same as doing or feeling it. It can't be measured. To an observer, you are what you appear to be. He wondered if this scientific principle applied to God: if he appeared to be praying, perhaps he would get some divine guidance.

He placed his hand on the back of a pew. Felt the softly splintered wood, the fragility of the legs. The musky incense drifted among the faithful, the soft clouds only dispersing against pillars and posts, wood and stone. Leme sniffed in a half-hearted attempt to join in with the communion. Guidance in any form is welcome.

He leaned against a pillar and relaxed. No one was looking at him. He had every right to be there, appearance or not. The priest shook the thurible and puffs of incense formed soupy fog in several half-time ejaculations.

He closed his eyes.

He thought about his mother. How his father had told him again and again about rescuing her from the *favela*. Rescuing her. He understood that now. After the kid with gold teeth. Not that he thought about it, exactly. It was just there, inside him now. It was a blur, like a half-remembered drunken memory – he couldn't be sure exactly what had taken place.

He moved round the church. Watched the people in prayer. And then it struck him: it had taken almost a year to find that kid. Carlos had said it was impossible. And then there was the incident in the *favela* when Leme was with the Militars. What was it Carlos had said to him? Leave it with me.

Leme froze. He'd questioned where the *bala perdida* had come from, suggested it had been one of the Militars. Carlos didn't want that, Leme realised now. He'd found him a scapegoat. But it had been corroborated. They *knew*, Carlos said. And the kid admitted it. He was a dealer. He was there. He'd shot at the police. Renata died. And now Leme was involved.

He'd killed.

Leme shuddered.

The pit of his stomach: black.

The pit of his soul: black.

What would Renata make of him now?

He'd done exactly what he always said he never would.

He'd killed.

His stomach: black.

His soul: black.

Renata –

But he had to tell himself: the kid was guilty by association. It was likely him.

It *was* him. It *had* to be him. He had killed and would again.

Would Leme?

His stomach: black.

His soul: black.

It was how they worked, the *traficantes*.

Carlos could not be blamed.

It was how *he* worked.

There was only one thought in Leme's mind.

It ricocheted wildly, like hungover paranoia.

His stomach: black.

His soul: black.

Renata.

He had to figure out what was going on. He couldn't do anything else.

There was nothing he could confess.

He would have to *act*. Move forward.

Why would Carlos let him become implicated in the death of Gold Teeth? Because he was, now. He wasn't sure it mattered. It had happened. Carlos was his friend and he trusted him. And he was protecting him. It didn't matter.

Except that it did, except that what he had done mattered.

His stomach shrank and the priest's whispers seemed distant, intoning some dreadful curse.

Her voice, whispering.

This time, he let himself listen.

At his desk, Leme nosed through the papers. His office was more dingy than ever before, but there was little point in requesting any sort of refurbishment. They'd even stopped cleaning the window. Now, a thick coating of dust filtered an opaque, mud-yellow glow, but Leme refused to turn on the light; he enjoyed the coolness of the dark.

The air-conditioning unit across the tiny courtyard spluttered into action, snarled and coughed, clearing its throat and settling into a low chug. Leme was looking for a particular story. He'd heard a rumour from Carlos that the PCC were going to make an announcement to the media. They'd consolidated their control across the city's *favela*s and were unhappy at the incursions of some of the braver police units. Carlos had sent him a text:

> 4 every drug dealer killed, 2 or 3 of us will die – stay away from the *favela*.

That morning, Governador Alckmin and Minister Cardozo had issued a statement against organised crime. A five-point plan to contain the PCC and stop the spreading violence. Political posturing. In Rio they declare war. In São Paulo they draw up a charter. They're going to have to get a move on. Leme looked at the calendar. A little over eighteen months to the World Cup and thousands of visitors descending on a city that wasn't ready. The problem with the PCC was the position of power they had. They had taken over all the other smaller gangs. This made negotiating with them extremely difficult as they didn't have any competition. Leme knew. In Rio, in preparation for the Olympics in four years, they were already paying off the gangs that ran the *favelas*, taking promises that there would be no street crime, no shit. But the PCC would not be bought and kept quiet. The Rio gangs were independent, separate, and it was an easy way to make money without the daily competition in their other business interests.

Fucking happy days – they'll probably ask for more as the games approach, and anyway, fuck it, what can they do if some *michê vagabundo* wrestles a Rolex off a rich yank and punches his fat wife in the cunt? Leme smiled: easy for a Paulistano to mock a Carioca, but even our gangs are more serious-minded, have more corporate ambition. That whole flip-flop/assault-rifle shtick was just childish. And no match for the BOPE any more. Pacification, meaning: invasion. They'd all seen the news when the *bandidos* had shot down the police helicopter with a bazooka. That had been a red rag. War-zone chic.

More reports were coming in of random acid attacks in Itaim. Nothing they could do about it. And how random were they, really? The desperate mutilating the rich. What sort of an accident is that? The attacks had a pattern: late at night, chauffer-driven cars, darker, back streets of the neighbourhood. Gangs of young men springing up from behind skips or disused taxi ranks. Shots rarely fired, but guns used as a threat. Heavy in a fist when brought down on some rich fucker's head, too.

Or his driver.

As Leme leaned back in his broken chair, put his feet on the desk and watched the dust twinkle above it, he realised that he had to go to the source. Ana didn't live at the address he'd been given. Nobody seemed to know where she was. Leme wanted to look further into Leonardo's death, talk to people who knew him, try and put a picture together of what might have happened, but Ana's was a case, an actual case, and for now he had to focus on that.

Leme looked through Ana's university email account. Once he'd made it clear that it was a genuine case, the university had been helpful. The IT department there had made available all her emails and any documents on their servers. The problem was that it looked like she was using her university account for exactly that purpose: university. The IT person had said that most students do: they all know full well that the authorities can access the accounts if necessary and with good reason. It was one way of preventing cyber bullying.

But it didn't leave Leme with much.

He scoured the inbox again. She seemed efficient with what she kept and what she filed. On top of things. Leme checked the dates: she hadn't used the account, it seemed, since the day after he had followed her and seen her go into the hotel room beneath the View Bar.

This, give or take, matched what Eleanor had said when she reported her missing. Obviously there was a little leeway, or for Eleanor to have made a slight error with the days. *That* was certainly possible.

All the new messages were university announcements. There were three other folders: admin, work, photos. He went through them in order, read every message in admin and work checking that they were exactly that: confirmation of her scholarship, important term dates, copies of essays emailed to herself as a back-up he expected, that sort of thing. It was only when he clicked on 'photos' that he realised there was a new message; some trick of the light and he hadn't seen the folder was in bold, the word 'photo' black: swollen, pregnant with something new.

He looked at the date: three days after he had followed her, the day before Eleanor came to see him. There was no subject. He opened the message. Sent from her iPhone. Sent to this account only.

Attached was a photo. Oddly fluorescent. Yellowing steps. A sunrise or sunset? What looked like the moon? A sort of black watchtower. The image was grainy, but there appeared to be figures some distance from the photographer. In the corner of the shot was a shadow, falling at an angle that meant it could not have been the person who took the photo. There were people with her. She had not been alone when this photo was taken.

He saved the image on to his desktop. He could get his IT guy to improve its quality, he thought. She took this photo after she'd gone missing. But why send it? Where was she? What was this photo *of*?

He looked at the other messages in the folder. Only half a dozen. Scrolled through them. They were all documents, taken as if for proof. A certificate. The odd quotation or set of notes, for back-up again, perhaps. Her RGE card and CPF documentation. Clearly she didn't file all of her photos here: there was nothing personal.

Then he understood: this was the only email account easily accessed by someone else. She had sent a message to whoever might be trying to find her. But what did it mean?

The two-tone ping of an incoming email – to his own account. He smiled to himself. There was a message from a name he didn't recognise at first: Luciana Camargo. Subject line: Leonardo Alencar. Leme opened the message.

You've been talking to Alex Santos. He showed me your card. I
cared about Leonardo. He didn't. Please don't reply to this address.

A number. Leo's ex, he remembered. Alex had told him. She was
now with Rafael Maura. Leme picked up his phone.

Luciana Camargo was already at the table when Leme arrived. She had that knack of drawing waiters around her and two hovered close. She ignored them – actually, Leme thought, she didn't even realise they were there, so accustomed was she to being waited on – and had left the menu closed and untouched.

She had chosen one of those traditional *chopperias* in Vila Madalena, the sort with pictures of ancient, lined Tropicália artists on the walls, and gravelly waiters in white dropping foaming beers in front of you without asking if you wanted another. Dangerous place, Leme thought.

Even at three o'clock in the afternoon.

He stood in the doorway and watched her. It had to be her: there were only two other customers and they were, typically, bulbous men involved in a slurred, recursive argument about football and looked like they had been there since the night before. She glanced at the menu and a waiter swooped. She gave him a kind, sad smile and placed her hand on his arm as she ordered. He moved away with a solemn nod and was quickly back with a beer and a bottle of mineral water. Her eyes darted around the room from her phone to her reflection in the large mirror that covered the longest wall. Leme smiled. Gestured with his chin at the waiter who followed to her table and placed a *chopp* in front of him.

'*Saúde.*'

He lifted his glass and she clinked hers against it. They drank down half to the sounds of glasses being stacked and shouting from inside the kitchen. Luciana's legs twitched. Leme scratched at his stubble, turned slightly away.

'So,' he began, 'about that email you sent me ...'

'Thanks for not replying.'

Leme opened his palms.

'It's just that my boyfriend ...'

'Your boyfriend.'

She grimaced and ducked her head. 'I think he checks my email. I can't be sure. But I think so.'

Leme raised his eyebrows. 'Change your password.'

She nodded. 'Like I said, I can't be sure …'

'Doesn't sound the best kind of relationship, Luciana.'

'Ah, he's Brazilian. *Sabe?*'

'So am I.'

She tilted her head to look at him. 'You're a man. He's a boy. Rafael …'

'Rafael?'

'Yes?'

'Maura?'

She nodded.

'Works for Mendes. Property. I know him.'

A puzzled look crossed her face and settled. Became troubled.

'How? I mean, why do you know him?'

'Routine, that's all. Talking to people who knew Leonardo. Bit of background.'

The look softened and her mouth relaxed into a half-smile.

'And that's why we're here,' Leme said, to reassure her further.

Luciana turned her beer glass around in her fingers. Although she appeared calmed by what Leme had said, there was a distance in her eyes. And it was clear that she wanted to help. In Leme's experience, people came forward because they had a conscience that needed satisfying, or because they had that slightly meddling urge to do good, to, as they saw it, help. He felt that Luciana fitted into the second category, though in her eyes he recognised something he knew not to be a desire to interfere, but to honour someone she was once close to. Or did that sound too fucking grand? Leme waited for her to speak.

'He'd always been naive,' she began, 'always had other people to tell him what to do. It's a legacy of those parents, *sabe?*'

'You mean he was easily influenced?'

'That's too obvious.' She leaned forward, eager to explain something more subtle than she had first perhaps understood, something she was only realising as she articulated it. 'Leo is, was, a sweetheart,' she said. She paused and smiled at a private memory Leme recognised as nostalgic and affectionate. Not love, perhaps, but something close. The fondness of an ex-lover.

'He was simple, and that was his problem,' she said. She nodded, emphasising the sentiment, as if she had reached the solution to a problem that no one else had really considered.

'In what way simple?' Leme asked. 'It's not the impression I've got from anyone else.'

'You wouldn't.' She checked herself. 'I don't mean that I know him any better or anything as trite as that.' She gestured across the table as if embarrassed at using a word like trite. Leme smiled. 'I mean I know a different side. *Sabe?*' Leme nodded, encouraging her to go on. 'He had a private side that he only showed to a few of us. That's all.'

'You said he was simple,' Leme prompted.

'His goals in life were, that's what I'm trying to say.' She nodded again. 'Yes. His goals. What he hoped to do.'

'He was helping his mother with something,' Leme said.

'And that was a good thing!' Luciana banged her glass down on to the table and waved for another. 'I mean, fuck, finally he was putting his name to some fucking use, *sabe?*'

She ran her hand through her hair. Leme flicked at a wood chip with his finger. Pressed it under his nail, felt it bite and turn a soft, meat-red. Leme raised a finger and a waiter splashed another *chopp* on to the table. Outside, a *manobrista* was shunting cars around, fitting them into ever more unlikely spaces. Laughing and shouting at his customers.

'But his mother … she has a lot to answer for. There are things … well, you probably already know.'

Leme shrugged. Feigning indifference normally encouraged people to share more than they otherwise might if you pressed them.

Luciana's mouth twisted into a scowl. 'She's not the fucking martyr she wants people to think she is. That's one thing I can give Alex, he never lied about all that. And he never accepted it. He got what he fucking wanted because he found out.'

'What about Leonardo's work with her?' Leme felt Luciana's emotion shift from unnamed sadness to a specific target. Grief plays out like a competition: if your own seems inadequate, attack someone else's. Someone with more to lose.

'He was helping with the scholarship applications. I was pleased he was. After we broke up … well, he drifted. He was drifting while we were together, even. The work seemed like something he could be proud of doing, which is all he ever wanted. That's what I mean by simple. He just wanted to feel that he could be proud of something that he *did*, not what he *had*.' She grimaced and swallowed hard. Washed the thought down in a thirsty gulp. 'Problem was, it was his mother that got him the fucking work. And that ate him up. Like it was meaningless as a result of the fucking nepotism.' She bowed her head. Leme sniffed and looked away.

'I wanted to tell him that he could, you know, be proud of what he was doing. I tried to, one day, when I ran into him at the club.'

'What stopped you?'

'Something my boyfriend told me.'

'Rafael?'

'Rafael. He wasn't my boyfriend then, though he was trying. I hadn't long finished with Leo.' A thought occurred to her and an expression of confusion formed comically slowly. 'Wait. I mean, I guess he might not have been telling the truth.'

'This is the same boyfriend you think might be monitoring your email?'

Her expression deepened; her eyebrows a tight knot. 'He told me something about what Leo and Alex were doing with these scholarship candidates. The girls.'

'When did he tell you this?'

'At the club. I'd already spoken to them and was going to go back, but was so disgusted with what I had heard that I didn't. I didn't speak to Leo again.'

'What did Rafael tell you exactly?'

She glanced around the bar. Still the same drunks talking that touch too loudly. How waiters must wish for a mute button.

'He said he had seen Alex and Leo at a *balada* with one of the girls. He met her. Ana, I think. Apparently they were acting pretty badly. I don't know. Like she was working for them, *sabe?*'

'Working? What does that mean?'

'Like an assistant, you know, bringing people to the table, fetching drinks. I don't know.'

'And Rafael told you this?'

'Yes.'

'And he was interested in you, right? So discrediting Leo would be a good thing?'

Luciana shook her head and smiled. 'Yes, that's right, I suppose,' she said. 'Rafa told me that a while later the girl turned up at his office with some gringa journalist doing a piece on his boss. He pretended not to know who she was, he said. But ... I was angry, right? Didn't think it through.' She dipped a finger into the head of her beer and sucked it dry. 'Thing is, it really doesn't seem the sort of thing that Leo would do.'

'And this is why you wanted to meet?'

'I was just going to tell you what I knew, what I'd heard, and what a fucking arsehole Alex can be. And not to trust him. But now ...'

She exhaled slowly and shook her head. 'I know Alex and he is manipulative.' Leme raised his eyebrows. 'Oh, I don't mean you wouldn't be able to spot that, it's just that his reasons for protecting Leo might be different from what he claims.'

'So might yours.'

She laughed and spat. 'Yeah, right, and we're all so fucking solipsistic that Leo didn't ever even exist outside our narrow conception of him? *Ne?* Fuck that, right?' She gave a bitter little cough. Leme smiled.

'Just saying,' he shrugged. 'But you're right. He only exists in our versions of him now. Which is why I'm listening to several of them.'

'You said you've spoken to Rafael?'

'I have.'

'Can you tell me what you think of him?'

Leme picked up his glass and wiped foam from the rim. It was probably worth trusting this girl. Not sure though if she was here for her own conscience or for Leonardo's. Either way.

'I don't trust him,' Leme said, looking Luciana in the eye. 'He's full of it. He's selfish and he works for a man who will turn him from a naive rich playboy into a force for bad.'

'Sounds dramatic.'

Leme shrugged. This was the reaction he had hoped for. 'These men,' he said, 'they don't see the city as anything more than a playground. And it takes an incident, or a person, to push a young man in that direction. Rafael thinks he's a hustler. He's not. He's just another boy following a well-worn path.'

'And you think the same about Leo?'

'Do you?'

She lowered her head again. 'No. I don't.'

'And Rafael?'

She breathed out and her brow tightened. 'I don't know. Maybe.'

'Just think about what he had to gain telling you that story about Leo.'

She nodded. 'I hope you're wrong.'

'You came here to warn me about Alex, right?' Leme leaned towards her. 'Remember, people will do desperate things more easily than we'd like to believe. And that includes Leo.'

She nodded again. Leme offered his hand and she took it. He studied her face and she looked away, embarrassed, the beginnings of a tear swelling in the corner of her eye.

This was the moment for Leme to ask: he wanted to know exactly what these jumped-up fuckers were doing.

'Do me a favour,' Leme said. 'Talk to Rafael about what was going on that night in the club with Ana. But do it casually. Then call me.'

She nodded. 'I'll try.'

Leme smiled. 'I think I know what Alex was doing with this girl Ana,' he said. 'I *think*, *entendeu?* Doesn't necessarily reflect on your Rafael, *certo?*'

She shook her head and grimaced.

'But I don't know why Leonardo was in Paraisópolis.'

He let it hang in there.

Luciana said nothing and sipped at her drink.

'OK,' he said. 'I think we're done.'

He dropped a few notes on the table and waved the waiter over.

He squeezed her hand and left, unsure as to how long she would sit there alone, disturbed, thinking through what she had just worked out for herself, as if that – the self-realisation – made it harder to bear.

Leme swung his car off Giovanni. He chuntered down pockmarked Clementine towards the *favela*. He slipped round the roundabout and parked at a clumsy angle. He jumped out and slammed the door.

A stale-booze, rotten odour hung in the heat, like a cloud.

A couple of *mendigos* called after him: *E aí mano*, what have you got for me? then cackled with laughter. He walked through the gates of Cemitério Gethsêmani, and the space stretched out in front of him, a green blanket. The air cleared where the flowers and plants and shrubbery breathed in cool shadows. He took the path north and stopped at the Aviary. It was built, he remembered, a few years before, and the birds all arrived a month or so later. Yellow heads with orange cheeks, long grey bodies and yellow-green tail feathers. The older birds perched on the wire-mesh surround while their young crouched in circular nests. Leme poked his finger through a hole, made a kissing sound with his lips. The birds looked over but ignored him.

He carried on down the path. A tearful *enterrado* was in progress. Two women veiled in black clung to each other in a desperate embrace, crooked-backed and shaking. Leme stopped at a respectful distance. Groups of young men in badly fitting, nylon-shiny suits slouched about, kicking their shoes into the grass, hands in pockets. The circle tightened and Leme heard the priest intone a blessing. A large black-and-white photo of the victim was raised above the grave. Smiling face. A graduation photo, perhaps. Can't have been more than nineteen. The priest's voice got louder as he condemned the senselessness of the act that took the young man's life. A *tiro-teiro*, a *bala perdida*. An accident. An accident of birth, really. The young man was born into this situation and his destiny was inescapable. Choice had nothing to do with it.

It had been Renata's choice to work pro bono in the *favela*. But that too was inevitable. Once again, he reflected on this choice. She'd been helping a man with a dispute over land. The man had visited her office to bless her and offer his respects. He'd talked for a long time and she was late leaving the office, locking the front gate as it started to get dark.

It's called a *bala perdida*, a stray bullet.

But the euphemism doesn't change its impact.

As he rearranged the sun-scorched flowers and brushed dirt from the glass picture frame, he heard his own voice.

That remains, he thought.

The compulsion to make São Paulo a better place was long gone. But he felt the old itch returning. What choice was there but to carry on?

He drove back up to Giovanni, and headed into town to meet Eleanor again.

'Why are we here, Eleanor?' Leme asked.

'Will you just trust me,' she said. 'Stop being so difficult. And call me Ellie, everyone else does.'

Leme smiled.

They approached an impressive-looking condominium in Perdizes, not far from Avenida Paulista.

'Ellie,' Leme said, 'it's not really fair to demand I do this.'

She had called him half an hour earlier, hysterical, said she had something she *had* to show him. He'd relented. He realised he'd set a bad precedent with her.

'What?' she said. 'I'm wasting police time? Ha. You got so much else to do, *ne?*'

Leme shrugged. This might be a lead, he supposed.

'Just tell me where we're going?' he said.

Ellie stopped, tilted her head into a smile, opened her palms like an flight attendant giving instructions. 'Right here,' she said.

Leme expected the *porteiro* to stop them, but he didn't. Ellie just flashed him a smile and flounced passed. He smiled back, looked pleased to see her.

They took the lift to the top floor, Ellie tapping her foot in time with the music that filled the small space. The bright light seemed to crack her rough make-up, whiten further her pale legs, bounce off the grease in her tied-back hair. Leme felt bad thinking this. He wondered how he must have looked.

'Ding,' Ellie sang out with the lift. 'This one,' she said. She pointed down the hallway.

The door was unlocked. 'It always is,' Ellie said.

They went inside. They heard music playing – low. Some hip hop Leme thought he recognised.

'Love this,' Ellie said. 'It's BNegão rapping about having lots of ideas in his head but no money in his pocket,' she said. She rolled her eyes. 'In this flat, there's plenty of money.'

Leme flinched. 'This song?' he said. 'I know it. So does Ana.'

Ellie gave him a funny look. 'O ... K ...' she said. 'How do you know that?'

'It was on when I met her. In the university canteen. We talked about some of the lyrics. Same ones you just mentioned, actually.'

Ellie smiled, impatiently. 'That's lovely,' she said.

Leme shook his head.

'Fuck,' Ellie said. 'Fuck.'

'What?' Leme edged past her and he saw for himself.

Another empty flat. Nothing but a small stereo. Whitewashed. Disinfected. Another one.

'You better tell me why you brought me here?' Leme said.

Ellie nodded. She turned circles in the enormous living room, stepped over towards the balcony.

'Don't touch anything,' Leme said. 'Wait.'

He went over to the sliding door and, with his handkerchief, opened it.

'Let's talk out here,' he said.

'Why?' Ellie gave him a look, pulled a sarcastic face. 'Might it be bugged inside?'

Leme shook his head. 'Fuck knows,' he said. 'I just need a cigarette.'

They went back inside. Leme paced the room.

'The last time I was here,' Ellie said, 'there were clothes strewn across the sofa over there, glasses on the table. It was lived in, know what I mean?'

'Who lived here?'

'Alex, at least I thought he did.'

'Why did you think that?'

'Well,' she grimaced, 'he brought me here, didn't he, *ne?*' She gave him that look again. 'We were fucking, after all. That alright?'

'Tell me about the last time.'

'We were fucking?'

Leme glared at her. 'You know what I mean,' he said.

She took a deep breath. Leme smiled. He knew she liked to talk. He tried to remember if he had anything to do. He looked out at the city below. Estadio Pacaembu was down the hill. Trees crept up towards him, leaves waving at him in the breeze. Another private university campus stretched out to the right, dots of affluent students flirting. Behind him, Avenida Paulista growled and barked, steam dispersing in the heat.

'OK,' she said. 'I remember. The door to Alex's bedroom was slightly open. There were sounds coming from inside.'

'What kind of sounds?'

'Murmuring. A low voice. Alex came out, pulling the door closed behind him. His hair was messed up and the buttons of his shorts were open, a T-shirt tucked roughly inside. He was barefoot. I remember that. When he saw me, he was taken aback for a second. He regained his composure pretty quickly.'

Leme believed that.

Ellie went on. 'I stamped and sort of snorted and gave him a look that I couldn't quite control and I hardened, shook with anger. I knew he was a playboy, but still, you know? If he was with Ana, too, I'd be livid.'

Leme raised his eyebrows.

Ellie looked at him. 'Yeah, yeah, that's right, it's hilarious. So I said to Alex, I wanted to see you. Thought I'd surprise you. He'd recovered completely and flashed one of his toothy grins, trying to be charming, the cunt. Well, you succeeded, he said and laughed. Don't you English knock? See, the thing is, I didn't have to knock, did I? You saw me with the *porteiro*,' she said to Leme, 'they know me here. What the fuck, right?'

Leme was poking around on the balcony, gloves on. There seemed to be nothing.

'So I asked him who was in his room,' Ellie said. 'And he told me it was Ana. I asked him why. He said she had come to see Leo but wasn't feeling well. What's wrong with her? I said. He said it was a fever and that I could see her if I wanted.' Ellie paused, looked back through the doors at the room. 'I thought he was either testing me, you know, making a show of his innocence, or he was telling the truth.'

'So what happened?' Leme said.

'Well, first he kissed me, and I tried to see if I could taste my friend. Oh, don't look like that, it's normal. Fucking grow up.'

Leme shrugged. 'Come on,' he said. 'Inside. Show me the room.'

They went into the bedroom on the right. Empty. No bed.

'This is where she was,' Ellie said. 'She was lying on her back dressed in a thin white vest and what looked like a man's boxer shorts. No bra. I touched the hem of the shorts and slipped my finger inside.' Ellie shook her finger at Leme. 'Don't fucking judge me,' she said. 'No knickers, either. Alright? She was damp between her buttocks, I remember that. Sweaty. Really sweaty. And there was a faint vomity odour. And rubber. She groaned and rolled on to her side. Her legs twitched. I felt her forehead. It was pretty hot, with a thick, slippery film of sweat. She breathed heavily. She looked beautiful, though, fragile.'

'Sounds like she was ill,' Leme said.

'Just wait, will you? "*Quem é?*" Ana was whispering. "*Não quero, não quero mais. Quem é?*" I didn't really know what was going on, but she sounded delirious, know what I mean?'

Leme nodded.

'Ana said, "Ellie? *É você?*" I felt cold. It was weird. Like she was expecting someone else. That old jealous taste rose up my throat. Betrayed by a friend. Again.'

'Then what?' Leme asked.

'Alex appeared in the door,' Ellie said. 'And Ana looked confused. I don't remember exactly what he said, but he got me out of there. I was furious. It was unfair. The little *puta interesseira*. She was more beautiful than me, younger, too, but I was her fucking mentor. She shouldn't be the one displacing me. I told Alex I had a deadline, that I was hoping he'd be alone. He did that long, lazy, Paulistano-male full-body shrug that indicates utter indifference. Know it? Course you fucking do. Then I hurried out the door and into the lift. And I didn't look any less of a mess than I do now.'

They went back into the living room.

'So you came here a lot, did you?' Leme asked.

'A few times. Enough.' Ellie laughed. 'Alex told the *porteiro* to always let me in.'

Their voices echoed in the empty space, like in an art gallery. Not that Leme went to many these days.

'Where's the bathroom?' he asked.

Ellie pointed.

He walked over to it and nudged the door with his foot. He tensed, not sure what to expect.

It was dark inside, no windows. He breathed out, wrapped his hand in his handkerchief and flicked on the light.

Nothing. He felt relief mixed with disappointment.

He went back out to Ellie.

'What do we do now?' she asked.

Leme looked around the room. 'I don't know,' he said. 'I don't know what this means. But you're going to give me a statement.'

She nodded.

Leme walked over to the stereo. The song was on repeat. Using his handkerchief, he stopped the music and opened the CD drawer. It was a blank CD with something scrawled on the front in spidery handwriting in one of those thick, black marker pens. He held the CD by its edges in the handkerchief. Studied the words. Looked like it had been written quickly. He wrapped it in the handkerchief and pocketed it.

'Come on,' he said.

On the way out he asked the *porteiro* who owned the flat and wasn't surprised to find out that he didn't know, and had been told never to ask.

'Who told you that?' Leme said.

'You know,' the *porteiro* shrugged. 'Not my business.'

Leme agreed with him and gave him his card. 'They didn't take everything,' he said. 'Who was the last person to leave?'

'A girl,' the *porteiro* said. 'People moved her stuff out. I saw her leave myself. Oh wait, there was a guy outside the door. Said something like, "OK, all done." Then they got the lift. Couple men were waiting for her downstairs and she left in a van with them.'

'Who?'

'Removal guys. Fuck should I know?'

'Next time someone goes in there, call me,' Leme said

The *porteiro* smiled and gave him a look. It said: we'll see.

Leme sat at his desk and looked again at the writing on the CD. Two words, two numbers. Like an address. But where? The song he and Ana had talked about was on repeat. She had been the last person in the apartment.

He traced the letters on to a piece of paper.

Estrofe 2, *Verso* 4.

If this was a place name, he didn't recognise it. He put the CD into his computer and played it again. He didn't generally listen to hip hop, but this was classic, so to speak. He sat back. Listened. He wasn't really sure what it was about, but it was railing against something, urging purity. The second verse was rapped by a man with an odd voice. The second verse. Fuck, he realised.

He googled what he guessed to be the song's title: '*Funk até o Caroço*'. *Estrofe* 2, *Verso* 4: second stanza, line 4. He'd been thrown by '*estrofe*': but of course it wasn't a fucking address!

He found the line.

What was it Ana had said? Something like advice after the fact isn't any good. Like medicine after a burial. Very profound, he thought. The singer's name was BNegão but Leme knew his real name was Bernardo Something.

He looked him up on the internet. He'd been around a while, played in various bands, one of them called The Funk Fuckers, which made Leme smile.

Bernardo Santos.

Leme shook his head.

He read the lyrics again.

He wrote down the name Bernardo Santos.

He'd let it marinate.

The day after his wedding, Leme woke up afraid. And remained so. But each day, the fear dissipated. Each year, things got better. And they'd started well enough. The lessening fear was a comfort, a sign of progress. On their honeymoon they'd gone to an island off Salvador. Some kind of car-free utopia, an anti-city. He'd felt itchy, struggled to understand what it was to be in the present, to freeze his life for the sake of pure enjoyment. It was supposed to be a celebration.

'There's no such thing as the future,' Renata had told him on their first night there, chewing on lobster in the heat. 'You can mock, *querido*, but it's true.'

On the last day on the island, Leme was struck down with food poisoning, vomiting prawns cooked in old oil on a deserted beach.

He missed her thinking, her need to scrutinise, to avoid complacency. She was a heavy and committed smoker, and rationalising her habit was a means of exercising her powers of reason and her legal brain.

'Smoking is a singular existential act,' she'd say. 'Almost political. It says "I am aware of my mortality and yet I am going to live in the present, as the future doesn't exist yet". There is no deeper, habitual, basically prosaic action that shows understanding of our transience and the world's brutal indifference to our fates. And it is delicious, which in itself furthers this understanding. Fleeting pleasure is all we will ever have. The trick is to find what makes us fleetingly happy and repeat it. "For me," she'd say, "those things are smoking ... and you."'

Hearing this for the first time – she would often repeat it to amuse and scandalise at parties – Leme had never felt such validation.

Repeating those fleeting pleasures, and finding a practical way to do so in our lives, she concluded, is how we achieve permanence.

Leme knew that the permanence they had found went beyond her clever justification. And even though she was gone, that permanence – as by her definition he supposed it should – remained.

He slept, drunk, in a chair, BNegão playing on repeat.

At 5.30 a.m., he woke up, the song playing quietly.

And then it hit him.

He knew where Ana was.

When he'd woken in his chair it had clicked. BNegão was Bernardo Santos. Ana and Ellie were to visit a site in São Bernardo. Alex's surname was Santos. And then the line in the second verse: the word medicine and then burial. There was a famous cemetery in São Bernardo – Cemitério Baeta Neves. He'd buried his parents there. And next to it, he knew, was an abandoned warehouse, part of an industrial estate that had once housed a funeral parlour.

He drove to São Bernardo immediately.

Pre-rush hour, it took a little under half an hour.

The cemetery was quiet and a thin layer of dew lay on the grass as he crossed to the estate. The air was fresher, cleaner, in this southern part of the city and Leme felt it scratch the back of his throat as he breathed, tug and rasp at his lungs.

The industrial estate was deserted. The fence was rusted and had been torn open in several places. Leme squeezed through, stamping the loose chain-links to the ground. The main entrance was padlocked shut, though the windows were mostly smashed, so it would be easy for anyone to get in. Leme circled the building. Two high storeys; warehouse space. He saw no one.

Round the back, he heard a door banging against its frame. A garage.

He slipped inside down a dark corridor, walls of concrete. He used the light of his phone to find the switch. He groped for it. The bulb flashed several times, like a strobe. Time slowed. The light bit and held. The room settled in a dawn half-light.

He didn't want to be there. The old anticipation came back in sharp waves.

And there she was.

Like medicine after a burial. Too late, Leme thought.

Ana had known what might happen to her.

The single naked bulb struggled to fill the space. It didn't matter. The body lay directly underneath. In the corners, ropes like coiled snakes. Leme circled.

The smell – and he was surprised – was not overwhelming. The space had been cleaned and recently coated in white. Toxic paint and disinfectant layered the air as if trapping the decay at its centre.

Leme breathed hard and steadied himself. Felt a shudder of emotion, like a moment of passion when you catch sight of a loved one unexpectedly. He had never got used to this: he didn't really like to feel anything at all. Human impulse, he'd always said to Renata. For some, a dead body is an affirmation. Confirms their own vitality.

He'd always thought that a form of narcissism, which offers its own kind of faith and optimism.

Death turns our fleeting lives into something permanent.

He'd felt it would be like this. But seeing her face didn't lessen the shock. Ana looked peaceful. Her hands were folded respectfully across her chest. Her legs drawn together. Her hair had been swept back from her forehead and tucked behind her ears. Her nakedness was fresh, clean. Leme knelt beside her. Another smell. The memory hit him like a low blow and he gasped and fell back. Turned away and vomited into his mouth. He spat acrid chunks. He had last breathed that smell while bent over his wife's body in the crematorium. He steadied himself, stared up at the light.

Ana looked at peace.

Girl became mannequin.

On the front page of the newspaper, an article about the Mensalão trial and the imprisonment of someone or other. Leme glanced at the article. In the last paragraph, a question: how did they hide the money? In the same place they hide everything. Property. Leme switched on the television. News channel. And there it was, right in front of him. A press conference. Mendes in the middle. Aline Alencar to his left. A couple of others Leme didn't recognise. The state governor. He turned the volume up.

Mendes was speaking:

'... this is an opportunity for the Alencar foundation as much as it is for us. We are thrilled to be associated with such a prestigious foundation. This marks six wonderful months. Our project – as well as bringing our great city forward – will provide prospects for the ethical venture capital projects that the foundation has pioneered ...'

Aline Alencar appeared flustered. She didn't want to be there. The governor maintained a fixed, toothsome smile. Leme shook his head. Mendes was immaculate. In the TV lights, his cheekbones sharpened, eyes hollowed. Forehead pulled Botox-high in a look of controlled surprise.

'Our *centro* has been neglected for too long. The involvement of the Alencar foundation demonstrates our commitment to sustainable and ethical development.'

He stopped, lifted his chin and looked down his nose at the audience of hacks and broadcasters. A question from the floor. The camera swung around and Leme choked on his drink. Francisco Silva. He was supposed to be in Brasília. Might be interesting.

'Sr Mendes.' Silva spoke slowly and the room quietened. 'Can you tell us where the investment for this project has come from? And can you make public the list of investors?'

There was some talking, cameras flashed.

'I think,' Silva was shouting now, 'it is in the public interest, don't you, Sr Mendes? Give us the list.'

On the TV, Mendes was whispering to a colleague.

'I'm sorry,' he said, eventually, 'I couldn't hear the question.'

The camera panned back to where Francisco had been standing.

In the corner of the screen, Leme saw him manoeuvred through the door.

Another question. 'What about the creative communities that are springing up in the *centro?* There are artists, writers, theatre companies making incredible use of the old buildings, fashioning innovative galleries and performance spaces. It's exciting. This project will signal the end of that.'

Mendes smiled. 'What's more important? Art or progress?'

'A thriving culture is a sign of progress, Sr Mendes.'

'Our project shows economic progress. More significant. And provides, as I said, opportunities for entrepreneurs who might not otherwise have them.'

'By tearing down buildings that once characterised our city?'

'We're making a far more creative use of the space than any bohemians. Next question.'

Leme turned it off. The black screen crackled, settled in the silence.

Leme felt responsible. He'd told himself that he had arrived too late to prevent what had happened, that it had already passed from predictable to inevitable, but it was of little comfort. Not in his nature to shrug it off and put it down to some occupational collateral.

Lagnado was ignoring his emails and avoiding him. His secretary had actually blocked Leme from going in to see him just that morning. He received a terse memo half an hour later.

Autopsy at 12. Accidental overdose. No questions. No press.

Accidental overdose. Right. The doctor had been a colleague for years, but Leme wasn't sure if he could trust him to tell the truth. Easier to be a cog if you are only the messenger, especially when there was no one crying foul or desperate for justice.

Leme looked on from the back of the room, the air thick with disinfectant-haze. Ana was laid out, naked-smooth, caramel flesh taut and cold. This time though, there were incisions and organs, surgical instruments discarded on the table beside her body like a mechanic's tools around a rusting car. The senior doctor, Nogueira, talked quietly to a couple of assistants and made notes. Leme didn't even try to listen. Nogueira glanced over and dismissed the other medics. They closed the door on their way out and the two remaining men waited a moment. Leme felt the silence deepening and Ana's body settle into the middle of it. He longed to say something to break it. But he didn't want to dictate the conversation: it was important that the doctor did what it was he wanted to do without pressure.

'You know this was an overdose, then?'

'I'd heard.'

'Right.' Nogueira looked down at his notes. 'I'll keep this in layman's terms for you, *tudo bem?*'

Leme nodded. 'Sensible.'

The doctor indicated the torso with his pen. 'The internal damage is consistent with drug abuse over a period of months and then a fatal overdose.'

Leme shrugged. This wasn't going to help.

'It seems, though, that she was using intravenously. There are needle marks, and although she doesn't appear to have a very long history of it, the marks are clustered together, which suggests habit and pattern. I would say that she started using approximately three months before her death. This is enough time to establish dependence but also short enough to make a miscalculation highly likely.'

Leme smiled. Looked like this case was about to go away. Bile rose. 'What about the state of the body?' he said. 'She was naked. That's odd, isn't it?'

Nogueira shrugged, tilted his head from side to side. '*Sei la*, it happened. But, it did make me look a little more closely though,' Nogueira said. 'This is not in my notes, but the needle marks are on her legs. Nowhere else.'

'And what does that mean?'

The doctor gave a grim laugh. 'Think about it.' He lifted Ana's leg to show the neat punctures. Pencil marks. Full stops. 'She wouldn't have been able to do this herself. Angle's too tight. No way she could have reached around and operated a syringe. Unless she was a professional contortionist.'

Leme ran his hand through his hair. Placed it on the operating table, fingers curled in, nervous of getting too close. He could feel the cold escape from her thigh. 'So you're saying someone else was doing this to her?'

'I think so.'

'Which means someone else was controlling the dosage?'

Nogueira nodded and looked away. Brushed imaginary dust from the body.

'But that's not going in your notes?'

Nogueira said nothing. Turned his back.

Leme patted him on the shoulder. 'Thanks for telling me.'

Back in his car, the anger returned. Emotional dead weight was of little use, but it helped him to focus. He played back the recording on his phone.

So you're saying someone else was doing this to her?
I think so.

Nogueira would be all right if it came to it.

The guy from the tyre shop called. Leme had pretty much given up hope that he would. He wasn't looking forward to another visit to the *favela*.

'*Fala*,' he said.

'Some news you didn't hear from me.'

'Right.'

'The playboy had been in before. Several times. Asking around for some woman. A seamstress. Never found her.'

'This during the day?'

'Think so.'

'Alone?'

'Yeah. But it was the same SUV. A couple of times in the month or so before the accident.'

Leme considered this. 'You think he was looking for this woman at four o'clock in the morning?'

'I doubt it. Doesn't fit the pattern.'

'So. You need to do a little more digging.'

'*Caralho*, Mario. *Chega, ne?*'

'And find out who this woman is. I want a name.'

The guy sighed into the phone. 'There must be a hundred seamstresses in Paraisópolis,' he said.

'Well he was only looking for one. And I'm sure you're more capable than he was.'

The guy whistled. 'Mate, you are a fucking pain.'

'But you'll do it for me.'

He sucked his teeth. Leme hung up.

Leme looked carefully at the photograph he'd recovered from Ana's email. He hadn't really had a proper look: quality was too poor. His IT guy had reformatted it and blown it up and he could now scrutinise it properly.

Perhaps a landscape in the interior? The moon surrounded by a circle of yellow light. A black house. Figures working. A shadow. Could have been any holiday portrait. Or representation – there was something artificial, staged, about it. Perhaps not even an actual scene? Leme imagined a vacationing couple walking, eating, drinking. Fussing over the little differences to their own home back in the city. Making love and sleeping under a light sheet, an ancient fan juddering and banging.

Leme called the IT department back. 'Having problems with the image?'

The IT guy stood in the doorway.

'Just wanted an opinion.' Leme waved him over.

The guy leaned over the desk and studied the screen. 'There's something odd about it.'

'That's what I thought. The light, right?'

The guy traced the corner of the picture with his finger. '*Cara*, the dust doesn't help.' He wiped his hand on his trousers. Gave Leme a sardonic look.

'Save the lecture.'

'You're right. It *is* the light. Move over a second.'

Leme grunted and stood up. The guy sat down and tapped and clicked away. The image became sharper still and he zoomed in on the shadow.

'That's where you can see it, the difference.'

'What do you mean?'

'The light is in contrast. It's a different type. See?'

He indicated a patch of shade. 'Look at this. It's a different … what's the word, texture, to this.' His finger circled the yellowing glass.

'Odd.'

Leme nodded. 'What might have caused it?'

'Hang on.'

More tapping and clicking. The edges of the picture were amplified, stretched out. They seemed to taper off, turn bright. He pulled one into focus.

'There. Look. The light changes again at the edge. It's the same as in the shadow.'

'So, it's like two different places?'

The guy ignored him. He spoke slowly. 'Yes, I suppose so.'

Leme raised his eyebrows. Looked across the room impatiently. The office was murky, the windows coated in dirt. He stepped over and ran his finger across it, wiping it clean. The glass shone.

'It's a photo of a picture,' Leme said. 'The light is refracted through the glass frame and that's why the edges look different.'

'Fuck me, that might be right.'

The guy scratched his head and adjusted the contrast of the screen.

'The shadow is someone else in the room, looking at the picture.'

The guy was nodding now. 'Makes sense. The light is artificial, that's why it doesn't match up.'

'Question is,' Leme said, 'where are we going to find the picture. Wherever it is, Ana was there not long ago.'

'Ana?'

Leme smiled. 'Don't worry. You can go now.'

The IT guy pushed the chair back and stood. 'There'll be a database. For the image, I mean. I can find it, probably. Might take a couple of days?'

Leme looked at him and smiled. 'Research, right? Your wife wants to buy some art.'

'I'm not married.'

Leme smiled. 'OK, your fucking boyfriend wants to buy some art.'

The IT guy laughed. 'I like art. Cool. I got it. For your girlfriend, right?'

Leme sat back down. Smiled. 'Yeah,' he nodded, 'I'll tell her.'

Leme and Antonia sat up in her bed eating pasta from bowls, a film turned down low on the television, the light from the screen flickering in the dark. It was the most comfortable thing they had done together.

They didn't talk while they ate. Antonia's legs were draped over Leme's under the covers, and she rubbed her foot against his.

'I'm curious,' she said, placing her empty bowl on the bedside table. 'About your parents. You've never really spoken about them.'

Leme nodded. He rested his own bowl in his lap. 'There's not much to say,' he said.

'There's always something to say about parents,' Antonia replied. 'And often it's not very good.' She gave a rueful laugh. 'My own,' she said, 'don't understand my life.'

'They're dead,' Leme said. 'Died when I was young. *Então*, not much to say.'

She rested a hand on his shoulder. 'Sorry,' she said. 'I didn't know.'

Leme sighed, smiled. 'I don't really have anyone left, I suppose. Family wise. I was an only child. My father, too. My mother ... well, I don't really know what happened to her family. When she married my father, things changed for her.'

'What do you mean?'

Leme shifted slightly, turned towards her. 'They had different backgrounds,' he said. 'My father was middle class – he worked as an administrator in a company that sold electronic goods. Lisboa's dad was always more of a role model, to be honest.'

'Your partner?'

'Yes, Lisboa. His father was in the Polícia Civil. He encouraged us to sign up.'

'So you did.'

'Yes. He made a good case.' Leme laughed.

'What about your mother?'

Leme said nothing for a moment. He had never really told anyone about his mother. Only Lisboa and then, later, Renata. And he only knew what he did through his father.

'She grew up in Paraisópolis,' he said. 'I believe she had sisters, though I'm not sure. My father always used to talk of rescuing her, as if he had plucked her from poverty, gave her a life. It was something Renata found strange. She worked in the *favela*. She never believed that you *couldn't* have a life there.'

Antonia nodded. 'How did they meet?'

Leme breathed out heavily. 'You know? I'm really not sure. My father's story is that he saw her one day on the street, knew she was the woman he would marry, and whisked her off her feet.'

'How romantic.'

'Quite,' Leme said. 'It never really fitted my conception of him, to be honest. He wasn't a romantic guy.'

'Well,' Antonia laughed, 'I didn't think you were either until you told me how you and Renata got together.'

Leme smiled. 'I suppose so.'

'And your mother never said anything?'

Leme shook his head. 'I don't know,' he said. 'What I think is that she preferred his version, too. I never even knew what she used to do. When I was growing up, she stayed at home. She never said much, really.'

'That sounds like a blessing,' Antonia said. 'My mother never stops talking.'

Leme laughed.

'How did they die?' she asked.

'They were old. Illness. They were old when they had me.'

'What sort of illness?'

'It doesn't matter.'

'Do you think that their age made it harder to feel close to them?'

'I don't know.'

Antonia reached for his neck and turned his face to hers. 'Kiss me,' she said.

He did. It felt warm, soft, tender. Her tongue played lightly in his mouth. She sucked, bit down gently on his lips. He felt a surge inside and pushed himself on her a little harder. This was desire and relief.

They broke off, smiling.

'Maybe you're right,' Leme said.

'About what?'

'About age and distance.'

'Explain.' She propped herself up on her elbows.

'I grew up in a quiet home,' he said. 'The only reference to any kind of affection was this story of my father's, how he met my mother. But it never rang completely true. They didn't really *connect* – is that the right word? – with me in the same way that Lisboa's father did with him. I was a little jealous. I just wasn't used to expressing anything beyond the most obvious necessity. When I met Renata, I understood this.'

He waited for Antonia to tease him. She didn't.

He went on. 'I'd never had to think about what I felt before I met her. No, that's not right. I didn't *have* to think what I felt – I knew what I felt – I mean I'd never had to *confront* it before. And that's why it was both exciting and confusing.'

Antonia kissed his shoulder.

'I really am a soppy bastard,' he said.

She laughed. 'Well, I didn't *want* to say it …'

Leme kissed her and they wriggled down under the covers. Until then, he'd only really thought of this thing as distraction. Now he wasn't so sure, and he wasn't unhappy about that.

Waiting to hear from Silva was beginning to feel a lot like falling in love, Leme thought: the restlessness, the not knowing. He had news, apparently, but news he didn't feel necessary to share in the email Leme had received a few days earlier. Something one of the convicted lowlifes in the Gabriel case had said. About Mendes's influence over Magalhães. About quite how far-reaching it was. Something Leme would be very keen to hear, apparently.

Just like Silva to set up a narrative.

He didn't doubt the Gabriel killers knew more than they had let on at the trial; they had accepted their sentences with a grim smile, as if the promise of some reward lay at the end of the stretch, like a house in Bahia, an American car and a pension.

'*Entregou*,' Silva had said when the hearing was done. 'Foul play.'

But there was nothing to prove this. Manslaughter didn't seem to cover what they had done, but conviction rates and all the other legal bullshit meant it was inevitable. Plus, the neighbourhood was a good one, full of low-rise mansions, diplomats and old money, and the pressure to reassure the residents was considerable. Leme understood that. A one-off opportunistic accident was preferable to targeting from a *favela* gang. And that was how they played it. The killers thought the owner was out. Said they saw him leave. Were walking past. What were they supposed to have done?

So what was new? Silva had claimed a while ago that the transcripts of his interviews with one of the convicted would be enough to reopen the case, and Leme had pointed out that if you are employed to kill, there is little in the way of manslaughter. But that was where they were stuck. It was difficult to know where they could take this new evidence.

Leme paced Ibirapuera Park, circled the bench where they had agreed to meet. There were shouts and swearing from the futsal and basketball courts. Runners in Lycra and headphones pounded past, puffing in time with their feet. He could see the spray of the fountain as it rose from the lake above the trees. A sun-smog haze filtered a green-yellow light. Not long until dusk. The heat rose in relief from the concrete floor, dissipated. Too cool to rain. Too hot to relax.

Silva shuffled into view. A flasher's raincoat. Red-faced. Christ, he looks awful. His tie crumpled and hanging loosely from his shirt, not bothering with any of the buttons. A hairy thatch poking from the bottom of a shirt-flap, trousers somehow slipping despite his girth. His suit glinted in the sun – cheap and worn.

He sat down and Leme wandered over, opening a newspaper as he joined him. Silva lit a cigarette. Leme shook his own soft pack and one came loose. He turned to Silva, who, he thought, enjoyed this little espionage game. Entirely unnecessary. Everyone knew they were working together.

'*Tem fogo?*'

Silva grunted in reply and handed over his lighter. 'Nice day. Not too hot.'

Leme smirked. 'Alright. *Chega, ne?*'

'*Você que sabe.*' Silva opened the document folder that rested on his lap. 'This is for you. It's a copy of the transcript from one of the convicted in the Gabriel murder. Not sure what you can do with it now, but worth a look, and definitely of interest.'

Leme took the file. 'And what are you going to do with it?'

'I'm working on it. Can't take it to my editor as it is, but maybe soon … *quem sabe?*'

'Why exactly are we meeting?' Leme asked. 'You've told me all this on the phone. You said there was something else.'

'Have a look at the last page.'

Leme shrugged and flicked to it. A single sheet, ten or so lines of text. 'What's this?'

'Read it. I've kept it separate from the rest. You'll see why.'

Leme raised his eyebrows and sighed. He'd done enough reading for the day. In moments though, he felt his chest contract and his tongue become fat and cumbersome in his mouth. Time slowed as his heart quickened. He realised he was reading what looked like a confession.

There was another job. A year ago. An issue in the favela. *Paraisópolis. Some bitch lawyer causing trouble about kicking the residents out for that project in the* centro. *You know? That fucking massive building thing Mendes is doing. She was working to have the whole project put on hold, they told us. Human rights shit, apparently. They were moving the residents on illegally and she wasn't having it. Her husband was a cop, too. They said he might know about some shit we'd done. Which means they would tell him if we didn't do this. That it could all be connected. All we had to do was organise a few wide boy dealers to shoot at the Militars on a particular corner at a particular time. The kids were well up for it – any excuse for a scrap. Those assault rifles are not very accurate in the hands of a fucking child. Stray bullet. That would be the excuse. Easy. And plausible. Some kid dealer with gold teeth, they say. Easy money. We didn't have to do hardly fucking anything.*

'I'm sorry, Mario.' Silva turned to him. Placed his hand on his shoulder. 'I thought you should know.'

Leme nodded. He felt a taut ripple of relief. Now he knew. If she had only stayed in her office a little later. If she had only had an appointment at the beauty salon. If she has just done one thing differently that day. The guilt at letting his wife work in the *favela* was always counterbalanced by the idea that she would laugh if she ever heard him say he *let* her do anything.

'What are you going to do?' Silva asked.

'Does anyone else know about this?'

Silva shook his head.

'Let's keep it that way.'

'If there is anything I can do …?'

Leme let the offer sit in the space between them. Fill it. He leaned forward. 'Help me,' he said. 'What we've got will never be enough. We both know that. And that's why you're here.'

'You're probably right.'

'This dead girl, though, and this dead playboy. We might be able to use it. I don't know yet. But if we can, we fucking well will.'

Leme straightened, rubbed at his eyes with his sleeve and looked across at Silva.

There was the hint of a smile. 'No disrespect, Mario,' he said, 'but I was hoping you'd say that.'

Leme snorted. 'Why am I not surprised? I'll call you.'

He stood quickly and walked away.

Once he had turned the corner, his legs buckled.

He stopped and leaned against a tree.

Mopped sweat from his brow.

Vomited in three urgent heaves.

The bark was rough to his touch and thin strips crumbled through his fingers as he picked at it.

The runners went round and round.

The shouts were louder.

The air was thicker now and wrapped him like a heavy coat.

His breathing steadied.

He spat and wiped his mouth.

He should get to his car before the traffic got too bad.

Leme walked the campus with Aline. It was tucked away from the mess. The air felt cleaner as he stepped through the gates. The students and professors had that healthy sheen lacking in the majority of people in the city.

Like Leonardo, Leme guessed, most of the students had never taken a bus.

Cracked leaves blew past, sun-baked and shrivelled, like the cleaners. A group of boys sauntered and swaggered, a rainbow of polo shirts.

'When Jorge outlined exactly what it was he wanted me to do,' Aline was saying, 'I realised the seriousness of the situation and understood that there was no choice, really. When a threat is imminent, it's sharper, like a knife. Alex made me understand that.'

Leme was confused. 'Alex?' he said.

'Yes. My son's best friend. He sat in my office with his feet resting on the chair to his right. Barely looked at me, as if – no, *because* – he knew the persuading had already been done.'

'Persuading?'

'To attach my name to the project. The foundation, too.'

'Right. And why was *Alex* talking to you?'

'Mendes sent him. I think Mendes approached him as he thought he might know something, you know, due to his friendship with Leo.'

'And did he?'

'Yes.'

'What exactly?'

'Two things. Firstly, that because of my marital agreement, the revelations about my private life would leave me with very little.'

'Why?'

'We married young. I was idealistic. I didn't think.'

'And the second?'

Aline grimaced. Leme said, 'Come on. You need to trust me. This is why you called me, right? Because you have a conscience. I know you do.'

Leme smiled. The flattery seemed to work. He was a little confused though. This seemed like a departure.

She nodded. 'The Singapore Project,' she said. 'Remember I told you I rescued it? Well, I did, but that was only as I knew – because of a deal I did with Mendes – that it would *need* rescuing. A whole reputation based on a lie. I'll be honest with you: we all knew what would happen to those buildings. I was lined up to do the rescue job, which would secure my reputation, make me philanthropic, benevolent, and make me money. A lot of money. He could expose all this. And sending Alex made it clear I really did have no choice.'

'Why?'

'The thing about my private life? It involves Alex's father.'

'Aha,' Leme said. 'Mendes is a clever fucker.'

'Later that day after Alex had left, I instructed the press officer for the foundation to prepare a release pledging our support. Then I called Eugenio – Alex's father – and told him that things had changed. He didn't take it well. I know, I know, I threw my hand in with the enemy. But it was easy to convince myself that I was helping my city.'

'Well you can now,' Leme said.

'I don't know,' she said.

'I thought you wanted to do what's right. Make amends.'

'I do. There is a way. But you'll need to go to the site in the *centro*.'

'OK.'

'I can't tell you much more, but …'

'I need more than that.'

'Well …'

'When I'm at the site, what do I look for and where can I find it?'

'There's one of those Portakabin offices behind the main construction. It's sometimes empty in the afternoons. There's a filing cabinet with a false bottom drawer. What you need is in there. A package. It'll help. For now, I can't do anything else.'

'What's in the package?' Leme said.

'Names,' she said. 'And numbers. OK? Understand?'

Leme nodded.

He decided to go the very next day.

The location that Mendes had chosen for the project was a smart one. Leme could see that straight away.

The Estação de Luz was visible from all sides and likely the Pinacoteca, too, from the tower blocks at least. It was close enough to the Sala de São Paulo to offer an illusion of culture and sophistication. The tree-lined, surrounding squares were already being spruced and cleared of junkies, with Militars posted on each of the corners. The *michês* had drifted off and wouldn't be back. Working Rua Augusta fleecing tourists outside strip clubs. Pimping silicone-heavy, violently waxed whores. The top end of Augusta had undergone something like gentrification, but the bottom end remained dark, neon and dirty. Would stay that way, too. The visitors for the football needed a seedy district. This was the one they had decided to retain, Leme had heard from Silva. Old-school glamour: the flesh darker, the mouths bigger, the drugs more sulphurous, cheaper. More chance, too, of waking up naked and penniless. Though Silva had also heard that even that was being evaluated: no petty crime against gringos with drink-swollen cocks, whores included, as he'd put it. No back-alley beatings. São Paulo was going to be a fucking playground. And the bullies were being sent home. Just like that Cazuza song Renata enjoyed in those wonderful, anti-establishment moments she sometimes had: the whole country turned into a brothel, as there's more money to be made. Some days we survive without a scratch. Others, we don't.

A few months after Renata died, Leme had been dragged along to Love Story by a well-meaning colleague. The girls – sequinned and heeled – whispered, tongues in his ear, cupping his balls and stroking his cock through his trousers. He'd recoiled in shame, rushed to the bathroom and masturbated painfully, coming in an urgent spasm into his hand.

He edged around the perimeter of the site. The post-colonial architecture of the buildings considered valuable enough to remain just about peeped through the graffiti: swirls of blue and green, sneering boasts, defiant signatures. Renata used to praise the ingenuity it took the artists to do their work. Leme didn't.

Leme skirted the main entrance. There were three security guards mooching about. They talked briefly into walkie-talkies, unsmiling. He had made an appointment to see a woman called Selina who ran Mendes's publicity. He was, he'd told her, representing a potential sponsor of the project, using a discreet friends association with an investment bank to provide credentials. That the bank was considering becoming involved was true, and Leme had worked his cover into a sort of independent consultant situation, so that it would be difficult to trace. Still. The security guards might pose a problem and he was prepared to reveal his identity if need be on the basis of cleaning the area of undesirables. A colleague in Vice was ready to back that up should it come to it.

After a nervous moment as his ID was run through the system, the burliest of the guards waved him in.

The site was bigger than it looked from the outside.

A vast, shallow pit lined with steel girders and surrounded by diggers.

Dust was puffed into the air like a smoker exhaling ... ·

Groups of helmeted, boiler-suited men pointed and shouted over the noise. Leme marvelled at the sheer foreignness of the construction, of the courage. How do they do it? Who has the confidence to say this will work, this will not fall down? The city was unrecognisable from the one he had grown up in. Construction was currency and the growth rate exponential. So what if some of them were left unfinished and derelict? There was always more money to plough in, more people who needed apartments, shopping centres, offices. Or thought they did. We're all conditioned now, he thought. The great ambition: to lay a stake in the city, even if it meant aspiring to a bigger debt. The instalment payment schemes and the independent developers working outside of the banks facilitated that. Defaulting on payments was an opportunity. Sue, and find another family to bleed. There are plenty of them.

'Sr Leme?'

Leme turned to see an attractive woman in her forties hurrying awkwardly towards him in her heels, shielding her mouth from the dust, ducking slightly at the noise.

He smiled. '*Prazer.*'

They shook hands and kissed once on the cheek.

'Why don't I show you around and then we can go to the office to talk?'

Leme nodded. She gestured for him to follow.

They took a turn around the eastern side of the site where it was quieter, Selina giving a running commentary, like an enthusiastic tour guide who took pleasure in the historical details that brought the tour to life. In fact, though, she was doing the opposite: her pleasure was in the removal of these historical details, their replacement. She pulled a map from her briefcase. 'This,' she pointed at a curved line, 'is where the shopping centre will be. Over there,' she indicated the far side, 'close to the main site entrance will be three residential blocks and a luxury hotel. The idea is to create an entire and ultimately self-sufficient lifestyle community.'

What the fuck does that mean? Leme smiled inwardly.

She continued. 'Of course we are offering the full *centro* experience. Our residents and guests can enjoy the regenerated area from the safety of a secure home. There will be restaurants and leisure facilities, too. This will be a vibrant and culturally significant part of the city and the legacy will last long beyond the World Cup and the Olympics.'

Centro experience? Leme wasn't sure there was one any more. He nodded. Adopted a thoughtful expression. His friend had told him that the best way to behave in these kinds of situations was to say little and maintain a neutral outlook.

Selina added, 'But I'm sure you know all this.'

Leme gave a tight smile. 'Perhaps we could talk somewhere less noisy?'

Selina made a show of returning the map to her case. 'Oh, absolutely. Of course.' She bustled towards a cluster of temporary buildings. Leme followed.

Despite their transient nature, the offices were cool and sophisticated. A scale model sat cased in glass on a high table. Leme paused by it, examined the generic corporate design. This was the new city – curved, sleek, modern. Isolated. It was a lifestyle, not a home. Inside the glass, tiny lamps lit the swimming pool and recreation areas. In this complex, the sun always shines.

Selina sat down and gestured for him to do the same across the desk. She shuffled some papers. She eyed Leme, seemed to consider her words.

'We're excited about your involvement,' she said.

Leme nodded. 'It's an exciting time for the city. *O mundo esta olhando.*'

'*E verdade, ne?*' Selina smiled. 'And we're right in the middle here. This is a pioneering project. Sr Mendes is taking the steps we need.' She gestured at the scale model. 'To show the world,' she said, 'that we are a force to be reckoned with and a place to enjoy the very best.'

Leme raised his eyebrows. He looked at his watch. Any moment now. He had to stall a little longer.

'We're thankful that the Alencar foundation approved the plans,' he said. 'We've given our *theoretical* support.'

Selina thinned her lips. 'We feel that you might help to convince them, *sabe? Da direção? Mostra o caminho certo.* We'd be very grateful and there are ways that Sr Mendes can show that gratitude. *O cafézinho, ne?*' She paused and smiled. '*Entendeu?*'

Cafézinho. Little coffee. Bribery. A neat, very Brazilian euphemism.

Leme sniffed. Smiled. 'I think I understand,' he said. 'I can pass the message on, you know, in the proper fashion.'

Selina's phone buzzed, rattled against the glass-topped desk. '*Da licença.*'

She stood and turned away. Spoke quietly with her hand covering the mouthpiece. She glanced back at Leme a couple of times as if deciding something. She nodded vigorously and Leme heard her say '*já tou indo aí*'. It had worked.

'I need to pop out for a few minutes,' she said. 'That was Aline Alencar wanting me to check on something.' She gave a pained, amused expression that said: what can you do?

Leme feigned displeasure. 'If you must.'

'*Eu volto já já.*'

She grimaced an apology and left.

Leme sprang up as soon as she was out of the door and arrowed straight towards the filing cabinet at the back that Aline had described to him. He opened the bottom drawer, which was empty, and reached in up to his shoulder, removing a false panel and pulling out a package not much thicker than a paperback book. He stuffed it into his shoulder bag and sat back down. Moments later, Selina returned.

'She called back. False alarm.' Her look said: stupid bitch.

Leme smiled. 'People like her think the world is to order, *ne?*'

Selina laughed. 'Where were we?' She smiled naughtily.

Leme stood and looked her in the eye. 'I think I have what I need,' he said, adopting what he imagined to be a business manner. 'I'll talk to my people. I'm sure we're all going to be very happy.'

As he left the site and headed quickly back to his car, he felt the package knock against his hip.

Leme sat in traffic. A low fog of exhaust pulsed and eddied amongst the cars. The air conditioning struggled to offer respite from the heat. He felt the small of his back sticking to the seat, sweat trickling slowly between his buttocks. Classic rock on Kiss FM made an unlikely soundtrack, he thought. 'You Give Love a Bad Name'. 'Paradise City' – he raised an eyebrow at that one. Translation: Paraisópolis. 'Enter Sandman'. 'I Don't Want To Miss a Thing'. Such lazy platitudes, Renata would say when he insisted on leaving the radio tuned to the station. Maybe. But an Aerosmith love song takes on new meaning when there is nothing left to miss, but everything. Leme barked a grim laugh: Renata would not be impressed with that. Then, 'Wild Horses', but even The Stones failed to distract him from the tired, resigned looks of the other drivers and the *motoqueiros* haring and beeping and swearing between the lanes, middle fingers ready.

He remembered the PCC attacks in 2006. He had been appalled and surprised by them, considerably more than he would have thought possible. Partly, he later understood, this was a selfish position. He and Renata were just beginning to form their relationship, and she had close ties to a number of the organisations affected. There was no personal tragedy – thank God – but for a few weeks at least, she was preoccupied and distant. Leme had felt the disturbances almost as a direct affront: how dare these *vagabundo ladrões* make her feel like that and, consequently, how dare they jeopardise his place in her heart! He felt genuine pain and trouble at the event – and was involved in the clear-up – that was true, but more than that he resented how it had risked displacing his burgeoning friendship, his love. When something external and uncontrollable happened to someone he cared about, Leme felt a deep desperation to help, even somehow solve the problem, as if he could return things to the status quo, obliterate the effects of bad news, then he could once again be sure of his place in that person's affections.

Every day, he longed for a problem to fix for her.

Now he had Ana. But he hadn't been able to fix any of her problems. He remained unsure that it had even been possible.

He pulled off towards São Bernardo. The industrial estates looked different in the middle of the day. At dusk or early morning, there was something about their potential that gave them gravity. If you could forget who owned them and saw them as the workplace of hundreds of honest Paulistanos, Leme thought, there was a sense of dignity. A member of the forensic team met him at the entrance. Tape surrounded the room where Ana had been found. The forensic's name was Victor, but everyone knew him as Bambino, because that was what he called everyone else. Leme had known him for years; he was scrupulous on the job, and decidedly unscrupulous off it. That's what comes of investigating murder scenes.

'Sorry to drag you down here,' Victor began, 'just thought there was something you should see.'

Leme shrugged. 'Not much else to do, *cara. Sabe?*'

Victor gave him a pointed look. They crossed the tape and entered the room. In the bright, temporary lights it looked like a photographer's studio, white and clean and empty. Leme looked at the spot where Ana's body had lain. He felt a beat of regret.

'Thing is,' Victor was saying, 'there are no traces of anything that we can make out. The whole place was whitewashed and bleached and we've found no fingerprints.'

'Any way of knowing how many were here?'

Victor smiled. 'This was a suicide; we both know that.'

Leme nodded. '*Então.*'

'That's why I called you.'

Victor led him to a door at the back of the room, which had been obscured in the gloom of Leme's last visit. He pushed it open.

'This is the only thing we found.' He pointed at the ground, which was made of loose cement.

'What am I looking at?'

'Track marks.'

Leme bent down and squinted. Faint, irregular lines marked the floor. 'These?' he pointed.

'Yes. And we think they are recent. And one of my guys is sure that they are consistent with a trolley. A hospital trolley, something like that.'

Leme nodded. 'So this is how she was brought in?'

'We think so. There's nothing at the other entrance. Cars come and go here, right? Bigger vehicles, too, so its hard to pinpoint what they might have arrived in. But there were some flecks of black paint – the type used on an SUV, you know, expensive, supposed to help protect it – dotted about near the back door through there.' He pointed at the end of the corridor. 'It's possible the trolley may have scratched the vehicle when they removed it. Something like that.'

'But we're talking about a number of people?'

Victor arched an eyebrow. 'According to my guy. If it were one of those trolleys I mentioned, then it would have to have been folded up inside an SUV, meaning, the body would have been placed on it when they arrived. That's a two-person job.'

'Not necessarily.'

'You tried doing that on your own?'

'You'd be surprised.'

Victor smirked, not entirely pleasantly.

'There's another option,' Leme said. 'She was alive when she arrived.'

Victor whistled. 'OK, but then why the trolley?'

Leme nodded.

'What do the medics think?' Victor asked.

'She was drugged over a period of months. The last injection could have been administered here.'

'And this is a suicide. We're just clearing the scene, to be honest.'

Leme smiled. 'A trolley. *Maybe*. An SUV. There were a few people here, right?'

Victor nodded. 'They did it here. Not that you heard it from me, *entendeu?*'

Back in his car, Leme considered the implications. Whoever was responsible needed help. Collusion. And resources. And there was likely some other threat, not physical. And there were at least two of them. Perhaps more.

As he started the engine, his phone buzzed.

His contact at the tyre shop.

I've found that seamstress.

But before he could pursue that, Leme had to have an awkward conversation with Gerson, one of Renata's devoted colleagues.

Gerson didn't like Leme much.

Leme wasn't looking forward to it, but he needed to ask him a few questions.

Old Gerson might know exactly how Renata had been trying to help the *centro favelados*.

'Why are you only telling me this now?'

They sat on Leme's balcony. A storm had threatened briefly, but the winds that circled the apartment buildings like hawks had softened, and the air was clear and cooler. Leme hadn't seen Gerson since Renata's funeral service, and they both, he thought, felt a palpable discomfort at the memory. While Renata hadn't exactly compartmentalised her life, her work colleagues in the *favela* had always seemed to retain a residual suspicion of Leme, partly, he hoped, due to his job, and partly, he feared, because they had never really believed that he was good enough for their saintly boss.

'You never contacted me before,' Gerson said.

'You didn't think it might be important?'

Gerson shrugged. 'We're not all in the business of solving crimes, Sr Mario. And I promised her I would keep it to myself. That was understood, by all of us, Sr Mario.'

The insistent formality pained Leme. It was false and confirmed his feeling that he wasn't trusted.

'Well,' Leme offered, more softly, 'I'm glad you came. It's good to see you again.'

Gerson bowed his head. No way of turning this relationship around, Leme realised. May as well get to the point. 'Tell me exactly what happened,' he said.

Gerson took a nervous swig of beer. 'Dona Renata was looking into the rights of residents in the *favela* in the *centro*,' he said. 'There were rumours that the site was going to be cleared for a new development. A group representing the *favela* came to see her. They had heard she had experience in the area.'

This was true. She had been involved in trying to smooth over and facilitate the changes brought about by the Singapore Project. She had also advised on social housing projects in Paraisópolis itself, ensuring the residents were treated fairly and understood the intricacies of property laws and responsibilities.

'Go on,' Leme said.

'She discovered that the rumours were true, and she also found out who was heading up the project.'

'Mendes Construction.'

'*Isso.*'

'Then what?'

'She looked into the land ownership situation and thought she had found a way to prevent the project from happening and keep these families in their homes.'

'But these families were being offered compensation, weren't they?'

Gerson raised his eyebrows. Leme noted the implication that he was being naive. 'The compensation wasn't guaranteed and was minimal,' he said. 'Also, it was financial – there were no promises to re-house. Essentially, they were going to be kicked out with a small amount of cash and told to move on. Many of them worked in the area. Relocation means starting everything again. Not easy with young children.'

Leme nodded, unsurprised.

'And that is pretty much what happened,' Gerson continued. 'After Dona Renata passed.'

'What was she planning to do?'

'She approached City Hall. They stalled her. Told her to help the families. *After* they had been moved on.'

Leme thought about the package from the site in the *centro* – names, numbers. Might be connected, somehow. He'd need to get Aline properly on side.

'Did she ever tell you that I wasn't aware of this?' he asked.

Gerson looked down again, reluctant to speak. 'Yes.'

'Do you know why?'

Gerson looked at him. 'No,' he said.

Leme knew he was lying. They didn't trust him, so Renata would never get him involved. It meant something, but he didn't know what.

Leme bit down on his bottom lip. 'We could have helped each other,' he said, quietly.

'No.' Gerson was firm. 'This was not something you could have helped with, Sr Mario.'

'Did anyone from Mendes's company ever contact you?'

Gerson nodded. 'There were some phone calls. Nothing sinister. Simply explained we were on the losing side. All very matter of fact.

They said they were from a place called Podemos, but we never found out exactly what that was.'

Leme tensed. So he *had* heard the name from Renata. He had been sure he had and that, in fact, she had fudged her explanation when he'd asked her what she was talking about. Was he remembering that right? Does it matter? He'd come this far.

It looked like the confession Silva had shown him was true. It didn't make it any easier to swallow.

He looked at Gerson. 'Anything else?'

Gerson paused and frowned. 'There was a young man,' he said, 'who came to the office a couple of times, knew something about one of the guys working for Podemos.'

Leme tensed. Alex? he thought. The cocky sod seemed to get around. 'What was his name?' he asked.

'I can't remember.'

Leme eyed him. 'Try,' he said.

'He wasn't involved with Podemos,' Gerson said. 'I remember that. His friends might have been. He had lunch with Dona Renata once. Not long before ... well, not long before.'

Leme remembered the receipt. Over a year ago. Leonardo.

'His name Leonardo Alencar?' Leme asked.

'Leonardo?' Gerson nodded slowly. 'I think so. That sounds right. It was only couple times and he only spoke to Dona Renata.'

'That's all you can remember?'

'Yes.'

Leme's expression softened. 'Thanks,' he said. 'Maybe you should go.'

Gerson nodded, ducked away from Leme and let himself out.

Although drunk, Leme wasn't worried about being stopped by a Police blitz. He eyed the garage entrance on Leopoldo, sitting in his car a short way from Mendes's headquarters. A phone call to Aline and he had found out Mendes was still there and when he was expected to leave. Should be any time soon.

A Jaguar pulled out and Leme followed it down towards the Marginal. He kept a sensible distance and couldn't be sure who was inside – the windows were darkened considerably more than the laws allow. Then again, anyone buying a car like that is generally not subject to those kinds of laws.

They ghosted through a back street shortcut.

Public tennis centre in disrepair: making way for another luxury block, no doubt. Rubble and advertising: mocked-up model apartments.

Taxi ranks –

Empty.

Leme's eyes peeled. Never knew at this time, off the main drag.

He'd heard the stories.

The car-jacking, acid-throwing lot. Robbery with a moral twist.

The have-nots fucking over the haves something proper.

Leme saw shapes, shifting shadows –

Nothing more.

They crossed Cidade Jardim and began the crawl up the hill towards the São Luis hospital, the white and red headlights like Christmas decorations. They turned left into a widening, mansion-lined cul de sac, climbing the steepening roads and heading right opposite Clube Paineiras. The Jaguar turned sharply and stopped at an electric gate which groaned and yawned, swallowing up the car. Leme drove a little further on, stopping on the far side of the cross-roads that led to his own apartment. He parked and walked back to the gate, taking in the house behind.

Lights were switched on and off at the top of the house. Perhaps Mendes was getting ready for bed, kissing his son goodnight, idly chatting with his wife about his day. Perhaps looking forward to climbing into bed with her, feeling her soft flesh under her night-dress. Perhaps she would give a giddy, exhausted sigh and let him slip his hands under it, remove it. And they would luxuriate in the warmth their bodies gave off as they drifted to sleep. And the next morning, the family would share breakfast, Mendes's wife glowing affection for her successful and brilliant husband. And Mendes would get back into the Jaguar, head to his office and the whole thing would start again.

Leme lit a cigarette. He spotted one of the security guards peering out of the booth window.

He sneered and walked away, back to his car.

At home, in his own bed, he sweated and slapped as mosquitoes whined by his head, his legs stretching to fill the empty space.

The package was filled with paper: names and numbers. Aline had known exactly where it was, but not, she claimed, *what* it was. Her idea to distract the press officer with that phone call. A good one.

The typeset was small, ordered in tight lines, like it had been done on one of those old-fashioned bookkeeping machines. It didn't take Leme too long to work out what it was.

There was a repeated list of names he recognised: Ribeiro, Bastos, da Cunha, Lemos da Silva, Sá. And then: Magalhães. Lagnado. Beside each name were figures, six digits most of them. In the final line, a list of first names: Barbara, Isabella, Kadi. And, most often: Ana.

The first group had a clear connection: these were politicians, several of whom were involved in the Mensalão investigation. Two of them – Ribeiro and Bastos – had been recently charged and tried. Magalhães was most likely the Delegado Geral of the Polícia Civil. The same man who had put a stop to the enquiry into Renata's death. And who had sidelined Leme and Lisboa. Lagnado was the Superintendent of Leme's Delegacia. It was he who had signed off the case notes on the Gabriel killing. He who had warned Leme off the case.

The girls' names were less clear. But they had done something, Leme thought. He remembered what Luciana Camargo had told him: that Ana was being used as bait. She'd called him back in the end, telling him Rafael had laughed at her. Told her he'd been fucking with her and that Alex and Leo were just showing off a hot new thing they'd found. She didn't believe him, she said. Leme told her to do nothing more.

The Mensalão payments had to go somewhere. Mendes had the means to hide the money in any number of projects. Was that what he was doing? Funnelling the money, washing it, and providing, essentially, an investment service for his crooked friends. That had been Silva's thought from the start.

But how were the girls involved?

And why then was Ana now dead and not the others?

On the final page, there was that word again.

Podemos

He found the number stored on his phone. After three rings, an assertive voice spoke.

'*Quem fala?*'

'I'm calling on behalf of Sr Bastos. Want to set something up for him.'

'No problem. Who?'

Leme looked at the names of the girls. Picked one. 'Kadi. Tomorrow if possible.'

'Hang on.'

He heard a rustle of paper.

'That's fine. Two o'clock?'

'*Perfeito*. New location though.' Leme gave an address in Morumbi. 'That OK?'

'Don't see why not. Send Sr Bastos our regards.'

Leme hung up. Dialled Aline's number.

'I need to get into Mendes's office.'

There was a pause. She sighed and measured her response.

'*Podemos*,' she said.

Leme smiled at her choice of word. We can do that, it meant.

Leme's IT guy poked his head round the door.

'Got a minute?'

Leme waved him in.

'I've found out what that picture is.'

'And?'

'A painting. Modern. Called *Off Duty Militias*. The artist's name is Priscilla de Carvalho. This is a copy.'

He handed Leme a printout.

'You can see why we weren't sure what it was. Poor-quality camera phone. That's why it looked like it might have been an actual place, I think.'

Leme looked thoughtful. 'Just need to find out who the hell has a copy of it hanging on their wall.'

The IT guy shrugged.

'I need to get into a phone. Can you help me with that?'

'I've told you I can.'

'Right. So what do you need?'

'Number, RGE, name, email address. That should do it. What are you looking for?'

'Photos.'

'Not a problem. That's easier, actually. Might be uploaded in a number of places, you know, back-ups, the cloud, that kind of thing.'

'*Você que sabe.*'

Leme wrote down the details on a piece of paper and handed it over.

'Might take a little while.'

'Don't worry about it.' Leme turned to his screen. '*Valeu, eh cara.*'

The seamstress worked in the Mosteiro School in Paraisópolis. Leme knew there would be a permanent ring of Militars surrounding it while Operaçao Saturaçao was still in progress. Should be safe enough. Still. He called Carlos. Told him he needed to go in.

He refused to help.

After what had happened to the boy with gold teeth, Leme should go nowhere near Paraisópolis.

But Leme insisted and Carlos relented, made some enquiries.

'You fucking appeal to my sensitive side, or something,' he'd said.

Leme had barked a grim laugh.

They picked a time when there was unlikely to be anything going on and Leme called the Mosteiro and made an appointment. Carlos took him to the door and waited outside.

The seamstress showed him to a classroom and she stood behind the teacher's desk, facing him.

'Do you know what happened to your daughter?'

She barely flinched, a flicker of something across her eyes. Leme scanned her face. Regret? Sadness, yes. Curiosity, too.

'I know enough.'

'When was the last time you saw her?'

She shook her head. 'She is very, *was* very stubborn.'

'What about her friends?'

'I don't know any *friends*.' She made the term sound distasteful, undesirable.

'I heard there was a young man. Came to see you a couple of times.'

She sighed with impatience. 'He tried to speak to me.'

'Know what happened to him?'

'I don't care. *Nem tem interessa.*'

'He's dead. Died just outside the *favela*. Car accident.'

She gave him a look: And? 'Drunk.'

Leme shook his head.

'So. Driving like an idiot.'

'No.' Leme leaned back against a desk. Felt it wobble slightly under his weight.

'What then?'

'He was looking for your daughter.'

Leme didn't know if this was true.

'Well, he wasn't the only one,' she said.

She took a deep breath and softened, saddened.

'He came to see me because he was worried about her,' she said. 'I don't know why.'

'Did you know what she was doing?'

'Yes. Well, sort of. *Mais ou menos, né?*'

'And?'

'She was working for a company involved in property – that's what she said. She was a runner, a *despachante*. Running errands, processing documents. Buying certain people … *cafézinhos, sabe?*'

'And what did this guy want?'

'To talk to my daughter. He said he was trying to stop it.'

'Stop what?'

'He wouldn't tell me.'

'When did you last see him?'

'It was … early. *Madrugada.*'

Leme made a quick calculation. 'That was the morning he died,' he said.

She leant forward and gripped the desk. The light caught the glasses perched on her nose.

'How did he seem to you that morning?'

She thought about the question. 'Distracted.'

'And?'

'A little panicked.'

Leme heard the shouts of children playing outside. Caught the dense smell of food from a nearby kitchen. Rice and beans and stewing meat.

'How long was he with you?'

'Not long.'

'What did he say?'

She glanced at the door. 'He wasn't making sense,' she said. 'Something about a friend of his, who might have been following him, and who might come and see me. And then about a girl, too, a different person. A colleague of Ana's.'

Leme realised this was the first time she had said her daughter's name. He had all he needed.

'And did he come, this friend? Did *anyone* come and see you?'

'The friend? No. No one did.'

Leme nodded. 'That's good.'

She looked shaken. Leme thought about comforting her, leaning over and touching her, but feared she would recoil, patronised. She wasn't to know that grief was second nature to him.

'Do you still think your daughter was just a *despachante*?'

Her look hardened. 'My daughter was capable of many things,' she said.

Leme waited for her to finish the sentiment. She didn't.

He turned and walked away, hoping she might stop him. But she didn't do that, either.

Carlos hustled him into the squad car and in ten minutes dropped him off at a bar outside his apartment building. He ordered an orange juice and watched as two mangy, sad-looking dogs licked each other, sprawled in the sun. He poked the ice in his drink with a straw and stirred the pulp. It was a chewy drink. His stomach tightened as he swallowed, forced it down. What is it with non-alcoholic drinks, he thought, that makes them feel such a waste of time? This was a joke of Renata's. He ordered an espresso, satisfyingly bitter. It came with a small biscuit, which he tossed to the dogs. They barely looked up at it as it fell by their feet. The sky darkened in thick cloud. He heard laughter from the taxi rank across the road.

He looked at his watch.

He decided to stay there until his maid had left his flat.

Leme spent his evenings in silence.

The apartment was big enough that the empty spaces in the different rooms had their own distinct hum and character.

He felt the pressure change as he went from one to the next.

He walked barefoot.

The scratch of the carpet, worn, frayed, ridged.

The cool of the kitchen tiles.

The loose dirt on the balcony between his toes, knocked from the plants his maid insisted he keep.

The quiet.

The groan-rattle of the fridge.

The crickets.

The toilet's pipe-juddering after-flush.

He had always liked to be alone, but had never before been lonely.

Before he met Renata, he disguised this with music. When she moved in, it became an accompaniment to their evenings. And he began to understand why that was important. A soundtrack provides a critique, yet reassurance.

Leme stepped into the lounge. The wooden floor was warped and splintered and in need of attention. He skated over it, let the cambered slats rub roughly on his calloused heels.

The stereo hadn't been switched on since Renata's death, apart from to listen to BNegão. He preferred the honesty of silence. Sad songs and alcohol are artificial influences.

Tonight he felt different.

He looked at the piles of CDs.

She had that infuriating female habit of not really caring if the disc matched the case in which she put it. Perhaps Leme had that infuriating male habit of caring.

He fished out a Tim Maia record. Turned the volume dial far to the right.

Brass and strings bounced upward and rolled, filling the room, lifting Leme's lips into a smile, bringing his head nodding forward and then back, in time, eyes closed.

I don't want money, (I just want love).

He smiled. They had listened to this song over and over as it affirmed their commitment to what was important. Like a contract: this is what matters to us. Only this.

Now, it made sense again.

Lisboa had insisted on coming, too.

'Someone needs to check you don't do anything stupid,' he'd told Leme, placing himself, again, as his burly chaperone.

They decided to use the Vice cover that Leme had prepared for his visit to the site. Aline set it up, telling Mendes that she wanted to go over the security arrangements with representatives from the Polícia Civil. It was, she told him, essential to her involvement in the project that the area was completely free of crime. Little point, she explained, in creating a self-sufficient lifestyle community, if the residents and guests are going to feel threatened the moment they leave the gates, in their cars or otherwise.

'He'll do it,' she told Leme. 'I mentioned your name.'

'They've been in touch with a colleague in Vice. He's vouched for us. Told them we're part of the team.'

'Could've brought him, too. Added some credibility.'

'Wants nothing to do with it.'

'*Faz sentido.*'

Leme paused. 'What are you going to do, Aline, if we can prove any of this?'

She gave a reluctant smile. 'Let's see what we, what *you*, can prove first, then I'll think about what I'm going to do.'

A young, very attractive woman showed them into Mendes's office.

'*Que filezinha,*' Lisboa whispered. Only half-ironic. Meta-misogyny, Renata called it. Leme shook his head. He hadn't seen Lisboa for days and realised how much he missed him.

Mendes welcomed them like family.

'Dona Aline.' He pulled her into him and kissed her with a show of considered affection. 'And these must be our friends in the Polícia Civil?'

'Detectives Leme and Lisboa.' Aline turned to them. Stood aside and let Mendes greet them. He gripped their hands and arms and looked each of them in the eye. '*Prazer.* You must send my regards to the Delegado Geral. We were college mates.'

Leme smiled thinly. 'We don't see him too often.'

Mendes waved this away. 'Well, when you do next. Shall we sit?'

He guided them to a large conference table. Leme glanced out of the window. The tops of Itaim out towards the park, the Marginal and Jockey Club in the other direction.

He examined the walls. There it fucking was.

Lisboa whistled. 'Quite a view, Sr Mendes.'

'Thank you. It's why we chose this building.' He ushered them to sit. 'Help yourself. *Fique a vontade*.' He indicated a decent spread of coffee and breakfast. Lisboa was first to pour coffee, took a sip, and popped two empanadas into his mouth.

'Dona Aline tells me you can explain how the clean-up is going.'

Leme nodded at Lisboa. They had decided that he would do the talking as the more sociable of the two of them. They'd both been briefed by their colleague and had a good idea of what to say.

'That's right,' he began. 'We've moved on the beggars and home-less and they won't be back.' He winked at Mendes. '*Entendeu?* They're taken care of. Permanently. Not that they posed much of a threat, but the place smells better now, *ne?* Wouldn't do to sully the new neighbourhood, am I right?'

Mendes gave a solemn nod. Brought his fingers together in a pyramid in front of him. Lisboa went on. 'The bigger problem has been the pimps and *traficantes*. We explained to the pimps that the sort of clients they are used to wouldn't be coming back any time soon. I know,' and again he winked, 'that your clientele would prefer a better calibre whore that was on offer down there until recently. Am I right?'

Mendes lips pursed into a half-smile, but his eyes were blank. Aline looked down in genuine embarrassment.

'Better type of person, *ne?*' Lisboa continued. Leme thought he might be overdoing it. 'Anyway,' he gestured with both hands, 'it shouldn't be a problem. They've all fucked off to Augusta. We cut them a break on the filthy hotels they use, which were supposed to be shut down. Quid pro quo, right?' Leme raised his eyebrows. Their guy in Vice had used the same phrase. 'After all,' he said, 'still some demand up there.' He laughed. 'I mean ... so I hear.' His eyes widened in faux-innocence.

Mendes gave Aline a pointed look.

'The *traficantes* were probably the hardest. They're all connected to the PCC and they're pissed off with us and the Military lot over the business in Paraisópolis. Don't want to play ball. They know trade won't be the same, but they just want to fuck us off.'

Aline spoke. 'That's my concern. Why I wanted to meet.'

Mendes looked sharply at her. Nodded. 'So what's the plan?' He paused. 'We must make sure we keep Dona Aline happy.'

'Only one way, really.' Lisboa leaned back, shirt stretching across his chest. 'We make a considerable donation to the PCC development fund.'

Leme hadn't taken his eyes off Mendes. He watched as his feral, spiky features settled, satisfied. He ran his hand over the crisp gel that held his hair in place. Stroked his freshly scoured cheeks, clean jaw. This was a solution he understood. This is what they had planned to do: demonstrate how corrupt they were prepared to be, show what they were prepared to *do* to facilitate Mendes's plans. Mendes raked his top teeth over his bottom lip and his eyes narrowed like a vulture on a low fence, a dying animal gasping below, enjoying the anticipation of a feast.

'And they'll leave us alone if we do?' he asked.

Lisboa nodded slowly. 'Should do. But, hey, these fuckers don't like to feel they're being pussy-whipped, *sabe*, so there's no guarantees.'

'We can't make any guarantees?'

'More *dineirinho* the better, I'd say. *Entendeu?*'

Lisboa shuffled forwards. 'There's a power vacuum in Paraisópolis. There's been a lot of violence. They want things to go back to the way they were – and they'll be more discreet the more you can provide. They're saying they'll give us the *centro* if they're kept happy enough, *entendeu?*'

Mendes crinkled his nose. 'Collateral consequence.' He looked at Lisboa with a smile. 'Am I right?'

'So you'll do it?' Lisboa asked.

'I think I know who needs to be persuaded.'

'*E isso ai*.' Lisboa sat back, glanced at Leme.

'This is –' Aline made as if to stand.

'Sit down.' Mendes placed his hands flat on the desk and pushed himself up so that he was above her. 'This is how things work, nothing more. Deal with it. After all,' he smiled, 'this will create more projects in Paraisópolis for your little, quote unquote, ethical venture capitalists. Your small, medium-sized enterprises.' He looked at Lisboa and winked. 'Opportunities. We all win.'

'My husband –'

'Your husband has left you, I heard.'

Mendes seemed to enjoy the ensuing silence. Ignored Aline's glare. She, Leme guessed, was not used to that sort of treatment.

He decided to speak. 'Make sure you're careful.'

'What?' Mendes had been staring over at his desk. 'Who are you talking to?'

'You. Your company. We don't want anything from the past to be … unhelpful.'

'I don't know what you mean.'

'Condominium on Gabriel.'

Mendes looked at Lisboa. 'This relevant?'

Lisboa shrugged.

'No secrets there. All above board, legitimate sale. Tragic circumstances, yes, but the situation was resolved. No way it can be,' and this time he stood, 'unhelpful.'

'Not yet,' Leme said. 'Manslaughter convictions are often based on – what was it you called it? – a collateral consequence. Easy thing to misinterpret.'

Mendes smiled. 'I think we've settled everything we need to, don't you?' He looked at Lisboa who nodded and pushed back in his chair.

Leme stood and turned, wandered towards the wall behind the table.

'This is nice,' he pointed at the large painting hanging there. 'Priscilla de Carvalho, right?'

Mendes breathed out, grimaced with impatience. 'I believe so.'

'Know the title?'

'I don't recall. It's been there for years, my assistant chose it.'

'*Off Duty Militias.*'

'What?'

'The name of the painting. What you're proposing, actually.'

Mendes cleared his throat. 'Actually, I think it was you that made the proposition.'

'*Você que sabe.*'

Leme took out his phone. 'You mind?'

Aline stepped towards him. 'Detective Leme, now's not the time,' she said. She placed her hand on his arm. Pulled it towards her. He shook her free.

'Really. There is no time for this,' she said. 'It's just a painting.'

Leme gave Mendes a look: well?

Mendes shook his head, exasperated. 'Go on then,' he said, forcing a smile.

'I –' Aline began, but Mendes glared at her.

'Humour him,' he said.

'Detective Leme, we really must go. I don't understand why you're insisting on doing this. It's hardly a well-known painting.'

Leme looked at her quizzically. 'I like it,' he said. 'That OK?'

She grimaced but nodded. Put her things together to leave.

Leme took several pictures, trying to capture the correct angle.

'You can do it, you know that,' Mendes said. 'What we talked about.'

Leme looked away from the painting and smiled. 'Yes,' he said. '*Podemos.*'

Lisboa made a flicking motion with his fingers. '*Embora.*'

They moved towards the door, which opened as they approached.

Selina came in, talking on her phone.

She looked first at Leme and then Aline.

Aline looked at Leme.

He ignored her.

Lisboa tugged at Leme's sleeve. 'Mario?'

Selina's expression darkened: confusion, understanding … anger.

'I'll call you back,' she said.

'*Vamos.* Now.'

Leme hurried them out. He turned back as the door started to close.

Selina was talking animatedly, waving her arms. Mendes was staring hard through the narrowing doorway, nodding, registering, Leme guessed, who he actually was.

In the lift, Leme said to Lisboa, 'You were good.'

'Get what you need?'

'Think so.'

Aline said nothing. Leme touched her on the shoulder. 'You, too. You did well. It's nearly over.'

She smiled sadly. Leme understood why.

Leme parked outside the condominium and headed into the small bar across the road. Converted garage. Ordered a beer and a whiskey and gulped them down. Ordered another. A table of men argued about politics, paunches exploding from tight tennis tops.

He reached for his cigarettes. He opened the package he'd lifted from the site. He looked again at the names. Tomorrow he was due to meet Kadi. Wondered what he would learn.

One of the men at the table came over. Nelson.

'*E aí, Marião. Como vai?*'

'*Grande*, Nelson.'

They shook hands and he slapped Leme on the back. '*Então?*' he said.

'You know. It's going.'

He leaned down over Leme, his hot breath soured by beer.

'Come. Join us.' He waved over at the table. '*Saideira.* Those *babacas* don't know when to stop. It's been a while, *ne?*'

His face broadened into a leer. 'Time to move on, *não e?* Come and have a drink.'

Leme smiled. 'I'm leaving soon.'

He gestured with the package.

'Thinking about something.'

Nelson shrugged.

Soon, the men left in a chorus of drunken cheers. Leme ordered a final round and watched as the owner tidied up around him.

Nodding, he drained his glass, paid up and left.

Halfway across the road, the roar of a motorcycle.

He turned into the noise, headlights blinding.

Something swung out from the side, connected with the back of his head.

A flash of pain, he tasted blood, fell forwards.

He felt hands in his pockets: the package.

Then everything went black.

Leme felt hands on his shoulders, but this time soft, less urgent.

'Sr Mario? *Tudo bem?*'

He heard the voice of a *segurança*. It wobbled in his mind, as if a cassette tape was jamming as it spooled.

'Sr Mario?'

He grunted and swallowed, gasped. He reached to the back of his head, which throbbed.

'*Tudo bem*,' he said. 'What happened?'

The *segurança* sighed. '*Não sei, exactamente,*' he said. 'There was a bike. It looked like you were hit. That's all I saw.'

Leme tried to sit up. 'Yeah, OK,' he said. It was dark enough for that to be a possibility, he thought. Clever of them.

'You need to go to hospital, Sr Mario.'

'Ah, I'll be OK,' he said. 'It's happened before.' He stood and patted down his pockets, slowly at first, and then frantically.

'*Caralho*,' he said and spat.

'*Que foi*, Sr Mario?'

'I've lost something,' he said. 'Something important.'

He gathered his senses. They knew he had the book, the list, the names. And now he didn't. He had nothing.

'Can you call me a cab?' he asked the *segurança*. 'I'm going to go to hospital.'

The *segurança* scuttled off.

At least he had the appointment with Kadi the next day. He better get some sleep. They'd patch him up quickly enough.

'The fuck happened to you?'

'Drunken accident, *entendeu?*'

Leme's head was bandaged and there was bruising around his eyes. His brain contracted, ached.

Kadi raised her eyebrows. Crossed her arms. 'Where's Sr Bastos?'

Leme had taken a risk and asked that only the girl came to the meeting. They were standing in a hotel room in Morumbi, the bed between them. Tower blocks clear through the windows. Standing plants creeping over the tops of balconies.

'He's not coming.'

Kadi shot him a look and picked up her bag.

'Woah, mate, I'm not into this.' She fumbled for her phone and stepped towards the door.

'Wait.' Leme pulled his badge. She stopped. 'Sit down.' He indicated the sofa. 'Just some questions. I've got a couple of uniforms outside. Nowhere to go, *querida.*'

This was a lie, but it worked.

She sat down. Pulled a packet of cigarettes from her purse. 'You mind?'

'*Fique a vontade.*'

She lit up and exhaled. Her hand shook.

'Tell me what you're doing here?' Leme asked.

'I came because I was sent.'

Leme smiled. 'Let's not do this. No point in wasting any more time.'

'What do you mean?'

'What is it that you do exactly?'

'You haven't got a fucking clue, have you?'

She drew hard on her cigarette. Leme poured them both some water and pushed a glass across the coffee table towards her. 'Here. *Toma.*'

She spilt water down her chin as she drank. Leme watched her. Young, early twenties, perfectly made-up, elegant. Beautiful. Feminine. But with an edge, hardness barely contained by her soft, inviting body.

'So. Why are you here?' Leme repeated.

'It's my job.'

'And what does your job involve?'

'Advocacy work.'

'In hotel rooms?'

'Our clients like the privacy.'

'I'm sure they do. What else?'

'There are sensitive documents. I run errands. Process things.'

'What, like a *despachante?* Sounds vague.'

She shrugged. 'It is what it is.'

Leme heard vacuuming in the next room. Ran his hand over the crisp folds of the white bed sheets.

'Who do you work for?'

Leme saw she was thinking about lying to him. Thought better of it.

'It's part of the development of the *centro*.'

He gave her a sardonic look. 'So you're in property?'

'Look, I've told you. It's advocacy work.'

'You help secure investors then?'

'Something like that.'

'And what if they need persuading?'

'We show them the benefits of cooperating.'

'We?'

'I'm part of a team.'

Leme nodded. 'That's why I wanted to talk to you.'

She made a face as if to say: well, get on with it then.

'What do you know about Ana?'

'Ana? Haven't seen her for a while.'

'I don't suppose you have.'

'Huh?' A worried look.

'Tell me what you know about her.'

She sighed. 'Pretty girl. A student, I think,' she said. 'She does the same thing as me. We work alone, but we occasionally meet for strategic planning.'

Leme smiled at this.

'You think this is a joke?' Kadi asked. 'It's complicated stuff.'

Leme laughed. 'What's Ana like?'

'Nice enough. Bit stuck up. Seems smart. She's Men ...' she

composed herself, '… she's the boss's favourite. So I've heard. I don't know. *Sabe?*' She waved smoke from her face and folded the cigarette end into the ashtray on the table. The filter lipstick smudged. Blood-red.

'What does that mean? The favourite?'

She arched her eyebrows. 'You know.'

'More advocacy work?'

This time it was Kadi who laughed. A bitter snarl, more like.

'Ana's dead, Kadi.'

Leme watched her expression change. Like her stomach had dropped.

'Murdered. We think.'

She lit another cigarette. Both hands shaking now. 'Why?'

'That's what we're trying to figure out.'

'Why are you talking to me? I haven't done anything wrong.'

'I'm sure you haven't. At least not intentionally. I just need to know more about what Ana was doing.'

Kadi looked reassured. 'Like I said, we were helping with the project, the investors.'

'What kind of people do you meet?'

'Politicians, police, powerful people. Never know too much about them.'

'And you help secure their investment?'

She nodded. 'Like I said.'

'Why do you think it's done this way?'

'No idea. It's a job, right?'

'Not a conventional one. How did you find out about it?'

'A kid I know contacted me.'

'Name?'

She sighed again. 'Do I have to?'

Leme leaned closer. 'This is confidential, right? Anyone asks, Bastos cancelled and you went home. Tell me.'

'Name's Rafael Maura. He works for the property company. Said he needed people to entertain … to do advocacy work. No questions. Great money.' She gestured at the room. 'What was I supposed to do? Expensive city, São Paulo.'

'Word Podemos mean anything to you?'

She shook her head.

'Paid in cash then?'

She nodded. Looked down. 'What happens now?'

'Carry on as normal. Call me if you need anything.'

He gave her his card.

As he left, he glanced back at her.

That look he had seen before:

Self-realisation.

The IT guy was nodding.

'Same picture, no doubt,' he said. 'Different time of day, I'd say, but you knew that. The three images from her phone show it, anyway.'

He'd got into the phone and they'd found three photos of the same painting Leme had got from her university email, taken before she went missing.

'And, let's not forget,' Leme pointed at the images with exaggerated emphasis, 'the times and dates are in the top corner.'

'You're the detective,' the IT guy said, a little huffily.

'Calm down, dear,' Leme joked. 'I just meant they match with what you've said,' he added. 'It's important.'

'Gee. A compliment.'

'*Ah, vai tomar uma, eh?*'

'So it looks like she was there at least three times before that final photo was taken, right?'

'I'd say that was clear,' Leme said. 'Her phone records show she was making calls and sending messages during this period, too. Easily checked.'

'So the difference in the final photo is the time of day, right? That's what we think? That explains the change in light.'

'Think so,' Leme said. 'You're the expert, *querido*.'

'And the fact that there appears to be someone with her in the last one.'

'Yeah,' Leme said. 'That, too.'

Leme stepped through the office and out on to the fire escape to smoke. It looked like they could place Ana in Mendes's office after she had been reported missing. She was his favourite – that was what the other girl had said. He didn't doubt that, but what did it entail exactly? He had an idea. And not a very pleasant one. Being in Mendes's office that night might not mean anything at all. He'd have a reason for her being there. No one had made a fuss about her going missing – she was working, binned school for a couple of weeks. Easy. Must have a legit front for the job she was doing. But if the job she was doing was advocacy for the Mensalão lot, then there was something to hide – the funds for Mendes's project, for a start.

Leme leaned over the railing and looked down into the narrow alley between the buildings, the city's non-space. Recycling bins and junk. How much was this land worth? One day, there won't be any gaps at all – just tower block after tower block lined up, like soldiers tight on parade, all air finally squeezed out. The lifestyle promised by the property developers played out under transparent domes harnessing the light but not the UV rays. That little cunt Rafael had said that São Paulo is the future. That we're already there.

But he was wrong.

Long way to go yet.

Six a.m. The sky bled orange.

Lanes of traffic shuffled right and left over the bridge.

Buses loaded with passengers, dark faces locked into grim smiles.

Men hanging from the outside doors.

Hypermarkets and building supply stores.

Manual labourers sat over coffee and shots of *cachaça* in roadside bars.

Exhaust fumes filled the air, trucks shunting angry through gears.

Helicopter buzz.

Leme checked his phone for the address that Silva had given him. Out past the university. The good one, Leme thought, not the rich kids' waiting room Aline ran. Trying though, give her that.

He skirted the university. The air thinned and he saw the expanse of green roll away from him, dense, like clouds gathering for a storm. São Francisco Golf Club.

It was an odd venue. Hardly anonymous. The car park was almost empty. He parked right by the front door of the clubhouse, in the bay reserved for the president. Small pleasures. He grabbed his notepad and slammed the door behind him. Circled his car with amusement. The parking space was designed for something a lot bigger.

A boy in white overalls came bustling over, struggling under a coffin-sized bag of golf clubs, wagging a finger. 'You can't park there,' he called out.

Leme looked from his car to the boy and back to his car again. Tossed him his keys. The boy tripped as he stepped to catch them, the clubs clattering on to the tarmac.

'Looks like I can,' he said.

Standing on the driving range, watching a middle-aged man trying to hit balls across a lush, close-cut meadow towards the impressive buildings that fringed the course, Leme felt immediately ridiculous.

He cursed Silva. 'Mate, what the fuck?' he said when Silva approached.

Silva laughed. He looked even more out of place in his cheap suit and egg-stained tie. 'Follow me,' he said.

They walked down the range to the final spot. There, a younger man in chinos and polo shirt hacked away with little success. Can't be that hard, Leme thought. Distance he's hitting it, he could probably do this in his back garden. Be a lot cheaper.

They stood behind the man, who swore as another ball trickled feebly a few metres to his left. Silva coughed. The man turned.

'Good. You're here.' He looked at Leme. 'Who's this guy? Christ, your head OK?'

'Detective Leme, Polícia Civil. Related case. He may be useful. Drunken accident, so he says.'

Leme liked the way Silva had turned it around. He might be useful to them. They had discussed at length that the opposite was true.

The man nodded. 'So. Let's get this over with. Tell me exactly what you need.'

Silva looked at Leme. 'We're interested in this company Podemos. What exactly it does, and what it is connected to. We're pretty sure it is Mendes's company, but don't know what it's for.'

The man glanced down the range. The nearest player was thirty yards away, and geriatric. 'I know the company,' he said. 'It's a paper company. A name. No concrete assets. No real ones, at least. They claim they're in real estate in a very small way. You know, doing up old flats, selling them on. They don't do anything though.'

Leme thought about Ana's apartment. 'How do you know this?' he asked.

The man looked irritated. Jerked his thumb at Leme. 'This guy? Helpful?' he said.

Silva gave him a look meant to placate him. 'Mario,' he said, 'our friend here works in Brasilia. For Ribeiro. His fucking PA. Know what that means?'

Leme nodded. Sr Ribeiro was about to spend his evenings and weekends in a secure facility for the next ten years as a result of his involvement in the Mensalão scandal.

'OK,' Leme said. 'Noted. Why are you telling us then?'

The man snorted. 'More people implicated, more distance from me. I'm fucking complicit, some are saying. Not true, actually, so I thought it'd help to stir things up a bit. Francisco approached me at a good time, shall we say.'

Silva bowed. Leme raised his eyebrows. He really was a resourceful fucker.

'Go on,' Leme prompted.

'It's pretty much what Francisco thought. The guys who were getting the Mensalão payments needed somewhere to put the money. Even they're not stupid enough to stick it in their trousers and leave the country. Mendes knew this and offered a service.'

'Podemos.'

'*Isso*. He took the money and "invested" it in the apartments the company owns. Set up the paper trail so it looked like the "investors" were private individuals after part-ownership. Like a classic instalment scheme.'

'But the money wasn't used like that.'

The man laughed. 'Those apartments are empty. Nice, true, but empty.'

'I've seen one,' Leme said. 'The girl who lived there is dead.'

The man shot a look at Silva. 'I don't know anything about that,' he said. 'Let's stick to what I do know, *certo?*'

Leme nodded. 'Just giving you some context.'

'Right.' He paused. Looked down the range again. 'Hang on.'

He took another swing. This time the ball travelled low and right, at least fifty yards. He grunted his approval. Leme wondered why.

'Point is, Mendes offered a *feijoada completo* and he wasn't prepared to lose out. The money he took went straight into the *centro* project. Six-figure monthly payments for years add up to a lot. Mendes started this a long, long time ago. Very clever, actually. Saw it coming. Also – and this was the stroke of genius – he got the political clout he needed from the men he was protecting. They fucking lobbied for him. And won. Bringing in that stupid bitch Alencar was a condition – instigated by *Mendes*. He realised it would give the project credibility.'

'He was right,' Silva said.

'Yeah.'

Leme looked across the course. A plane rose silently between the towers out of Congonhas airport. Banked left, curving away from them. Rio-bound. He breathed in the clean air, fresh on his bare arms and neck.

'Who knows about this?' Leme asked.

'Those involved. I'd say a couple of others.'

'Tell me again how you know.'

'My boss asked me to destroy some documents. He thought I'd just do it, as I'd always been loyal. I knew something was up and looked into it a bit. Gave him a choice: keep me out of it and tell me everything or I'll take what I do know to the press. Or police. He agreed.'

'Good deal,' Leme said.

He nodded. 'Leaves me in a decent enough position. He won't honour his side of the agreement – guy's a fucking snake. This is insurance.'

'What about the girls?' Leme asked. 'What were they doing?'

'Told you. I don't know about that. Don't want to know.'

Leme considered this. Felt he was telling the truth.

'And you'll go on record, if you have to?' Silva said.

'Yeah, anonymously. If possible.'

Silva nodded.

'There is one pretty major fucking problem though,' he said.

Silva and Leme leaned in.

'This company, Podemos, isn't linked to Mendes by anything other than word-of-mouth, you know, by people like me.'

'So whose name is it in?'

'Not long ago …' he smiled. 'You're going to love this.' He looked away from them out at the course. 'Not long ago, it was reverse-merged with an arm of the Alencar foundation.'

Leme flinched. The swish and crack of a successful shot nearby. About time.

'Fuck. So it's in Aline Alencar's name?' he said.

The guy shook his head. 'No. Milton's. Her husband. The foundation's all in his name again, after he got suspicious, protective. She just runs it, *ne?* Word is, though, Milton doesn't even *know* about this merger.'

Silva was making notes. Leme thought about what Aline had told him, that she had no choice. So this is what she had been forced to do. That's how she knew where the package was kept.

Now she's trying to make amends, Leme thought. And now they had confirmation of what exactly these names and numbers meant. This, Leme realised, was the bigger story, in which Ana for sure, and probably Leo Alencar, had been caught up.

'So, what does that mean?' Silva asked.

'It means that the same foundation that gives the project its credibility also provided the funds, which in turn, it helped to raise from private investors. Legally speaking. Perfect cover. All accounted for.'

He twirled his club and knocked dirt from his spikes.

'Ribeiro was careless.' He stopped. Smiled. 'Thinking about it, he was really fucking stupid, actually.'

Leme and Silva walked back towards the car park. The clubhouse was filling up with breakfasting members.

'Doesn't leave us in a great position,' Silva reflected.

Leme wasn't sure. 'I think Aline Alencar will cooperate, eventually, one way or another,' he said. 'She wants this resolved.'

'That would be a start.'

'I'll talk to her.'

Silva nodded. 'There's the Gabriel case, don't forget that. And, what happened with … Renata.'

Leme had been trying not to think about that. Even he understood that to confuse their purpose might be damaging. Trying to keep things separate.

'I don't think anyone will listen,' he said. 'That guy you've got is hardly a reliable witness.'

'Worth a try.'

Leme shrugged. They reached his car, parked now further away from the entrance, the keys under the front windscreen wiper. He opened the door and climbed in, tossing his notebook on to the passenger seat.

'Keep in touch,' he said.

Silva reached in, gripped his shoulder. 'Take care, Mario.'

As he drove away, Leme waved at the boy he'd seen earlier, hunchbacked like a crab, weighed down under two sets of clubs. The boy scowled.

Leme looked at Alex with undisguised disgust.

'Be nice,' Alex said. 'It's usually a girl who's giving me the daggers.'

'I can connect you with this company, Podemos,' Leme said.

'Podemos, Podemos.' Alex rolled the word around in his mouth. 'Yeah, I've heard of it.'

'You're the first person to admit that.'

Alex smiled.

'Alencar foundation, right?'

'It is now.'

'*Então*.'

'Why was Leo leaving the *favela* in such a hurry?'

Alex paused. Rubbed his chin and then his legs. 'I guess you could say that I got there too late.'

'Go on.'

'In essence,' he said, leaning closer, relishing this, Leme thought, 'it was largely about managing information.'

'Your best friend's death? Managing information?'

Alex narrowed his eyes. 'Not what I mean.'

He rocked back on the chair and looked around. They were in the *centro*. Alex sneered. 'These fucking cafés are so bourgeois with their distressed wood and their chipped tables,' he said. 'Does no one else recognise the irony? Ethical furniture used to hold up iPads and laptops made by Asian children.'

'Don't fuck around,' Leme said. 'I'm in no mood to listen to your bullshit.'

'Sorry,' Alex said, not meaning it. 'It's just I don't want an *experience* when I go to a café. Eight reais for a cappuccino, plus service? There's the experience: consumerism. Mendes is right to tear this all down. There's something more honest about a soulless, corporate shopping mall. It's the ultimate form of globalisation: you can be anywhere, *anywhere*.'

Leme leaned across the table and grabbed Alex by his T-shirt with his left hand.

With his right, he slapped him hard, twice.

He grabbed his hair and pulled him so their heads met in the middle of the table.

'Talk,' he said. 'Got that?'

Alex looked down. He breathed quickly. 'Alright,' he said. 'You can let me go.'

Leme leaned back.

'It was Rafael who got me into it,' Alex said. 'All you have to do is find girls, he'd told me. You're a fucking expert at that. He said his boss needed someone and he thought of me. His boss. Jorge Mendes, whom Leo hated. That was reason enough. And the chance to score points over that sour-faced *puta* Aline was a bonus.'

'So it was revenge?' Leme asked.

Alex ignored the question. 'And then another opportunity,' Alex said. 'Leo's scholarship programme. Ana's file. Why wouldn't a girl like that want to earn some extra money?'

'Go on.'

'Rafael told me: "Just remember one thing. These girls will have a job, right" – he was enjoying it, the cunt – "but, really, they'll just be the bait." I asked him for what. He said, "What do you think? What it always is." Rubbing his thumb and forefinger, *entendeu?* Money. But then Mendes couldn't behave and said too much and it had to be taken care of.'

'What happened?'

'Well, my father moved out soon after Aline committed to the Mendes project and told him she could no longer see him. I grew up with this woman. She was kind to me, cared about me. Her son is my best friend. I do not remember my life when they were not in it. And all the time she was fucking my dad. As my mother fed and bathed and looked after Leo and me, as we played football in the garden and swam and laughed, the snake had the old man's cock in her mouth. So it was a sweet feeling when I wrote to Milton and told him about his wife, and advised him to secure the foundation again in his name. I mentioned that we knew what she had done in the Singapore Project. Brokering a secret contract to repair the buildings when they inevitably fell down in a fait accompli with the corrupt developers who knew exactly how long their work would last. A clean-up that would make her look good, ethical, humanitarian. And a lot of money, too. Everyone wins. The bitch thought she'd got away with that. Mendes didn't give a fuck – just asked me to wait a little while, which I did. He had used the threat and he let me have the information. Like I said, that's what it was all about: managing information.'

'I said you were something,' Leme said.

Alex ignored that, too. Carried on not looking at Leme. 'Then Mendes called and told me Ellie had talked to him. She wanted to know about Ana's job. She told him that Leo was worried about her and was going to visit her mother in Paraisópolis.'

'But Leo didn't know about Ana's place in Pinheiros? About Mendes's visits?' Leme asked.

Alex smiled then. 'That was my own insurance, *entendeu?*'

'And how did you use it? What did Mendes want to do about Ana?'

'He just said that she knew something she shouldn't. And I told him to leave it with me. He said he had a couple of people in Paraisópolis. Reliable. Done stuff for him before, who'd make sure Leo didn't go back.'

'How would they make sure of that?'

'You know, scare him off.'

'Really?'

'That's what I heard. And it worked, didn't it? The *babaca* drove off so fast he fucking killed himself.'

'Not quite,' Leme said.

'What does that mean?'

'I was there.'

'What?'

'I was in Paraisópolis the morning that Leo died. It wasn't an accident.'

'I don't know what you mean.'

'I heard shots. He'd been shot. I saw his body when they got into the car. He wasn't just scared off, Alex.'

'Why has no one mentioned this?'

'That's what I'm trying to figure out.'

'It's official. It was an accident. Everyone knows. The funeral. Right?'

'No.' Leme shook his head.

Alex was quiet for a moment. He said, 'I ...'

'You've spoken enough,' Leme said. 'There's more. We know where Ana was the night she was found dead and we can connect you to –'

'What?'

'I said, we can connect –'

'No, about Ana.'

Alex looked like he'd been hit in the stomach.

His face grey. His hands shaking.

'We know where she was that night,' Leme repeated. He searched Alex's face. He'd made a mistake.

'I don't mean that. You said she was found dead?'

His face grey –

'Well, yes.'

There it is, Leme thought: panic. But why? 'Didn't you know?' he asked.

Alex shook his head.

His hands shaking –

He looked down.

'Fuck,' he said.

He looked up.

Wide-eyed.

Shocked.

His face grey –

'I didn't,' he said. 'I really didn't.'

Leme and Lisboa sat in Superintendent Lagnado's office. Paperwork sat between them on his desk. A request. Evidence, or supposition, at least. Leme wasn't sure.

'This again?' Lagnado's tone was fierce. 'Not going to happen,' he said.

He pushed the files across the desk and Lisboa picked them up.

'This is an investigation,' he said. 'Let us investigate.'

Lagnado shook his head. 'These are closed cases. Car crash. Accidental suicide. You're done.'

'We just want to bring him in for questioning,' Lisboa insisted. 'There's more to this than you think.'

Leme sat quietly. He seethed. Knew that it was pointless. Hadn't they learned anything? Apparently not. Did that make it any less worthwhile, then, what they were trying to do?

'What do you have exactly?' Lagnado said. 'Conjecture. A company that is a part of the Alencar foundation, which, I shouldn't have to remind you, is a respected institution. A couple of vague testimonies about a girl who was on drugs and a confused rich kid. Nothing concrete.'

'We can place the girl at Mendes's office on the night she died. Surely that's worth following up.'

Lagnado shrugged. 'This is a vendetta. You two are lucky to be working at all. You have to learn to leave it alone.'

'And that's your decision, is it?' Lisboa leaned back, scowled.

'Yes.'

'Yours alone?'

Lagnado smiled. 'Don't fuck about,' he said. 'Neither of you is that naïve. It's simple: Mendes cannot be brought in. Too much going on, too much invested in him.'

'So that's it?'

Lagnado stood, turned to his window. Adjusted the blinds so that light flooded the room. Leme squinted up at him.

'Either of you do anything with this and you'll be transferred to an office in the interior looking after traffic fines, all benefits rescinded.' He looked at Lisboa. 'You've got a family. It's over.'

Leme watched the building on Leopoldo. There was only one way left to do this. Alone and to his own satisfaction, which might bring some sense of resolution. He hoped. He couldn't tell Lisboa and he didn't want to, anyway.

He strode into reception, thrust his badge into the face of the security guard, pushed past him and vaulted the turnstile. Was in the lift before anyone had time to react. He heard shouted instructions as he was whisked skyward.

He was met at the lift by another *segurança*, who held firm. He led Leme through the open plan office and through another secure door into the inner sanctum.

'Sr Mendes will see you,' the guard said. 'Got to do this first though. Arms up.'

He searched Leme's pockets. Lifted his phone, his wallet and keys. Pocketed them. He smiled. 'You can have them back when Sr Mendes is finished with you. I'll be right outside.'

'I don't normally take unscheduled meetings with policemen.'

Mendes stood in front of his desk. Raised a crystal glass at Leme.

'Drink?'

Leme nodded. Mendes poured a large measure of whiskey from a decanter into another glass. 'Ice?'

Leme shook his head and took the glass.

'Quite right.' Mendes nodded at the sofas. They sat down, facing each other.

'We know what you've been up to, detective.'

Leme smiled. 'I was about to say the same thing.'

Mendes laughed. 'I'm not sure you can, really.'

Leme watched as he shifted about on the couch to find the best position, a position of strength, entitlement. Trying to find the higher ground.

'Maybe I'll clear a few things up for you,' Mendes said. 'My project will not be interrupted. I've spoken to the right people. The donation's been made.'

Leme nodded.

'I should thank you.' Mendes smiled and waited for Leme's reaction. There wasn't one.

Mendes went on. 'We know you think you have something on one of my sister companies.'

'Podemos.'

'Really doesn't matter which. That one though, is not mine. The funding for the project has been handled properly. I've met the conditions I was set.'

'It was an interesting list of names, in that filing cabinet.'

'Yes, well, that list was recovered, wasn't it?' Mendes gave Leme an ironic look. 'And it looks like you have, too.'

'And the trial?'

'Inevitable.' Mendes waved his hand at the room. 'Trade-off. Quid pro quo, right? Some sacrifices were made.'

'Ribeiro.'

Mendes smiled, his straightened, whitened teeth gleaming.

'We've had to let that girl Kadi go, unfortunately. Missed opportunity there. For her.'

'I have a statement.'

Mendes laughed again. 'Of course you have. Sadly, I think you'll need a lot more than that. And you're never going to find it.' He waved his hand again, this time in a circle around his head. 'Doesn't exist. Like it vanished.'

'Like Ana de Moraes.'

Mendes frowned, paused. 'I haven't visited … I haven't seen Ana for months.'

'But you know what happened to her?'

Mendes nodded. 'Like I said, several months.'

'What happened to her took several months.'

'*Então.*'

'She was here. There's proof, photos taken with her phone. Someone can corroborate.'

'And what exactly does that prove? She came here to do a magazine article, if I remember rightly.'

Leme said nothing.

'What Ana might or might not have been doing has very little to do with me. Her employment history and whatnot.'

'And Leonardo Alencar?'

'Boy with a crush.'

'Something scared him that night in the *favela*.'

'It's a scary place.'

'You'd know, I suppose. They did more than scare him. You know that?'

Mendes shrugged. 'I've read the reports. I was at the funeral. An accident.'

'Right,' Leme said. 'An accident. Then why had he been shot, eh?'

'I don't know what you're talking about.'

'The *favela*,' Leme said. 'You've had problems there before.'

Mendes raised his eyebrows. 'Really?'

'A lawyer. Representing the *favelados* in the *centro*.'

Mendes considered this. Leme noted a glimmer of understanding in his eyes.

'Your wife.'

Leme said nothing. His insides hardened. He felt a rush of anger spread in his chest, controlled it.

'A tragedy. My condolences.'

'It worked out well for you.'

Mendes leaned forward. Leme caught a whiff of his powerful scent, sweat and pheromones.

'What do you want me to say? Lie to you? Yes, it did. It was an accident. You know that as well as I do.'

'Accidents seem to have favourable consequences where you're involved. Life is cheap, right?'

'Opportunities, that's all.'

'Like the Gabriel murder.'

'Manslaughter. Another accident.'

Leme nodded. Didn't want to reveal they had a source, however unreliable. 'Like I said, favourable.'

They sat in silence for what felt like a long time. Leme stared down at his drink and finished it, the warmth of the whiskey dissolving his anger, leaving him briefly relieved, settled.

'Why are you telling me all this?' he asked.

Mendes narrowed his eyes. 'Confirming a position,' he said. 'Yours and mine. Mine is stronger. Unassailable, you might say. I'm just showing you what you don't know. What you can't find out.'

'Friends are important.'

'Mine certainly are.' He seemed to enjoy his wordplay. Smiled. 'You got the message, right?'

Leme nodded. 'It's been made pretty clear. By all of you.'

'*Então.*'

Mendes stood, taking Leme's glass from him.

'Next time,' he said, 'I hope we meet in more agreeable circumstances.'

Leme left.

Mendes wouldn't leave anything to chance, he was sure of that.

He would have to be very careful.

He didn't know what more he could do.

He didn't know if it even mattered.

Days passed. Leme spent them shuffling between home and work. Empty thoughts. Acceptance, or, more like, resignation.

Nights, he followed Mendes. He too spent his time between home and work. The similarities ended there. Lights and movement in his house. There was, Leme realised, only one key difference between his mornings in the *favela* and the nights watching Mendes: at night, he knew who he was looking for.

Everything else continued. As it always does. The corporate equivalent of the woman selling homemade coffee by the bus stop in Paraisópolis, structures raised, dust settled, nothing changed but the fault lines. An illusion of progress, of order.

Aline had gone quiet. Not a surprise. Leme didn't bother contacting her. She was as helpless now as he was. The funny thing was that they hadn't realised it sooner.

On the eighth evening, Mendes left his office much later than normal. Leme had been drinking from a hip flask, angry at this perceived slight, then feeling ridiculous for thinking it at all.

Mendes's car drifted down Leopoldo and made a left on to Garimpeiros.

Then left again on to Fernandes de Abreu, a dark side street that ran behind a decaying, abandoned public tennis venue now a building site.

Shortcut.

The car stopped and the back doors swung open.

Trees stripped of leaves leaned over the road.

Distant street lights, the hum of heat and traffic less intense.

Leme watched as Mendes and a large man jumped out either side, stepping towards his own car.

He sat tight.

Dimmed his lights.

Fuck.

They knew it was him, knew he had been following them.

Mendes's bodyguard reached into his inside pocket.

There was a glint of silver in the low light.

Leme gunned his car.

Looked over his shoulder and jammed it into reverse.

It stalled.

Fuck.

They kept coming.

He had known this would happen. There was no way Mendes would leave it as it was. He didn't leave loose ends, Leme had learnt that much. But it hadn't stopped him.

And now it was happening.

They were yards away.

Leme's car stuttered, the engine wouldn't catch.

Mendes was smiling, shaking his head.

They didn't make it much further.

Four young men swarmed out from behind an old taxi rank deserted since the building work began.

Shouting.

The inside of Mendes's car spilling light across dark faces.

The bodyguard raised his hand as one of the men came at him.

But he wasn't quick enough.

There was a flash, a bang.

He grunted in pain and fell, grabbing at his shoulder, his white shirt darkening.

Mendes stood with his arms raised.

Two of the men approached with a container.

Money. Wallet. Phone. Car keys.

They were shouting, making a threatening motion with the container.

Mendes shook his head. 'I've got nothing,' he said. 'Nothing of use. Please.'

'*Porra!*' The men shouted again. 'Don't fucking lie to us. You know what we want. Wallet, now.'

Mendes froze, shook his head again. 'There's nothing.' He opened his jacket. 'I have nothing for you.' He pointed behind him. 'Take the car,' he said. 'Please.'

'*Filho da puta. Você vai morrer, caralho.*'

Leme knew what was coming; he'd read the reports.

The fourth man pulled the driver from the car and brought a weapon down over his head.

Leme opened his glove compartment.

He pulled out his gun.

He opened the door and jumped out.

He stepped towards the men, but they didn't see him.

His arm shook.

This was not how he had imagined it would end.

More shouting.

Leme took another step forwards.

Then, a bitter, astonished scream.

Mendes was on his knees, clutching at his face and neck.

The men emptied his pockets, hit him three times over the head with what looked like handguns and kicked him.

Stamped on him. And again.

They rifled through the wallet, examined the phone.

Whooped with pleasure at the notes and credit cards in their hands.

Scrambled towards the car.

'*Vamos vamos vamos*,' one of them shouted. '*Ta feito. Embora.*'

Leme looked on.

He lowered his gun.

The instinctive need to act left him, muscles slack, eyes sharp.

Taking it in.

There was nothing he could do.

The men jumped into the empty car and accelerated away towards Juscelino.

Leme stood for a moment. He looked down at Mendes, lifeless. His mind clicked. He had to leave. This was not his fault, but it wouldn't look like that. He climbed back into his car. This time it started. He reversed the way he had come, pulled on to Leopoldo and carried on to the Marginal.

He felt nothing.

Mendes's funeral was fairly low-key, considering. More people seemed to hear the rumours, and the state was keen to distance itself. Best left unconfirmed. Wouldn't do to admit to one of their own acting as Mendes had. That became clear, at least. Leme went. Stood at the back. As he walked away, after the body was committed, he felt something settle inside.

He hadn't realised that he'd been seeking revenge.

And he knew that Renata wouldn't approve. But this time, he was happy enough to disagree with her. He'd passed Aline on his way out. She'd touched his arm gently and flashed a quick, soft smile.

'How do you feel about this?' he asked her.

She gave a quick shake of her head. 'Not now,' she said.

'I see,' he said.

'I guess,' she said, looking from side to side for fear of being over-heard, 'that this means it's over.'

He sighed, smiled tightly. 'Well,' he said, 'for me, maybe. You still have a lot of work to do.'

She nodded.

'Good luck,' he said, as she walked away. '*Valeu, eh,*' he said to himself.

He couldn't provide concrete evidence that Mendes had ordered Ana's death or had overseen the gradual poisoning, but he had enough for himself at least. No way Lagnado was going to reopen the investigation. He only had Alex's testimony that Mendes had planned to scare Leonardo Alencar, a fright that went further than Alex seemed to know. He hadn't told Aline that Leo had been shot and that that was what had killed him, because he didn't know how she'd react and he needed her. Or he had. He wasn't so sure any more. And Alex had begun to backtrack a little after he found out about Ana. Leme understood why. Alex was an arsehole, but not a murderer. It wasn't surprising. Give the boy a chance. Not too many opportunities left to be magnanimous.

The Mensalão trial, predictably, fizzled out, the prosecutors happy enough with a couple of big fish landed. Another illusion of progress. There wasn't the celebration of democracy and good governance that so many people seemed to think the country deserved. Easier to give them a party in 2014 and hope the *seleção* can get their act together and win a few games. Soon forgotten.

Silva dug about a bit, published a speculative piece based on his anonymous source, but couldn't write too much. More like a fucking blog, really, Leme thought, as he read it. He hadn't told Silva he was there when Mendes died, and anyway the piece was defined by the last paragraph, added, Silva said, by his editor.

> … *so another victim of the arbitrary injustice of São Paulo. The violence remains. A sickening, tragic end to a life spent serving the city.*

Silva was embarrassed. His editor stripped most of it away. Just fattened rumours further. Nothing doing.

Mendes's friend Magalhães introduced legislation in the Polícia Civil preventing a new investigation into the Gabriel murder. It didn't look legal, but it happened.

Leme had given up all that, anyway.

There was no need for it. That first step had been a need for justice. The next was a need for peace. And he was trying to take it. More time with Lisboa and his family, more time at home, by the pool, playing tennis, drinking less. Seeing Antonia. Treating the job like a job, one which enabled a life outside it. They were never going to get anything high-profile again, and that, he realised, was fine. Help with the smaller cases, effect change one person at a time. Murder was a tiring business and being shunted to robbery was proving to be a good thing. The victims are grateful, at least. And alive, too, on the whole.

It felt like he might be doing something right for once, despite the nagging voice whispering at night that there was so much unfinished business. Some people dedicate their lives to hopeless causes because they are right and somebody has to. Leme realised he was no longer one of those people, if he ever had been.

What he experienced, for the first time in a very long time, was relief.

He slid into a weekend routine. *They* did. He and Antonia.

They sat by the pool. Plastic table and chairs, loungers. The wooden deck hot under their feet. Umbrellas offered only a little shade.

Saturday.

Families with inflatable animals. *Seguranças* in shirts and ties. Waiters from the bar rushing about with cocktails and snacks. Crude banter with the men whose buckets of beer sweated and dripped. '*Mais uma. Não, duas. Tres! Falei quatro, bundão!*' Laughter as the waiter hesitated, stepped back and forth, not sure if he had the order right. Then he smiled and flicked his wrist in a lazy, coarse gesture. The men roared. Swore. Laughed. Perfect.

Leme and Antonia drank cold beer from cans and chatted to groups of women in bikinis and sarongs and large men in small swimming trunks. Not Leme. He wore shorts and a T-shirt. Sunglasses. The sun piercing, rippling the water, iridescent, broken by teenagers dive-bombing, and women gossiping and splashing themselves cool. The pool a pale electric blue. As he looked at the men and women who came over to say hello, to chat about inconsequential condominium stuff, they were outlines in the light; opaque, simulacra of the friends and neighbours he had known, slightly, over the years he had lived there. Sensitive, they noticed the easy affection between him and Antonia and said nothing. Even the brash, vulgar men, so quick to throw about casual misogyny, innuendo, left them to it. They knocked their beer cans with them, offered their cheese and their olives, shared their chips and their *pastel*.

Leme said little, but sat content. He felt like he had with Renata when they had visited Europe. When they drank in bars in London and then Spain with her friends, he was uncertain in the languages she spoke so well, and happy to soak up what was going on around him. Now, it was like learning his own language all over again, taking tentative steps to engage. And Antonia encouraged him. A word here. A hand on his arm there. A smile. Warmth. He was beginning to understand that he had thawed, that she had rubbed feeling again into his once-numb limbs, his chest. Inside, he felt loose, malleable, open; only weeks before he was still tight with fear and grief. This hadn't gone, but it was being managed now, and massaged into something more positive. The weeks after Mendes's death made him really understand for the first time that he wouldn't change a thing. That he couldn't. How can you regret meeting the love of your life whatever the outcome? Just the very fact of it was a source of wonder. The pain was a consequence of something he could not control. He had to accept that. And he did. He was trying, finally, to view their relationship as the best thing that had ever happened to him. And to take comfort in that. *He* was the best thing that ever happened to *her*. They would both always have that.

'*Fala Mario!*' Lisboa bellowed from the other side of the pool. He marched towards them, a torn plastic bag stiff with more cold beer. He swigged from a can as he negotiated the sunbathing women, the wobbling toddlers, nodding and slapping hands with the men he'd come to know over the years.

Leme smiled. Looked at Antonia.

'You asked him, did you?' he said.

She smiled back. 'Ah. Why not, *ne?* He's your friend. Forget he's your partner for a few hours, *certo?*'

Leme nodded and Lisboa pulled up a chair.

'*Puta, ta quente, eh?*' he said. He leaned back, turning his face to the sky. '*Que sol, meu.*' He slapped Leme on the thigh. 'How are you, *garanhão?*' Winked at Antonia. 'He behaving?'

She smiled. '*Mais ou menos.*' Paused and winked back. 'Not *too* well, obviously.'

Lisboa laughed. Whistled. '*Caralho, bicho,*' he said. Then looked at Leme. Made a face. 'Don't worry I won't stay long,' he said.

Leme laughed shyly. He hadn't exactly told Lisboa what was going on with Antonia as he wasn't sure how he'd react. He should have known that he'd be happy for him. It was progress: that's how he would see it. Lisboa was one of those men who thought it didn't really matter how you *felt* – it was all about momentum. Better to be with someone you quite liked and *doing*, rather than moping and waiting for the great love that didn't really exist. And this thought – and the fact that he felt the opposite – sharpened Leme's reflection on Renata: he, *they*, had been lucky. He clung on to this idea like a drowning man to a life raft. The difference was that not long ago he had been slipping from it into the water; now he was on top, perhaps precarious, but safe enough.

'You seen the news?' Lisboa asked.

Antonia clicked her teeth. 'Really? You want to talk about that?'

'What is it?' Leme asked.

'Mensalão,' Lisboa said. 'They've overturned some of the convictions. Racketeering, apparently. Fuckers are going to get away with it.'

Leme nodded. Felt little. He said, 'No change there then, right? It is what it is.'

Antonia nodded. 'Yes, that's right. It was a step. It'll take time. *Chega, ne?* Let's talk about something else.'

Lisboa grumbled something about wanting an adult conversation and Leme laughed.

'What's so funny?' Lisboa said. 'You try living with two children and a wife whose only fucking concerns are what I should be doing to help.'

Leme gave a sympathetic sigh. Antonia touched his hand.

'Sorry.' Lisboa brightened. He dipped his hand into the plastic bag. '*Mais uma?*'

They nodded. They cracked their cans. '*Saúde,*' Lisboa said. 'Here's to … *you.*' He winked again. Leme knew that he was being as affectionate and supportive as he could and that it was a big deal.

The sun swelled, throbbed. A hum of chatter. A splash. A shout. A tennis ball hit down below on the court. The heavy hiss and slap of the freezing pressure shower in the sauna hitting the concrete floor.

Lunchtime approached and the families drifted off to their apartments. Younger children dragging their feet and whingeing. Bottom lips stuck out, towels trailing damp patches.

Lisboa smirked. 'This day off is fucking sweet,' he said.

Leme said nothing. He knew that Lisboa's mother-in-law was at his house so it was both guilt-free and double the relief. He let him have it. Lisboa didn't mean what he said about his family. You're only as happy as your unhappiest child, he'd once said. Leme understood that. It had been the same with Renata. He wondered if that was what happened when you had kids: your allegiances shift.

'Oh, this is funny,' Lisboa said.

Antonia and Leme shuffled forward on the loungers they'd moved to and leaned in to listen. They'd been comatose for the last fifteen minutes, the heat baking a sleepy, beery buzz.

'That Aline Alencar,' Lisboa went on. 'She wants to see us. Well, I think she wants to see *you*, actually.'

'Why are you telling me this?' Leme said. 'She has my number. Why didn't she call me?'

'Yeah, it was weird,' Lisboa said. 'She called the office. Said she'd been trying but hadn't managed to get hold of you. I said I'd tell you to call her.'

'What does she want?' Leme asked.

This was the first time Leme had thought about it all for what felt like a long time. He didn't *want* to think about it. It was over. Speaking to Aline Alencar was only going to make him feel bad again. He was resigned, had accepted things: it was what Ana had said to him when she'd described Aline's lessons, about how the whole system in the city is designed to make sure the rich, the privileged, stay on top. That there will never be genuine change. Seeing her again would hammer this point, this reality, home. It was something he could do without.

'What does she want? Fuck knows,' Lisboa said. 'Maybe she fancies you?'

Antonia gave Leme a playful slap.

Lisboa raised his eyebrows. 'But, ah, I doubt that, *ne*, Antonia?' Jerked his thumb at Leme. 'He's too old.'

Leme reddened. Shrugged. 'Did you ever get too old for this?' he said, gesturing at Antonia. '*This* is the only interesting thing, right?'

They all laughed and Antonia kissed him hard, twice, on his top lip, like she was aiming just below and had missed.

Leme touched her neck, felt his hand warm in its long crook. Pushed her hair behind her ears. Ran it through his fingers. She smiled deep from within.

He nodded, settled.

He decided he would call Aline on Monday.

Later, in Antonia's bed, Leme lay awake as she murmured and sighed, wriggled her legs against his. The warmth of her buttocks unknotting the dread that, once again, he felt in the pit of his stomach. Every time they shared a bed, she was able to do that for him.

Leme and Aline arranged to meet in a restaurant in Itaim.

He parked and staggered across Juscelino Kubitschek. Cheap, spluttering, exhaust-spewing cars with open windows swarmed around blacked-out SUVs, jostling for position at the lights and the entrance to the tunnels that ran to and beyond the park at Ibirapuera. A motorbike ran a red light just as he stepped into the road. '*Vai se foder*,' the driver shouted back at Leme, the bike bending into the curve and away, his middle finger raised. 'Go fuck yourself.' Leme shook his head. Tensed.

He was met by a blast of cold and a pretty smile in the restaurant doorway. It was 'international', all clean edges and mirrors, small, expensive portions and cocktails. Dark, glass tabletops and uncomfortable chairs. Tall ferns offered privacy by the tables at the window, in which the sun refracted and pierced the gloom in precise lines. He looked at the bar in hope, but saw her in the corner. She waved.

'I haven't ordered anything interesting yet,' Aline said.

She stood and manoeuvred her way around the table, squeezing sideways. They kissed on one cheek in that knowing, traditional Paulistano way. Sat back down.

She sipped at sparkling water.

'Agua?' she asked, tilting the bottle towards him in a question.

He shook his head and asked the attractive maître d' that lingered close by to bring him a beer. He always liked to slake his thirst with beer, not water. Seemed a waste to deny yourself that pleasure.

A table of boisterous young office workers were celebrating a deal or a birthday and toasting each other with champagne in braying good spirits. The restaurant shrank, the shouting intrusive, and Leme felt confined in its lessening space, the curiosity he'd harboured before the meeting sliding towards an undefined anxiety, which surprised him.

As Aline began to talk, the noise increased. Waiters, a buzzing irritant; other diners clattered cutlery, spoke in ghostly whispers.

'I wanted to thank you,' she said.

'Thank me? What for?'

Aline smiled, sighed. 'For making things easier for me,' she said.

'I'm not sure that I did.'

Leme's beer arrived. He gulped at it. Exhaled. 'I'll have some of that water now, please,' he said.

Aline poured. It cracked and spat against the ice in the glass. Fizzed up, like a soluble painkiller.

'It's not been easy,' she said. 'For either of us. You were sensitive to me, to my … situation. And I know why.'

Leme gave her a questioning look.

'I know about your wife,' Aline said. 'I found out. You could have used that, our … *meu Deus*, this sounds awful, our shared plight, I suppose.' She took a sip of water. 'What I mean is that you could have made me trust you for a personal reason. It would have worked, I'm sure. But you didn't. You kept everything professional. I appreciate that.'

Leme nodded. He remembered that the very thought had crossed his mind when they had first met. Said nothing.

'I'm still coming to terms with Leo's death,' she said. 'It's unlikely though that I ever will. What do you think?'

Leme considered this. He didn't have children. It was looking more and more like he never would. Could he possibly comment? Grief was a word with a thousand permutations, proliferations.

The waitress appeared.

'Saved by the bell,' Aline smiled.

They ordered. Pasta for her, filet for him. Salad to share.

'Well?' Aline asked when the waitress had bustled off. 'What do you think?'

Leme examined her face. Buried beneath the formality, the professional façade, was a longing for truth or reassurance, he couldn't quite tell which. What was it she needed to hear? That his own grief was only recently manageable, in part because he had met someone? She would never meet another Leo.

'I don't know,' Leme said.

Aline looked a little desperate. 'You don't know?' she asked.

Leme gave her a tight, sympathetic smile.

'OK,' she said.

'I think,' Leme began. Paused. It was hopeless, he thought. 'I don't know,' he said, finally. 'I don't know if we ever do.'

Aline breathed out. She leaned back in her chair and looked away from him. Her face was set. Her lips turned up; her mouth closed. In her eyes was sunk a well of feeling hovering between regret and hope. And something else, Leme thought. Shame? Couldn't be.

They sat in silence. The food arrived and it was a relief. Aline complained that the pasta seemed overdone and the waitress gave her a murderous look, which slid off her. Aline didn't even realise, thought Leme.

He ordered another beer, drifted in and out of the noises around him. Laughter. A dropped plate in the kitchen. A brief silence then the chatter resumed. Carefree. A squeal of pleasure. A deep, throaty chuckle. He skewered his steak and watched as Aline chased cherry tomatoes around her plate.

There was an awkwardness that hadn't been there when they had met before. It was disquieting for Leme. They had helped each other and now seemed unsure of how to move on from the episode that connected them. It was, he reflected, a little like the first time he had seen Antonia after they had slept together: aware that they were happy about what had happened, but uncertain quite how to move forward. But also aware that they would. That they had to.

'We're going to do something for Ana,' Aline said. 'A memorial. Something significant. It's been very hard for the other students. Some of them are a little lost, I think. We don't want them to feel like that.'

Leme nodded. 'That's good,' he said. He felt a pang of keen regret. Her face invaded his dreams from time to time.

'Yes,' Aline said. 'We're thinking of naming something after her. I mean ...' and she paused, looked Leme in the eye, 'we don't really know what happened to her, but we need to mark her passing.' She coughed. Placed her fork on her plate with a light click. 'No one else will,' she said, looking at the table.

'There's not much to know,' Leme lied. 'I'm sure you'll do the right thing by her. For her.'

Aline laughed, mirthlessly. 'We're experts now, right?' she said. 'In unfairness? That's what we do. It's our currency, *ne?*'

Currency. A word she *would* use, Leme thought.

'She said something interesting to me,' he said. 'About what you taught her.'

'Oh yes?'

'Yes. Something about the system. The way things work in this city.'

They had finished eating and they both pushed their plates to the centre of the table. Remains smeared in black and cream, tinged with blood.

'What do you mean?' Aline asked.

The waitress returned. They ordered coffee.

'She told me that you talked about the way in which things would never change. That everything was designed in such a way that those in charge would remain so. In São Paulo, at least.'

Aline nodded. 'That sounds like something I might say. It doesn't mean I think that it's right.'

'That's what she told me. She said that she was the only person in the room who didn't benefit from the system you described.'

Aline bristled. 'I think she benefited a little. Don't you?'

'I think she benefited from *you*, yes. Not the same thing though, is it?'

Aline shrugged. 'I'm a part of the system, so in a sense, that's wrong.'

'But by creating the scholarships, by helping these start-ups with money, expertise, aren't you at least trying to effect change? I saw what happened at Mendes's office. You wouldn't countenance anything that was going to harm the *favelados*. I respected that. Respected you for saying it, however hopeless it was at the time.'

Aline nodded. 'That's kind of you to say. But these are baby steps we're taking. The fact is that no, in my lifetime, we won't see a significant change. São Paulo is a conservative, mercantile city. Always has been. Right since its inception. It was a gateway to the gold, to the interior. It has always exploited the indigenous population. The men – and they are mainly men – that run it would have it no other way. And there are too many people too comfortable in their condominiums to take any kind of political stand. Condominiums like yours,' she added. 'It's why we keep voting in the same shameless politicos. They look after the interests of the money. And the money only goes so far. And besides,' she placed her hands on the table, 'nothing will change this year or the next or the one after, whatever we try to do.'

'Why's that?' Leme asked.

'There's too much riding on the World Cup. Then the Olympics. We're short-term thinkers in this country.'

'And what happened at Mendes's office confirmed that for me,' Leme said.

She opened her palms. 'That shows you the priority. Like in that painting in Mendes's office,' she paused. 'Well, you know. Money, right?'

Leme eyed her. She looked down at her plate. Fingered a loose hair behind her ear. 'Well, you were there,' she said, quietly.

Leme nodded. Remembered something. The way she had been so keen for him not to take the photos of the painting. Frowned.

He said, 'I knew all this, but I never understood it until I met Ana.'

'What do you mean?'

'Well,' Leme searched for the right phrase. 'She embodied something I didn't know existed.'

'Which was?'

'Hope, I suppose. No,' he paused, 'that sounds dramatic. I mean here was a young, intelligent woman given an opportunity. An opportunity that seemed golden. And so what if she were only one of millions? It was a start, right? But look what happened to her. They couldn't allow even one poor woman a step up. And she paid for it.'

'I don't know about that,' Aline said.

'No, you don't.' Leme smiled. 'And I'm not going to tell you. It wouldn't be right. Let's just say she was a victim of circumstance.'

'Aren't we all?' Aline said.

Leme sniffed. Smiled. 'It's been a character-building experience, right?'

Aline laughed a grim laugh. '*Querido*,' she said, '*life* is a character-building experience.'

When he got home, Leme opened up his laptop. He studied the photos of the painting that Ana had taken. Perhaps it wasn't a trick of the light. He took the clearest from the group of three and measured it exactly against the last photo. He tried to overlap them on the screen, connect them. He realised how amateurish he was being. Tomorrow morning he'd speak to his IT guy. He looked again and shook his head, couldn't see it.

He stood up and poured himself a whiskey.

Why had Aline mentioned the painting earlier? Yes, there was a sort of relevance, they'd even talked about it in Mendes's office, but … she hadn't wanted him to photograph it, had been adamant in fact. She had stopped short of actually telling him off, but she'd been embarrassed about the way Mendes was talking to her.

But why was it such a big deal?

He looked again. Too dark. He turned on all the lights in his living room, the standing lamps and the spotlights. He sat back down.

He played around with the computer's brightness, angled the screen, lifted it to the light.

Then he saw it.

They had been taken in different places. He was sure of that now.

'What is it about this woman that you keep accepting her invitations, eh?'

Leme sat with his feet up on Antonia's bed watching as she changed. She had a mirror on the inside door of her wardrobe and she held dresses up against her and tilted her head, pouted at them while she spoke, discarding them one after the other, piling them on a chair like a mound of twisted, spent corpses.

'I mean, you're a fundamentalist, right?' she went on. 'For you, everything is essentially reduced to one idea, one idea that you believe in. Thing is,' she stretched out a purple cotton dress, frowned and tossed it aside, 'you have different principles for different people, different situations. *Entendeu?*'

Leme smiled. 'Not really,' he said.

He couldn't tell her what he now thought about Aline, about what she might have done. It was a suspicion that needed confirmation and Antonia was not going to give him that. He had to see Aline and talk it out with her. He had arranged this meeting, but to avoid any difficult questions, he'd told Antonia that Aline had invited *him*.

'I'd say I was pretty consistent,' he added.

She ignored him. 'So, what I want to know is, what is the idea about *this* woman that you believe in?'

Leme laughed. 'I think you may be giving me too much credit, *querida.*'

She ignored him again. 'What you've got is hidden depths.' She measured the length of a pastel-yellow dress. Nodded at her reflection. Pulled it over her head. Flicked out her hair with the backs of her fingers. Gave him a look: see? 'And the thing about hidden depths is that they are never that well hidden. From people who know you, that is.'

Leme smiled again. Renata had said that to tell someone you know them is a tricky thing: it's never that simple. Saying that means you want something. And you'd better know what it is that you want when you say it.

He was beginning to understand why Antonia and Renata never quite became the friends they might have. His phone rang. The car Aline had sent for him was downstairs.

He kissed Antonia and looked forward to seeing her later.

He went downstairs to the car that Aline had sent. It was a Jaguar. He smiled appreciatively as he sank back into the leather seat. Depending on how the conversation went, he might not be travelling back in such style.

Aline lived in a two-floor penthouse apartment close to the university, where she'd been since her husband left her. Kicked her out, Leme had heard.

It was vast and minimalist, he supposed. Barely any furniture. What happens when you have to move quickly, he assumed. A man – a *butler*? Christ, he thought – handed him a whiskey and he stood on the lower level gawping through the floor-to-ceiling windows, an enormous goldfish bowl in the sky. The pollution seemed to stagnate in front of his eyes, like the dank, slow-moving water of the fat river far below.

The city crept up towards Avenida Paulista, tower blocks flanking the low-rise houses of Jardins. Through the other window: down to the river and Leme's own home. He could see Parque Burle Max and smiled at the memory of his and Lisboa's one attempt at exercise.

Aline swept down a circular staircase in the corner, drink in hand.

'Sorry to keep you,' she smiled. Let Leme kiss her on both cheeks, chin raised. He felt her make-up crack, soft powder on his lips.

They stood in silence, Leme slightly uncomfortable, rarely in a social situation without close friends or drunken neighbours.

'So,' Aline began, 'everything has changed. I'm glad we met those conditions. It's established things.'

Leme nodded. 'Well,' he said, 'in a sense, right? Things remain.'

'We have to continue with what was planned.' Aline tilted her head. 'Now we have the chance to do so … ethically.'

'That's what you're doing?'

'It's what we've been trying to do since we came on board.'

'You might have tried harder.'

Aline nodded vigorously. 'I'm aware of that. But you know why it took some time. Why I'm here, in this apartment, and why my son is … not.'

It was too easy, Leme thought, to forget the perspective that is a consequence of the death of a loved one. That little else really matters. He felt the warm, light touch of empathy.

'I should give you the tour,' she said, brighter. Flashed a smile. 'Upstairs, first. Apologies though. I haven't had a chance to really, you know, decorate. My things are ... elsewhere.' She smiled. 'Upstairs then,' she said.

Christ, Leme thought, *bedrooms*. He pressed his lips together and caught the faint taste of make-up. I didn't sign up for this ...

He followed her up the staircase. Tried not to examine her hips. Fucking power of suggestion. And grief can be a potent aphrodisiac, though it wasn't for him. Uncertainty flickered. He took a slug of whiskey.

'Bedroom, bedroom, bedroom,' she trilled. She was pointing and looking back over her shoulder. 'All guest. This one,' she said, pushing the door, 'is mine.'

Leme edged his nose around to look inside.

'Lovely,' he said. Took a step back.

'You should see the view from the balcony.'

She pulled open the sliding doors with a flourish. Ta dah!

Bloody hell, Leme thought. Up there, the reality of São Paulo was brought into clear focus: a plague of twenty million rats sniffing and scavenging. Ground zero. It's a wonder the rich ever descend into it at all.

He murmured something complimentary and she smiled. That middle-distance look of the privileged. Never sure what or who it is aimed at.

'It's a comfort,' she began and was cut off by a buzzing noise inside the room. 'Sorry. Need to get that.'

Leme looked at his glass. He was going to need another one. He stepped to the edge of the balcony and felt the dust of the railing, rubbed it between his finger and thumb.

Aline reappeared at the door. 'Really sorry. Something important. I'm going to have to take it in the office. Ten minutes?' She gave him a look. Gestured at the city. 'Stay here. Enjoy the view.'

Leme smiled and watched her disappear through the door. He felt the urge to pee and stepped back into the bedroom. This was a chance.

Two doors led from it. One of them had to be a bathroom. He picked the closest and tried to open it. It was locked. He crossed the room and turned the handle of the other door. Also locked. Fuck. He really needed to piss. He looked again at the door. One of those bars across the middle. Bolts at the top. Odd. He unlatched them and pulled at it. They were on the wrong side. To keep the door locked from the *outside*. On a side table next to the door was a small, elegant box. He lifted the latch and inside was a key. Bingo. He placed it in the lock, and the door opened with a click.

It was a bedroom annexe, small but elegantly furnished in white, like a hotel. He ran his hand over the crisp bed sheets; saw a television bolted high on the wall opposite, thought of a hospital room. A bathroom to the side. He went in and pissed. Something didn't make sense. He rinsed his hands under the tap and went back into the room.

There were drooping flowers, spotting pollen on the white doilies, either side of the bed. A book, which he picked up and examined. Machado de Assis. Raised an eyebrow. Someone still reads the classics. He dropped it back on the bedside table.

Then he saw it …

The painting. *Off Duty Militias*, cased in glass.

He was expecting this, but not here. He remembered the photo and nudged the glass. It opened and in the corner, the edge of a white bottle – the difference between Ana's photos. This is where she was when she went missing.

He went back to the door. No sign of her.

He stood in front of the painting. The glass case was not quite attached to the wall. *That* had created the odd angle in the photo. Leme pressed his nose almost against it. He nudged the edge of the frame again and it swung towards him.

Behind it was a shallow cupboard, two shelves like a medicine cabinet. Rows of bottles and syringes.

Ana had taken the photo alone. He had intended to confront Aline tonight. He had known when she mentioned the painting again. But he was not expecting to be brought to the scene itself.

He took out his phone and opened the map application. He swiped 'current location'. He looked at the door. He was starting to feel hot, panicky. The map kicked in and the blue circle tightened to where he was. He tapped 'share', then 'message'.

Leme took a handkerchief from his pocket and wiped where he had touched the painting. He breathed out and frowned. Fuck. His head swam. He felt hot, prickly behind the eyes, under the skin.

He looked at his phone. The map was loaded and ready. He tapped L-I-S-B-O-A and stopped, brought his hand to his forehead.

He looked at the door.

He looked at his phone.

He edged back through the door into the main bedroom.

The balcony was still unlocked.

He slipped outside.

He checked the signal.

The message had been sent.

There was that criss-crossed safety netting across the balcony.

He edged his phone through one of the gaps.

He watched it drop down into the city below.

He went back into the annexe.

He relaxed into a hot feeling of confusion.

He sat down on the bed, a sudden headache pushing against his temples.

He looked at his glass.

Fuck. There was a white residue gathering in the bottom.

He rubbed and massaged his head.

He lay back and dropped his drink.

He came to with a hot, sticky lurch.

Aline stood in front of the painting. The man who had given him the drink stood by the door.

He felt all his strength evaporate, his limbs like water. He tried to sit up, but he could only lift his head a few inches from the bed. He moved his hand to scratch at his head. It didn't get far. The headache pulsed. The feeling oozed back into his legs.

'How long was I out?' he asked.

'Twenty minutes.'

'Where am I? What is this?'

'We've … restrained you.' Aline poked at his leg.

Leme looked down and to the left and right. He was manacled to the corners of the bed. Loose enough to move a little. Soft leather around handcuffs.

She gave a thin smile and pushed the picture frame back into place with a click. 'This doesn't make any difference,' she said.

'Where am I?' Leme repeated.

'Ana was here, as you know.'

'Why was she here? What is this place?'

'She was … self-medicating. We needed to keep an eye on her.'

'We?'

'Me. Mendes. He'd told her the truth about what she was doing, the idiot. Mensalão payments. She was shocked, confused. It jeopardised everything.'

'For you?'

'Of course.' She sat down next to him on the bed.

Leme thought about Ana's apartment. 'This is one of those flats, isn't it?' he said. 'Podemos, ne? Empty flats. Whitewashed soon, too, I suppose.'

Aline ignored the question. 'My husband found out about my … private life,' she said. 'The foundation and its assets were transferred to his name. It had been a condition when we married over thirty years ago. Nothing I could do. And Mendes knew that, hence the threat.' She paused. Looked down and then back at Leme. 'And there was something else, too, that I had to protect. My reputation.'

Leme wiped his forehead, ran his heavy tongue around his mouth now furry and tart. He let his head fall back against the white sheets.

She continued. 'I made my reputation with the work I did on the Singapore Project. The recovery. We all knew the buildings wouldn't last. I made some deals. We were guaranteed the rebuilding long before it was done. We looked very good as a result.'

'And got very rich,' Leme added.

She ignored him. 'This project is the only way I can live, and it became quickly clear that the project itself can only survive with the money from the monthly payments.'

'So, what, Ana was sacrificed?'

Aline pouted, her eyes flashed. 'My son is dead.'

'Because he was worried about her.'

'Yes. He came to me. I told Mendes to have him followed, to keep him out of Paraisópolis. The accident was my fault.'

'It wasn't an accident.'

Aline gave him a sharp look. 'His car crashed,' she said, 'after he'd had a scare.'

Leme barked a grim laugh. 'No,' he said. 'There was more to it. The men in Paraisópolis, whoever they were, probably fucking Militars, they did more than scare your son. They shot him.'

Aline stood. 'You're serious?'

'I was there.'

Her face twitched. Her hands came up to her neck. She breathed uneasily.

'It's done,' Leme said. 'One way or another, it was an accident, right?'

She flashed him a look. A look that said: not now.

'And Ana?' Leme asked.

Aline regained her composure. 'She was malleable,' she said. 'It was straightforward. We were only hiding her, at first. After Leo … was killed, I made the decision. There are … discreet people. Always will be in São Paulo.'

The man behind her smiled.

'And this makes no difference?'

Aline smiled. 'You're a liability. Funny what you can get away with, right? Mendes is dead. My son is dead.'

Leme shook his head. 'Why did you tell me where I could find the Mensalão list in the site office?' he asked.

'Because I knew that you were after Mendes. I had nothing to do with that – it was before I became involved. It was a risk, certainly, but one I thought worthwhile. It proved to be.'

'Why have you told me all of this?'

'What exactly have I told you?'

Leme coughed, laughed. 'It's like you taught Ana,' he said. 'The system exists to protect those in power. And it's better for you all if it stays that way. I've never seen it so clear as these last few months. You killed Ana.'

'She died. Not the same thing.'

Leme shook his head. 'No. I suppose it isn't. And now it's my turn.'

Aline looked at the man and back at Leme. 'We'll speak again,' she said.

Leme pitched forward, felt his head snap back and then vomited. Bitter, thick bile spilled down his chin. His stomach heaved and he retched again. This time he managed to bend his head to the right and through glazed eyes he watched a white-yellow liquid spatter the sheets and slap against the washing-up bowl that was close by.

'*Ah, meu,*' the man said. 'Use the fucking bowl, eh?' He smirked.

Leme's brain seemed to slop back and forward inside his head, in time with his heart. He groped with his arms but they too snapped back into place. He had no strength. He tried to speak but couldn't.

'It'll get easier,' the man said. 'First couple of times always make you puke. You'll get used to it.' He smiled and nodded at the syringe in his hand, tilted it back and forth, watching the brown-red sludge slip up and down inside.

Leme reached towards the man in a desperate lunge. He was under water, pawing at the man, seeing him through the lens of a camera whose shutter opened and closed in rapid shots. Staggered, slow motion – click, click, click, click, click. Time stopped. Turned. Rushed back up inside him. He gasped and coughed an anguished cry filled with bitter, liquid chunks. A thick, toxic soup.

His lips were coated and cracked.

His head rocked back.

'You'll enjoy it the next time,' the man said.

Leme's eyes opened and closed. He breathed heavily, which felt like a relief. In the corner of his eye he saw the man leave, heard the door click shut.

He scanned his body from head to toe. It shuddered and settled in relief. He almost smiled. Yes, he thought. Yes. Yes.

He slept.

Hours passed. Or so it felt. He was pulled in and out of sleep, barely noticed when he slipped into consciousness. Thoughts were dragged though his mind like an anchor through sand. Where …? What …? Who …? He couldn't finish them, didn't want to.

His eyes rolled back in his head. Liquid gargled in his throat. He tasted blood, a metallic tang. His tongue lolled forward in a protracted stab. He gagged and black spots dotted the sheets. His mouth formed the letter 'O', contracted, formed it again, like a newly landed fish on a river bank, teeth speckled red.

His dreams drifted through him in distinct episodes, fragmented conversations, whispered words. Renata, but in a different shape. She came to him as his mother, as Antonia, as Aline, as her ex-boyfriend, even. As herself. A white background, sheets like waves of water lapping against him, sticky, damp. He felt the toxins oozing out of him and he shivered in pleasure.

Leme was pulled awake by what felt like a violent orgasm. He gasped, eyes wide, heart racing. Aline stood in front of him.

He said nothing at first. His throat cracked with thirst, the roof of his mouth sore with ulcers. He coughed and nodded at a glass of water on the table.

Aline picked it up and dripped some into his mouth. He choked and spluttered and felt the relief of water, and not blood, escaping between his teeth.

He lay back. 'I'm trying to understand why this is the right thing to do,' he croaked.

'We can't change what's happened,' she said, 'but we can control what happens *next*. It's an exciting opportunity, it really is. And we'll share it with the city. The *whole* city.'

Leme's eyes widened. 'I'm talking about *this*,' he said, nodding at his arms and legs. 'About me.'

Aline nodded. 'Like I said, you've become a liability. It's a risk, but all big decisions are.'

Leme tried to laugh, but it hurt. 'What are you doing to me?' he asked.

'I think you know,' Aline said. She pointed at the painting and the cabinet behind it. 'You now know what happened to Ana but no one else does. When they find you, they'll also find the same drugs in your apartment, money, too. And your connection with Ana, of course. That you were seen with her. That'll help.'

'And meanwhile you'll carry on.'

'That's right,' she said. 'I will. *We* will. This influx of money, this building, all this ... *preparation*. Some of the benefits will filter down.'

Leme was confused. 'You keep talking about the good you're doing,' he said. 'Who are you trying to convince?'

'Look,' Aline said. 'We're doing a lot of good. Like Mendes said, there is some collateral damage, but that's inevitable in São Paulo. We're engaging the start-ups that my foundation has been sponsoring and we're finding more. There's been a stranglehold on construction in this city, and that's something I have been involved in. It's important to start to redress this. That's what I'm doing. Building brings work – it's a stimulus. It's always been this way. I'm sorry that you can't see that.'

This time Leme laughed. 'It's a little hard to see *that* from my position,' he said.

He thought about what Alex had told him, what Aline had basically confirmed. About her role in the Singapore Project, in the secret contract she had brokered. And now she was taking steps to atone? It seemed like she really felt she was.

'We're on the edge of a precipice,' she said. 'We can turn back, keep things as they are, or plunge into something new and exciting.' She smiled. 'Like I said, I'm sorry.'

'I have to ask,' Leme said. 'How is Mendes's family?'

Aline looked grave. 'I don't know,' she answered. 'Money? Things? They'll be fine. He had a son. He had a wife. I don't know. They kept their distance with ... Leo. And I'll keep mine now.'

'How long is this going to last?'

'This? Oh, you mean you.' Aline smiled. 'You came on a Friday. Not long.'

'My ... my girlfriend knows I went to meet you,' Leme said.

Aline nodded. 'But she doesn't know where. I've been seen out and about, had meetings. By the time anyone looks for you ... well,' she said, gesturing at the room, 'this won't exist, effectively.'

Leme grunted. He wanted to tell her that she wasn't going to get away with it, but it felt futile, stupid. The city had won. She was a part of *that* city. A different part from the one that killed Mendes, a stronger part, a better part. A secure part, like she had taught Ana, like she was explaining now to him.

She had won.

'I need to go now,' she said. 'You're not going to see me again, which is for the best. For both of us.'

Leme said nothing. He lay back and watched her leave.

He waited for the door to open again.

Leme felt worthless, vapid, cold. To give up, or not. It made little difference. He was too weak to think. Moments of euphoria, then plunged into blackness and terror. The man came three times. Leme's arms pricked and tingled from the syringe marks. 'No need to worry where *these* holes go,' the man had said. 'You're a grown man, not some *favela pretinha* slut like that Ana girl.' He'd laughed.

The dosage was being upped, slowly. For how long, Leme didn't know, couldn't work out the time he'd spent there already. Felt like days. Felt like his whole life. And then, eventually, there'd only be one more dose, and it would all be over. In the moments when the injections wore off – and they were only moments – he didn't even have the motivation, or the courage, to feel frightened of what was next. He was flat, excavated: a greying corpse.

The man visited again. The drugs coursed through Leme in a rush of relief and terror. The man laughed as Leme stretched out to him.

He writhed, groaned. Renata lay next to him, smiled. A flash of gold teeth darkened by patches of blood. The teeth fell one by one and her smile widened into an empty chasm. He turned, screamed. Ana carrying a dead baby, its stitches opening, thread by thread, small plastic bags of crack dropping, disappearing in smoke. Ana's head turned and smiled. Her face melted and set in a mask.

He heard the thump, thump of a dead body hit with chair legs, like a carpet beaten clean. Thump, thump. His eyes opened, then closed. Thump. The body puffed dust, contracted, shrunk, grew. Thump, thump.

Air escaped from Leme in shallow breaths. The thumping got louder, more insistent. Hardened. A crack.

Leme rolled, sweated. The noise was sharper. Crack became splinter. Crack. A great rip and a bang. Leme's eyes opened.

'Mario,' someone said.

'Mario.'

Leme tried to nod, to speak.

'Mario. Look at me. Mario.'

Leme swallowed, his stomach knotted, then pulled free.

He felt a deep pit of nothingness at his core.

'Mario, it's me, Ricardo. Lisboa, you idiot.'

He felt hands on his face, pulling at his legs.

'Cut the thing, *porra*,' he heard Lisboa say.

He felt his arms and legs come loose and he floated up and looked down, saw himself, wretched and alone.

Three months later

Leme leaned back on his chair, adjusted his sunglasses and took another mouthful of *chopp*. He watched the horses in the paddock, some frisky, others placid, some proud. It was an early race and the crowd in the bar that faced the finish line was filling slowly. Dressed in slacks and hats and dresses, drinking champagne and cocktails. They think they're in Europe, Leme joked to himself. Can't they see the buildings on the other side of the river? The traffic?

He hadn't been in hospital long. The first couple of days he was on a drip because he couldn't take any solids. He threw up frequently until they managed to get his blood sugar levels back to something close to normality. The dosage had never reached a level that threatened his life, but it wreaked havoc with his insides, his mind. He was drained, almost literally, according to the doctors. It was like he had been flushed out.

The crack had been the door splintering, kicked in by Lisboa. Leme had been gone over three days before anyone looked into it. Before they even thought there was a possibility he was missing at all. When Antonia eventually called Lisboa on the Monday morning, almost seventy-two hours after the meeting with Aline had been scheduled, he was furious.

'Why the fuck didn't you call before?' he'd shouted at her.

She apologised. Later she'd tell Leme that she hadn't told anyone that he hadn't come home as she was jealous, paranoid, convinced Leme had done something he shouldn't have. With Aline, she supposed. Lisboa had said it himself: Aline Alencar fancied Leme. Antonia had been angry and hurt. She had been devastated, actually, and it was a surprise. She hoped that Leme could forgive her stupidity.

Of course he could. No damage done. And he smiled. He winced as he did, the insides of his cheeks raw, landscape ripped apart, ridges of ulcers.

Lisboa knew immediately that something was wrong. He hadn't

contacted Leme himself that weekend, which was a first, mainly as he had wanted to give him some space for Antonia. She understood that Lisboa took responsibility and thought no more of him shouting at her. Transference, she told Leme one morning when he was still propped up by hospital pillows. But Lisboa had received the message, the shared location. He'd ignored it, thinking it was some kind of dirty joke.

Lisboa was jump-started into life, energised. The energy had remained. He was at the apartment within an hour of his conversation with Antonia. Leme had been a clever fucker, Lisboa said, chucking his phone off the balcony.

Their IT guy managed to recover the photos and data: nothing lost.

When they discovered him, Leme was sprawled on the mattress, wearing only a shirt and underwear, all the sheets gone. The apartment was stripped bare when they arrived, no sign of anything – save the fixtures – or anyone at all, like its contents had disappeared into a tornado and were spat back out in another part of the city. Lisboa didn't care. It didn't matter if they never caught anyone; they had come to find Leme.

Leme took a careful swig of beer. The Jockey Club had long been a favourite Saturday afternoon escape. Drinks and snacks, girls coming round to the tables to take your bets. All very civilised and easy. A tenner a race and you're likely to win at least one or two if you bet the favourite every time. Covers it, at least. More like dog racing, the course is so short.

The question was what they could do next. Leme's word that Aline was at least partially responsible for Ana's death was not enough, and the evidence no longer existed. Aline had left the country. She was spending time on other projects in Europe and overseeing the work in the *centro* remotely, through the foundation. The rumours were that she was doing no such thing, really, that her husband Milton had basically taken over, and no one was unhappy about that.

He waited for Eleanor. She had done well. It hadn't been too hard to talk her editor round. Another one taking a risk. And Silva, too. The report and accompanying article was almost ready and there was international press interested, thanks to Eleanor's boss. But they may yet simply use it all as a bargaining tool. The only way they could bring Aline and anyone else to justice was to go outside of the system: to force their hands through external pressure. The truth should be enough, but in São Paulo it didn't always work like that.

He thought a better position might await him and Lisboa if this all came off. That they might head up a division, even. Leme was optimistic, but cautious. There was a long way to go, yet. But at least they were doing it, all four of them. Together.

He saw Eleanor and Lisboa snaking through the bar laughing. They waved. He smiled and waved back. Antonia would be joining them soon.

As he waited, anticipated the day ahead, he realised something, and his chest flooded with emotion.

He smiled.

He hadn't heard any whispering for a long time.

Acknowledgements

I'd like to thank the following:

Will Francis, Helen Francis, Angeline Rothermundt, Kid Ethic, Lucy Caldwell, Susanna Jones, Jenn Ashworth, Luke Brown, Sam Mills, Wendy Thomas, Danillo Aguiar, Karen Brodie, Rachel Mills, and, for everything, Isabella Lemos.